EXPIRED SECRETS

LAST CHANCE COUNTY - BOOK 2

LISA PHILLIPS

TWO DOGS PUBLISHING, LLC

Trade Print ISBN: 979-8-88552-031-7

Publisher: Two Dogs Publishing, LLC. Idaho, USA

Cover design: Ryan Schwarz

Edited by : Jen Weiber

1

———

Tate Hudson, private investigator, sat at the corner booth. Hotel bar. Thursday night. Most of the guests were at other hot spots, like the club two blocks over, so it was pretty quiet. Too few people, and he'd be spotted easily. Too many, and he'd never get what he came for.

He left the drink he'd ordered untouched. His phone kept his attention far more than the beverage, like so many other patrons. But what occupied him was not social media. He angled the cell against the edge of the table so its camera showed the man at the bar.

Blue suit. Brown hair, no discernible style. Middle aged. A few too many donuts around his middle, though not enough to indicate anything more than a bad habit. At least, Tate told himself, it was nothing a good New Year's resolution couldn't fix.

The subject glanced around. Getting the lay of the land. He turned to a woman as she slid onto the stool beside him. Red dress, blonde hair. A convention attendee, according to the badge hung around her neck. She flashed a white smile—dental health conference.

They were forty miles outside Last Chance County, where

no one knew the subject at hand. Not well enough to know he worked in management at the phone company. Or that he had a wife who'd hired Tate to find out whether her husband's night meetings were, in fact, him cheating on her.

The subject bought the red dress woman a drink. She laughed, though she was completely sober. The subject was into his fourth drink. If he got his keys and decided to head home, Tate might be tempted to intervene.

Most people would call the cops and report a drunk driver, or the bartender would take his keys and request that he call for a ride. The police department in Last Chance County had set up a text line, so folks could anonymously report the things they saw. Tate never used it. Probably never would, since he preferred a more *hands-on* approach.

Red dress was giving his subject the brush off. Too bad she couldn't see the potential there, because Tate would've been able to snap a couple of images, and then send his report to the wife.

Along with an invoice.

Tate got a couple of pictures, though it was plain to see, even from the cell images he took, that as hard as the subject tried, she just wasn't taking the bait.

Better luck with the next one, buddy.

Tate sighed. He sipped at his drink and watched the subject glance around, looking for someone else to try his lines on.

His phone screen flashed. It started to vibrate across the tabletop and a name illuminated on the screen. *Claire.*

Double sigh. He almost didn't answer it. "Hudson."

"I didn't think you'd pick up." Her breath crackled against the phone's microphone. But it wasn't Claire, it was her sixteen-year-old.

His body tensed in reaction to the tone of her voice. All thought of his subject was dismissed from his mind as he stood. "What's going on?" Tate pulled out his wallet, tucked a folded twenty under the glass, and headed for the lobby. He pushed outside. "Lex, talk to me."

She spoke again as he strode out to the parking lot. "It's mom. She won't wake up." Her voice tremored. "He hit her pretty hard this time."

Bile rose in his throat. "Call an ambulance."

"No. She said—"

"I don't care what she said." Tate hauled the driver's door open so hard he nearly pulled the thing off the hinges. "You know what? Forget it. I'll call Dean. Maybe he's close."

"He's on his way."

"Your first call?"

"Yes."

"Because your mom has the medic on speed dial?"

"Don't be like that." She sounded like an adult and a child, all at once.

He wanted to ream her for making excuses for her mom, as he would any of his peers who'd made a tough choice. But he didn't. She might look and sound like an adult, but Elexa was still a kid. A smart kid, independent and capable. Good grades. Held down a steady job at the ice cream shop. She might've been his kid in another life.

Tate hit the gas and tore out of the parking lot. "Where's your stepdad now?" His phone's Bluetooth connected to the car stereo, and he tossed the cell in the cup holder.

Her voice came through the car speakers. "He was gone before I got home."

"So you don't know for sure it was him who did this."

"Pretty good assumption. He was coming home for dinner." Elexa let out a long breath. "She was excited. They were gonna talk."

Elexa's stepfather, her mother's third husband, only talked one way. And it wasn't with words.

"A car just pulled up outside," she said. "That you?"

"Probably Dean but confirm that for me. I was working at the Sunrise."

She whimpered. "It'll take you an hour to get here!"

"No, it won't." He heard the doorbell ring. "Go answer it. Don't hang up."

"Okay."

He heard her talking, and then Dean came on the phone. "Tate?"

"What's the situation?"

"One sec." Dean spoke again, but Tate couldn't make out what the former SEAL said. Elexa answered a series of questions, then he came back on. "We're going to the hospital."

"Serious head injury?"

Instead of answering the question Dean said, "That's a good idea. I'm sure Lex will appreciate you meeting us there."

Tate pressed his lips together. He needed an answer, but if Dean didn't want to say while Elexa was listening…well. That was an answer in itself, was it not?

"Put her back on the phone."

A second later she said, "Tate?"

"I'm here." He said, "Text me when you get to the hospital. I'll meet you there. But you need to drive separate, and pack an overnight bag. Both for you and your mom. Can you do that for me?"

"Yes." She sounded relieved. "I've been halfway packed for weeks."

"Since volleyball camp." The teen had been gone four days over Spring Break.

"That isn't why." She paused. "I've gotta go. Dean is taking mom."

"See you soon."

He hung up and held tight to the wheel. So tight he wouldn't be surprised if it was warped when he let go. Tate had been Claire's first husband. After they divorced, she'd gone and gotten pregnant a few weeks later. Elexa's father hadn't married her, but up and left when he found out about the baby. All those years ago.

Claire and Tate had had a two year marriage and had agreed to disband it before things got too out of control. He'd been volatile back then. Fresh out of his short career with the FBI. At first, it had been a draw for her, his wild ways. Then she'd tried to "settle him down." That had been the beginning of the end.

Tate reached the gas station at the edge of town. He pulled over and loaded the app that would find Elexa's phone—something she'd willingly given him access to. She'd actually asked him to set it up. Just in case.

Maybe for some people, their relationship—whatever you might call them—might be weird. A forty-five year old man couldn't be friends with a sixteen-year-old girl. But he cared about her mom, and she knew she could always count on him if either of them needed help.

The little dot said she was on her way to the hospital.

He sent her a text to meet him in the lobby. When he walked in twenty minutes later, she said, "I kind of thought you'd have brought cops with you."

"Your mom decide to start filing police reports now?"

Claire never had before. She always said she could "handle" it, despite the fact he could see the pain she was in. Physical and emotional. Elexa didn't answer. "She should. If she wakes up."

"Come on. She's gonna wake up."

"You didn't see her."

"Dean knows what he's doing, and so do the doctors." He had to hold himself in check. "Besides, if Rob disappears later, I don't want my name involved in a police report. You know the first place they look at is the spouse, right? Second place is the ex who's still in her life."

Elexa rolled her eyes, but he didn't miss the edge of fear.

"She'll be okay."

"You don't know that," she said. "But thanks."

"Let's go find out."

She had to speak with the hospital staff, and fill out all the forms for her mom. While she did that, he made a call.

Tate wrapped up his call when she started towards him. "Thanks." He stowed his phone back in his jeans pocket. "All good?"

Given her look, he figured that was a "no."

She said, "They did an x-ray. She's still unconscious. The doctor said there's a fracture in her skull. She might not wake up for a couple of days, maybe longer." Tears gathered in her eyes.

Tate lifted a hand and squeezed the back of her neck, his forearm resting on her shoulder. She grasped it. Holding on for dear life while she got a handle on her emotions.

"I told her that she should leave as well."

He nodded. She'd been planning her exit for months, wanting her mom to go with her. Tate had encouraged them both to start a new life. He didn't know if Claire was just scared, or if she was so under Rob's thumb that she felt like she couldn't leave. Whatever it was, he was prepared to help Elexa get her mom to work through those feelings. Otherwise, neither of them would ever get free.

"I know you did." He let go of her neck. "Maybe this will convince her."

Elexa shrugged. "They said nothing's gonna change tonight. Maybe not for a couple of days. They said there's a spot where I can sleep, though. Cause I don't really wanna go home."

"You packed bags for you and your mom like I told you to, right?"

"I thought that was just for the hospital."

"You wanna sleep on an uncomfortable hospital chair, night after night, with the lights on and people everywhere?" The alternative was that she go back to the house, where she would be alone with her stepdad—after putting her mom in the hospital.

Fear washed over her face. "Can I stay with you?"

He shook his head. "That's not a good idea."

"Whatever. Everyone already thinks you're my dad."

He nearly choked. "What?"

Elexa made a face. "Literally *everyone* I know thinks you're my dad."

"And, of course, you told them that I'm not?"

"No way. Let them think whatever." She brushed at her hair, and he realized how exhausted she looked. "It makes me more mysterious. The town's super-hot, rogue private investigator might be my dad…or he might not be." She lifted her hands and wiggled her fingers. "Nobody knows."

"Tune in at ten for more fictional adventures."

She almost laughed.

"I'm not even touching that super-hot thing."

"You're old, but it can't be denied. All my friends think so, but I told them to quit talking about you like that because that's just gross. But even mom said it. Though, I think she still hates you for the umbrella thing."

Yet another thing he wasn't going to touch. "Let's go. Tomorrow you can get an update before school." Before she could move, he said, "I do need to know if he's ever touched you. Or hurt you in any way."

"Because you'll kill him?"

He would certainly want to.

"He's never even touched me. I already want you to kill him. That would just give me even more reason." She studied him. "I have money saved up."

He gently shoved at her shoulder. "Come on."

"Where are we going?"

"A safe place for you to stay."

Tate drove, and she followed him in her car across town. Set up as a shelter, Hope Mansion now took any single woman—children, too—on an application basis. They also had empty rooms for occasions like this. The owner, Maggie, was going to meet them at the door.

Anytime Tate called, day or night, Maggie picked up.

He got Elexa's bag off the backseat. "Maggie said she was going to make tea for you."

As they approached the side door, it flew open. A woman ran out. Tate caught the flash of a police shield on her belt right before she slammed into him.

"Easy." He grasped her biceps to keep her from knocking him over, and the bag banged against the side of his leg.

She looked up at him. Those blue eyes, blonde hair. Flustered. Breathy, as though they'd just kissed.

"Savannah." He sounded like they'd just kissed.

"Seriously, Dad? You're gonna flirt with a woman right now?"

Any other time it might have been funny.

With literally *any* other woman.

2

Savannah pulled up outside the victim's office thirty minutes later. She shut off the police lights and siren before also turning off the engine. The black and white car she parked behind was dark, but the gentrified office building was lit up and the officer was at the front door.

Don't think about Tate.

She climbed out and shoved the door closed. It slammed. Savannah pulled on her jacket like there was nothing wrong. Nothing but frigid spring night air, and the fact she hadn't seen the beach in far too long—or even a warm day, for that matter.

Her brand new partner, Mia Tathers—formerly ATF— winced. "What's so wrong that you gotta take it out on your car?"

Savannah said, "Sorry. What've we got?"

Mia didn't didn't begin to explain the situation at hand—a dead man. "He's not getting any deader." Mia folded her arms over her wool coat, and Savannah noted she'd curled her hair. "So explain."

Savannah looked down at her partner's red skinny pants, and her eyes continued down to the white-soled sneakers on her feet. "Were you on a date?"

"I changed my shoes. And you're avoiding the subject," Mia said. "But while we're talking about it, Conroy wasn't super happy he didn't get to the 'walking me to my front door' portion because of the murder I had to come investigate."

"So I hope you reminded him it was his idea you become his new lieutenant, and my partner. Which means, as the chief of police, he can't really complain, right?"

The whole situation was hilarious. Mostly because her boss had been uptight for so long. She was enjoying his game being thrown by his newfound emotions. The former chief had passed away a few weeks ago after an uncharacteristically long, drawn-out battle with pancreatic cancer. The interplay between Lieutenant Mia Tathers and new Chief Conroy Barnes was like watching a soap opera happen at work.

There was a police department poll circulating the office to correctly guess what month they would get married, even though Conroy hadn't asked her yet.

Savannah had her money on July.

Mia said, "He's uh…working on dealing with the fact me being his lieutenant means I actually have to be a cop sometimes."

Savannah grinned. "I'm sure."

Mia was taller than her, lanky like a volleyball player. Savannah felt like the sidekick—five-four and curvy. Older, by nearly ten years. On top of it all, her new partner was also a former ATF agent. Talk about an inferiority complex. A fed? Savannah loved her job, and she loved Mia. But if you took away either of those, she'd be back with the town shrink and something new to talk through.

Mia had also grown up here in Last Chance County, so people all over town knew her. They knew her story; how Conroy had dated her older sister—before she'd been killed in an automobile accident. Mia had forgiven Conroy for what she'd believed was his responsibility in the tragedy, while he'd worked to keep her safe from a crazy guy with a career terrorizing people.

Savannah, on the other hand, had been here two years, which meant she was about twenty-eight years from officially qualifying as someone "from here." She was a newbie in town, and she would always be the detective not born and raised here. An outsider.

Savannah said, "How's your hearing?"

"Some ringing on occasion, but generally good."

A dangerous man had fired a weapon next to Mia's ear only a few weeks ago. She was recovering better than the doctors expected from having a perforated ear drum. Still, she would never be back to full capacity. Mia had to wear ear protection to safely fire her weapon, which meant that in the event she had to draw— and fire—her gun on the job, she would be stuck with permanent hearing loss. One that would confine her to a desk indefinitely.

Savannah had already had the hard conversation with Conroy about Mia's hearing. She'd tried to convince him it wasn't worth it for Mia to take that risk. One incident was all it would take for her partner to wind up disqualified from field work. But, and for good reason, he wanted her to make the choice herself.

In the meantime, that meant Savannah had to report directly to him, regularly, on how Mia was doing. Loud noises were going to be a problem. Gunshots. Explosions. Maybe they'd had their fair share of those before Mia's injury—when that dangerous man had targeted her—and things were back to normal now.

Whatever that meant.

Though, she figured it at least meant no more Tate Hudson.

"What?"

Savannah said, "We should get inside."

"Yeah, no. Spill."

She decided to rip off the bandage. "I ran into Tate on my

way out of my place—where I live." She turned to head for the scene. "That's all. No biggie."

"If you're using the word 'biggie,' then it *is* a big deal." Mia snagged her arm. "What?"

Savannah sighed. "I literally ran into him. As in, slammed right into him. My face hit his chest, and he grabbed my arms."

Mia's dark brows angled together. "He grabbed you?"

"Not like that." They'd had a moment. As hokey as that sounded, she'd stared up into his eyes and just paused. "He was nice about it. There was this girl with him."

"A girl?"

"She called him 'dad.'"

"*No.*"

"So now you know, let's go. End of story. Time to work."

Tate Hudson, private investigator and one time FBI agent, had a kid. A full grown, beautiful teenage daughter.

Savannah made a beeline down the sidewalk at a strip mall in the low-rent end of town. The dead guy was a CPA, Kenny Aggerton. Well known in town as the owner of two businesses. One legitimate, and the other one that resided…under the table. Where he kept a second safe, literally, in the floor beneath the rug under his desk.

They checked with the officer stationed on the door. "You found him?"

Donaldson nodded. He was young, but he'd proven himself recently when he'd helped save Mia and Conroy's lives and detain the dangerous man. He said, "Call came in from a neighbor who works at the clothing store next door. She heard shouts and called it in. By the time we got here, the guy was DOA."

Mia said, "You ID'd him?"

"Photos on the walls, name on the door," Donaldson said. "It's him."

Mia nodded.

"Checked his pulse, but it was pretty clear he's dead. I didn't touch anything else."

The reception area was clear. Single desk with a computer and phone, a faux leather couch and coffee table. Side table and coffee pot. Water dispenser. "Donaldson, get the receptionist down here."

He said, "Copy that."

Savannah stepped into the office and saw what he meant about it being "pretty clear" he was dead. Her partner wasn't going to like this. "Mia, you—"

She nearly slammed into Savannah's back, though not like Savannah had slammed into Tate. "Good gravy."

"Yeah." It was gruesome. Just what Savannah needed to get Tate out of her head.

Sure, they'd worked together a bit during the time Conroy had been protecting Mia. They'd brought down Ed Summers, a local guy who'd been selling drugs—and other things—for years. She still didn't understand everything Tate had going on. It had been clear he worked according to his own rules.

Still, they'd finally gotten enough evidence to topple the empire, which then created a power vacuum in town among the criminal element. They weren't a big town, but big enough; the highway connected them between two major cities. Ed Summers had controlled what went through town, charging taxes on things transported across the state.

"Kenny Aggerton."

"Yeah." Savannah said, "Ed Summers's uncle, via his mother." She pulled paper booties over her shoes and moved to the body, donning rubber gloves. "Got your camera?"

"In the car."

"Once we have the preliminary look done, we'll get down to processing the scene." It was going to be a long night. She crouched. "Multiple stab wounds."

Up close and personal. Someone was angry.

Aggerton had been holding leverage over his nephew, Ed Summers. Now that Summers was in jail, pending his court case, could be he'd taken out his anger on his uncle for the man's part in the charges against him. Or he'd ordered it done.

He still had loyal friends on the outside. Even after a lot of his crew were swept up with him.

Then again, Aggerton wasn't exactly an upstanding guy.

Stabbings didn't just happen. Sure some people carried knives with them everywhere, especially in more rural communities like this. But it wasn't usually the top choice in weapons for a premeditated murder.

"Look around for a knife. If it's not here, we can widen the search to the surrounding area. Maybe the killer dumped it on the way out."

Trash cans. Streets and side roads. Storm drains. If they knew which direction the killer had fled, they'd be able to narrow the search.

"Okay." Mia's voice sounded funny.

Savannah glanced at her partner. "If you're gonna hurl, you should do it outside or you'll contaminate the evidence."

Mia glanced around, her face pale. "He certainly enjoyed staring at images of himself. This wall is covered with photos of him with all kinds of people." She wandered to one framed photo. "That's the governor."

The victim was a power player in town. A guy with known criminal ties, who made money through those connections. She stared at his body. Then she stood and looked around.

Who had he angered, and did it have to do with the case being brought up against Summers?

She turned around slowly, taking in the room as a whole. "The safe is undisturbed."

Because the desk was still where it always stood. Something Savannah knew from the last time she was here. It had been a few weeks ago since they'd served a warrant and removed evidence from the safe under the rug. Part of their case against Ed Summers—removing account books from Kenny Aggerton's office

On the wall, behind a painting, was another safe. The one his clients saw him use on occasion. That was also undisturbed.

She muttered, "He wasn't looking for something."

File cabinets were shut; the key turned so it was locked. Computer intact, switched off. His phone lay on the desk.

"But they argued, and he or she pulled a knife and killed him." Savannah pressed her lips together while she thought about it. "Means they brought it with them. Unless they grabbed a letter opener, or something else, and used that. But when you stab someone multiple times, things get slippery. Your hand slides down the weapon, and you usually end up cutting yourself and leaving DNA on it. Or prints if you don't get cut yourself."

Mia said, "So we really need to find it."

Savannah glanced at her partner. "I'll make notes if you get the bag."

Mia nodded, leaving Savannah alone with the dead guy. Too bad all she could think about was Tate. Last in a long line of things, and people, she didn't want to remember. Or dwell on.

Working cases was the only thing that made sense. Pieces of a puzzle she dug up that fit only one way. Solving crime was what she had been born and raised to do. *Thanks, Dad.* Not much she could be grateful to her father for, but that was something at least. After her mom had died, he'd done his best. She hoped he had, at least. The thought gave her only a sliver of comfort.

Her thoughts drifted again, to a different man.

Seriously, Dad?

The girl had spoken to Tate with obvious affection. He could have a family he'd never told her about, though she knew he wasn't married. Why did she care, anyway? They had sparks, but it wasn't a thing.

She was a cop. Just a cop, with no room in her life for complicated anything.

A man was dead, and she would figure out who did it. Then

she would arrest them. After that, there would be another case. Another victim, with their own suspect. That was about all the complicated she could handle. Adding in emotions and drama because she found out Tate had a daughter and he hadn't even—

"Whoa." Mia stepped into view in front of her.

Savannah realized she hadn't even noticed her friend and new partner had walked back in. "Just checking your reaction, regardless of circumstances. You passed."

Mia shook her head, smiling. "Yeah, sure."

Not fooled, but that was no surprise. Savannah needed to get her head together. If Tate wanted a relationship, or even had feelings for her, then he'd have said something. He hadn't, and that was fine. Because Savannah needed procedure. She needed investigation.

What she did not need, was more secrets.

Officer Donaldson appeared in the doorway.

"Security cameras?"

"Oh. I'll look." He came back a couple of minutes later. "One over the front door, another at the back."

"Call Ted. Have him come down here and find us the footage." Their tech guy was a genius, and Savannah had about as much patience for technology as she did for the US Postal Service.

"Copy that." Donaldson disappeared.

Two hours later, her hunch paid off. Ted called out to her from over at the receptionist desk. The woman had logged him into the computer, then she'd been escorted off the premises by the officer who had driven her here so she could answer some questions.

Savannah strode over from the CPA's office. "What is it?"

Ted shoved back the thick, dark hair that had fallen over his forehead. "I've got something you're gonna need to see to believe."

3

———————

Tate let himself into his office just before eight in the morning, set his mug of coffee on the desk, and fired up his computer. He rolled the chair in close, and it rolled back to settle into the grooves he'd made in the plastic chair mat.

His phone buzzed with a text.

Tate pulled it from his front jeans pocket. Elexa.

No change.

He sent a text back to ask if she was going to school. When she answered yes, he told her to be careful in case her stepdad showed up.

K.

Tate shook his head, his fingers swiping across the screen.

I'll swing by the hospital at lunch.

No matter that the doctors wouldn't tell him anything without consent, he'd ask anyway. Or at least make sure her husband wasn't hanging around. Soon as she woke up, he was going to ask Claire to file a police report. It was time for her to be done trying to domesticate that guy. Rob Gaynes was nothing but an animal, and she didn't need him in her life—no matter how civilized he acted in public. The truth was evidenced in what he'd done to her.

Tate checked his email and found a couple of new messages from people who'd filled out the contact form on his website. He sent the standard reply to set up an initial meeting on one, and answered the question the other had. Then he downloaded the images he'd gotten of the suspect from last night.

While that was processing, he got more coffee. He sipped and stared out the window.

Fine.

He was going to do it. Even though he knew he shouldn't, and even though every other time he'd done it, there had been basically no results.

Tate opened up his browser and typed *Savannah Wilcox.* Nothing else. He knew exactly that much about her and her life before she'd come here. Zip. Nada.

He scrolled down.

A museum curator in Boston was opening up a brand new exhibit.

In Los Angeles, a high school teacher had just been convicted of embezzling funds raised for the school.

Neither even looked remotely like the Savannah Wilcox he knew.

He typed *Savannah Wilcox, Police Detective.*

Still nothing. Just a local news article about taking down Ed Summers.

He sat back in his chair and blew out a breath. He'd already cashed in the favor owed to him by the woman he knew at the DMV from his last job. He couldn't call in another favor. Then he'd owe her in return, and he didn't like to work that way.

A chime sounded through his computer speakers. The window for his doorbell camera popped up on his monitor. He saw who it was and felt his eyebrows rise.

Tate clicked the button on his desk to admit her through the front door. Usually he got up and met the person in his reception area. This time he yelled, "In the back!" and didn't even stand.

He sipped his coffee so Savannah Wilcox—in the flesh—couldn't see his reaction when she strolled in. Acted nonchalant, like he hadn't just searched her name in his browser. After she'd been standing there a couple of seconds, he lowered his mug.

"To what do I owe this pleasure?"

Last time he'd seen her she'd slammed right into him. The feel of her, and staring down into her blue eyes, was something Tate couldn't let himself get too distracted over, or he'd be off his game. Nor could he let his gaze snag on her red trench coat, or the way her blonde hair spilled over her shoulders. He'd felt it between his fingers. It was as soft as it looked.

She jerked her thumb back over her shoulder. "You need a secretary, you know."

"I had an assistant. She got pregnant and quit."

Savannah said, "When? I've lived here two years. You haven't had a secretary in all that time."

"The 'when' was…" He counted his nephew's age. "Six years ago. She moved away with her husband. They live in Denver now."

She shivered.

"Don't like Denver?"

"There's even more snow there than there is here." She shivered again.

"Coffee's hot." He motioned to the row of low cupboards alongside the opposite wall. At the end was a counter-height refrigerator. "Or there are cold drinks."

She shook her head. "I'm not staying that long."

"Business?"

"You could say that." She tugged over one of his club chairs and sat. "Seriously, though. You need a receptionist."

She was stalling. He figured she didn't want to talk about whatever it was, so she was psyching herself up for what she thought would be a hard conversation.

He was a nice guy, so he let her do it. "I was going to ask

Mia Tathers to be my new receptionist, but Conroy beat me to it by hiring her as your lieutenant."

She blinked. "No way."

He shrugged one shoulder. "Not like she'll be a cop for long, given her hearing issues." She started to argue, but he cut her off and motioned to his reception area. "Plus, having a trained federal agent out there fending off angry customers?" He let that hang.

"You think Conroy will let her work here?"

"I think your new partner can decide that stuff for herself." He said, "Besides, it's not like I'm a threat. You really think I'd have a shot to come between them?"

Savannah studied him, as though trying to figure out whether he wanted that shot. He'd been trying to put her at ease. Could be he'd failed at that. She should know by now that being around him meant she needed to always be on her toes. Always.

Too bad for him, Savannah only allowed herself to get emotionally involved with people who were safe. Conroy, her boss, for example. She cared about him and they respected each other, maybe even considered each other friends. But only at work.

Mia was another—someone Savannah knew understood the job. Added bonus, Mia was preoccupied with Conroy so it didn't put pressure on them to hang out all the time.

Despite how Tate was drawn to her and the obvious sparks between them, he knew she'd never consider letting him into her circle. Tate was definitely not safe.

He took a sip of coffee. "So what did you want?"

"Oh." She pulled out her phone. "Just a few questions." She scrolled, probably longer than was necessary.

He fought the pull of a smile on his lips.

She looked up. "Can you tell me where you were, last night, between four and approximately seven-thirty?"

For a second he'd thought this was going to be about Elexa.

Four and seven-thirty? He considered where he'd been—taking a shower and catching up on this week's episode of his favorite TV show—before he realized what this was. "You need my alibi." He leaned forward in his chair. "For what?"

Someone had to be dead. There was no other reason she would be on the case unless it was a major crime. Tate knew only one thing about her past. Wherever she had lived, Savannah had been a detective.

But then, why could he find nothing about her?

"Just tell me where you were."

"At home." He pointed a finger at the ceiling. "Which is upstairs. Taking a shower."

She frowned. "Can anyone corroborate this?"

"Well, I don't have a cat. So…no."

She said, "Is there an alternative?" Not happy.

He couldn't fix that for her. They had very different jobs and lives. She followed the rules and enforced the law. Tate worked for people, not the rule of law. "It's been a long week. I was between things to do, so I decided to clean up and rest."

"And later that evening, when I saw you outside my place?" She kept a straight face, as though she thought nothing of it.

"With Elexa?"

"Is that her name?"

He said, "You don't know about her?" When she shrugged, he continued, "She's my ex-wife's daughter."

"Oh."

"Between the shower and bumping into you, I was working."

She was playing it close to the vest. He decided to do the same. Tate was pretty impressed, even if he knew she was only doing it for the sake of protecting herself. He wanted her to take a chance on him. But he knew if she did, he'd only wind up hurting her, which was the last thing he wanted to do. So, really, what was the point?

"Who is dead?"

Savannah blinked. She swiped across her phone and then turned the screen so he could see. "How about you explain this first?"

A black and white image depicted a brick wall and pavement. Savannah pressed 'play.' Emergency Exit. The door opened, and a man pushed his way out. Dark jeans and a black hoodie. It was pulled up over the man's head, obscuring the face in darkness. He turned and Tate saw the emblem on the back.

He knew who it was.

"That's your sweater," she said. "On you. Coming out of the office of Kenny Aggerton last night. Around the time he was murdered."

"Ed Summers's uncle?" That guy had terrorized good people in this town.

"Yeah." She shot him a pointed look. "Your friend, Ed Summers."

Yeah, he'd kind of made it seem like that. "To the extent it served my purpose. Which wasn't much."

"Didn't seem like that. Not considering I saw you with him multiple times."

"A few weeks ago," he reminded her. "When he was making Conroy and Mia's lives a nightmare."

"So you were doing it for the good of your friends?"

Tate said, "My work is my business. I don't ask about your cases."

"Ah, so it was a job." She swiped the screen of her phone.

"Yeah, jot that down."

"And you were working last night, when you visited Aggerton right before he died?"

Tate put his hands on the back of his neck, elbows out to the sides. He wasn't about to repeat himself. And he hadn't lied.

"How'd he die?" If she told him, he might be able to use the information to prove it wasn't him.

"Answer the question." She stared him down like this was a contest. "Was your contact with Aggerton case related?"

"You're assuming that was me." He motioned to the phone with one elbow. Her gaze strayed to his biceps, the outline of his muscle tight against the T-shirt he wore.

She blew out a breath and looked at the ceiling.

"My sweater was stolen from the backseat of my car recently." He nearly smiled, mentally filing away that little glance at his arms. Watching her shift off her game was one of his favorite past times, more so when he was the one poking her off balance.

Tate wasn't going to lie to her. "Aggerton and I have had dealings before."

"So you knew him?"

"In a business sense. It was mostly related to cases he had me work. Clients he wanted investigating, and information he wanted about people who worked for him. Or prospective employees."

"Anyone you can think of who might want him dead?"

"Like me?" Tate shrugged. "I have no idea if anyone wanted him dead. Not like we were friends. It was an agreement between two people, a contract he signed and the money he paid me. Just business."

"What about an employee, former or prospective. Someone you dug up information on who might want payback?"

He stood. "I can check my records. Let you know if I find anything. But the work I did for him was just basic background checks...looking for criminal history, pulling their credit."

"That's it? We're done here, and you're dismissing me."

"I didn't kill Aggerton."

Intellectually, he knew she wasn't accusing him, and it wasn't personal. That guy in the surveillance footage had been wearing his sweater, or at least owned the same one. Savannah was just doing her job. The one where she showed up only because of work, and only to fish for information.

"I'm glad to hear it." Her phone buzzed. She glanced down, and then paled.

"Something wrong?"

"No." She cleared her throat. "No. I have to go." She practically sprinted for the door.

4

———

Savannah entered the police station. "Where's the chief?"

The receptionist, Kaylee, looked up from her novel. "Out to lunch with Mia. You coming in?" When she nodded, Kaylee hit the buzzer.

Savannah headed for her desk, where she dumped her things and sat. It was fine. Everything was fine.

The adrenaline that had coursed through her body when she saw that notification on her phone was finally dissipating. The Google alert she'd set up—specific phrases pertinent to her past—had sent her a notification by email. It was letting her know someone had posted something that used those phrases. Usually it was just random stuff that didn't actually relate specifically to her past. False alarms.

For the first time in two years, the Google alert actually sent her something useful.

Savannah bit the inside of her lips together. *Everything is fine.*

"You okay?"

Savannah yelped and spun in her chair. It was just Kaylee. "I'm fine. Thanks." Her voice sounded breathy.

The receptionist didn't believe her. Not one bit. "Girl…"

Savannah cut her off. "I have a lot of work to do."

Kaylee waltzed back to her counter stool, to the novel she had flipped face down. Beside her book were the remains of a chicken wrap.

Across the other side of the room, Sergeant Basuto sat at his computer. If he was working, it was basically impossible to disturb him. The whole place would have to be on fire. Or under attack.

Like it had been just weeks ago.

She rubbed at her breastbone with the heel of her hand. Not a good memory, being hit point blank and thrown to the ground in the bathroom off the back hallway. A gunshot. The bruise had finally gone away two weeks ago.

Mia, on the other hand, had been bitten by a poisoned dog, terrorized in the middle of the night, kidnapped, and then to cap it all off, suffered hearing loss from a close range gunshot. Savannah figured Mia had at least earned a lunch break with her boyfriend, who happened to be their boss. She'd seen and heard about worse impropriety during her time as a cop than Mia and Conroy's eating together.

Last Chance was a small town where everyone just *had* to know every little bit of detail about every little thing. Eventually she would get used to those small town ways of doing things.

Eventually.

She'd *have* to get used to it. There was no chance of going home, and she had no interest in leaving here only to settle somewhere else. Starting her life all over again. For the second time.

Her mother had passed years ago. Her father...well, he didn't even warrant another thought. It wasn't like she would be making contact with him.

Last Chance County was her home now. It would be forever —or until her safe place crumbled into dust and she had to run again.

Her thoughts strayed back to her Google Alert and the news

it brought. Kind of like a rubber band stretched so far there was nothing it could do but snap back.

The district attorney in New Orleans had been killed. Gunned down in the street outside a restaurant. A tragedy. A senseless, meaningless murder.

Except that she knew the reason. That was why she'd driven here to the office—because she had a pile of cases to work. She couldn't access any information from her work computer. Not without someone noting it. Same for phone calls made from her work cell. If she went home, she would be tempted to drown in all the gory news and her mental state would go down like the DA did. Never to get back up again.

Just work, don't think about it.

Savannah wasn't in witness protection, but the way she lived wasn't far from that life. And now the one person who knew everything she'd been before, and everything that had happened to her, was dead.

Murdered.

Not tortured for information. Just gunned down and killed.

"You seriously don't look all right."

Kaylee's voice sailed over to her from where she was sitting. Savannah kept her head down and gritted her teeth, "I'm fine, Kaylee."

"Detective."

She looked up at the man who stood in front of her. "What do you want, Ted?"

The younger man, barely mid-twenties, stood by her desk. He was their resident technological expert. Dark hair, shaved close on one side and hung like a curtain over his right eye. He flicked his head so it swung behind his ear, but immediately fell back where it had been before. "You should apologize to Kaylee. That wasn't nice."

Savannah wanted to say something about his sensibilities. She bit those words back.

Frustration and fear weren't fuel for taking her powerlessness out on others. Her father had done that. And she'd sworn to herself. *Sworn.* She would never do that; she would never become him.

Savannah shut her eyes, took a few long breaths and tried to quickly process the tragic death of someone she knew and cared about.

"Did something happen?"

She opened her eyes and looked at him. The kid might dress and act like no one should get close, but Savannah knew something about pain that resided under the surface. About not letting people get close. Self-preservation.

"If it did—" She glanced at Kaylee. "—that wouldn't be an excuse to take out my bad mood on you." She looked back at Ted. "Either of you."

"Thanks, hon." Kaylee gave her a small smile and then put away her book, lunch break over.

"Don't let me be a jerk, Kay."

She didn't look over. "Don't call me 'Kay'."

"Yes, ma'am." Savannah smiled.

Ted gave her a tiny nod.

"Whatcha need, Ted?"

He slid into Mia's seat behind the desk that faced Savannah's. It had been unoccupied until a few weeks ago.

"Tired of solitary?"

He always sat there when he had something she needed to go over with him. Or when he was bored of sitting alone in his closet-sized office.

Ted tossed a flash drive over to her.

She inserted it in the USB port. "What am I looking at?"

"The contents of Kenny Aggerton's files, photos, web search history, and video library."

The way he'd said that was telling. She glanced at him. "Yikes?"

"Mega yikes."

She nodded. No one would want to sit by themselves after

watching questionable footage. She also would've sought out a colleague or friend.

"Jess isn't on today?"

The skin around his eyes shifted. It was an interesting tell, usually reserved for when he was irritated. Officer Ridgeman had recently lost her grandfather, the former chief. But that wasn't what this was about. There was something he wasn't saying.

They were both the same age and single. They worked together, but Savannah had thought that maybe they should expand their relationship a bit. Not that she would meddle in their love lives. That would be weird. But she could see them together. That shouldn't be a problem, since the chief was dating his lieutenant.

So, what was bothering Ted?

Savannah decided to put him out of his misery. "You should play poker. Or get into undercover work." She interlocked her fingers, elbows to the desk. "Or undercover poker."

He flicked his hair back with his hand this time. It didn't stay. "Sure. In all my free time."

"Recommendations on where to start with all this?" she asked. "Aside from just searching 'Tate Hudson' and going from there."

He almost smiled. She could see he wanted to. He said, "Not much in there about Tate, if anything. There is, however, a file I labeled 'hate mail' which is exactly what it sounds like."

"Thank you."

"You really think Tate is the one who did this?"

Savannah shrugged. "Not really." Before she could jump too far too fast, she stopped and thought about what she wanted to say. "It's his sweater in the surveillance. Whoever it is, they were there around the time of the murder. Given we can't see their face, it really could be someone else. Someone with the same sweater and the same build."

Ted made a face.

"Yeah."

The fact was, Tate had been in the house with Ed Summers when she'd shown up to ask about a suspect—a very dangerous killer who'd come after Mia. Seeing him, of all people, walk out onto that porch with a known local criminal, a man they were trying to take down, had made quite the impression. And not a good one. She just couldn't forget that. The sudden rush of surprise. Feeling like he'd duped them all, and she'd fallen for it. Suckered in because of her feelings for him.

No. Whatever Tate had done, she was going to find the evidence. If he deserved prison, then she would do her job. It was that simple.

Ted sat quietly. "There's more on Aggerton."

"Yeah?"

He nodded. "Poison in the whiskey bottle."

"He was stabbed."

"Aggerton was also being poisoned."

She felt her eyebrows rise. "We know that already?" She hadn't heard that they'd gotten any of the lab results back.

"I figured it out the moment I smelled it, though the lab will confirm. Someone put poison in his drink, just a small amount. Probably figured he would ingest it slowly, get sick, and then die."

"Wow. The smell?"

He shrugged.

"You've smelled poison before?"

"Enough to recognize it under the regular whiskey musk. Don't even know why I checked it, except that we were bagging everything for fingerprints. One of those glass containers, with the fancy stopper you know?"

She nodded.

"I figured I'd get a whiff of what the good stuff smells like." He started to smile, then his eyes flared. "Don't tell Dean about the whiskey. And *don't* tell him about the poison."

"Okay." She wasn't sure which he seemed to think was worse. "It didn't affect you, right?"

"No." He coughed. "No way. Tell Dean that, too."

Sure, since he didn't even know about the whiskey or the poison to begin with, she should also tell Ted's brother he wasn't affected by either. She looked at him cross eyed. That made perfect sense. His brother Dean was a former Navy SEAL and the unofficial local emergency medical tech. She'd gathered that he was overprotective of his younger sibling, but it sure seemed like this was more than that.

Alcohol and poison. Why did the two things immediately raise red flags with Ted and why did he want to keep it from Dean?

Savannah reined her thoughts back to the case. "Poison *and* a stabbing? What, was it taking too long?"

"That, or he had multiple people after him."

"At least two," she said. "One who tries to slowly poison him, the other who, in a rage, stabs him multiple times."

"Why a rage?" Ted tipped his head to the side.

"A gun can kill a person easy enough," she said. "You bring one to the meeting and pull the trigger. Bang, they're dead. It's done. With a knife you've got to know what you're doing, or it's just a hand, stabbing at them over and over and—"

Ted swallowed. "I get it."

Savannah shrugged one shoulder. "People who want maximum carnage in order to get maximum satisfaction out of it? Aside from the obvious allure of an explosion, which is hard if you know nothing about bombs, a knife really is the best choice. Especially if you're angry enough."

"Wow." He didn't exactly look impressed. More like ready to be sick.

"Guess I'll start with the hate mail."

He seemed pleased she made that choice. Savannah caught the edge of something. "You okay?"

He pushed back the chair and stood, shoving that swatch of hair back. "Yep. Gotta get back to work."

Ted headed for the hallway that led to his office and the bathroom where she'd been shot. Savannah shuddered in her chair. She'd been wearing a vest that day but had gotten knocked unconscious from the force of the bullet slamming into her. Tate had been shot in the vest that same week, as had Conroy.

It wasn't like she was special. But, she'd thought that maybe it would gain them solidarity of some sort. Apparently not.

She still had yet to go down that hall since the shooting. She only used the front door now.

Halfway through her reading of the hate mail, Conroy and Mia headed back in. He shot her a two fingered wave, looking pretty happy with himself after their lunch date. Savannah stood up, done wading through the mire of hate mail for the time being. She grabbed her weapon in its holster from her top drawer and slid it onto her belt.

"Are we going somewhere?"

Savannah said, "You're clocking back in?"

Mia narrowed her eyes. "I texted you. You said you didn't want me to get you a sandwich to go."

"I didn't." Savannah pulled on her favorite red coat. She had a picture on her clean phone back at home. Her mother, wearing one that looked almost exactly like it. "We have work to do."

They didn't say anything during their short walk out the building and into the station parking lot. Savannah drove.

"Where are we going?"

"To talk to the wife." She typed the address onto her dash screen.

Mia looked at the GPS, then said, "No. Freelander is always backed up this time of day. We should take Benton." She canceled the directions. "I'll tell you where to go."

Savannah turned where Mia directed her, keeping her frustration to herself.

They found the house number. A two-story that looked at least three thousand square feet, even though Aggerton and his wife had no kids or pets to help fill the monstrosity.

Savannah spotted the wife. "Well, look at that."

Standing in the driveway, Aggerton's wife lifted a suitcase and shoved it into the back of a luxury SUV.

"Making a run for it, probably." Mia grasped the handle.

Savannah got out, and together they walked up Mrs. Aggerton's driveway. "Somewhere to be?"

Bernice Aggerton yelped and spun around. She wore wide-leg, pink pants, a tent-like white blouse that draped over her, and enough gold to pay Savannah's rent for six months. With four-inch platform heels, she split the difference between Savannah's height and Mia's.

"Don't got no time for no cops."

"Like I said." Savannah planted a hand on her hip. "Somewhere to be?"

"Yeah. My cruise ship." She slammed the back of the SUV closed and waved her fingers. "Laters."

5

Tate paced his office, then headed out the back door. He walked through the neighborhood, past businesses that ran alongside his and through residential streets. Long enough his leg muscles started to ache and his stomach began to rumble, though not nearly long enough for his head to quit going over and over the particulars from cases he had open. Not to mention everything he knew about Aggerton.

A school bus passed him. It wasn't the end of the day already, was it? He wore no watch—who did these days?—and he'd left his phone back on his desk, which wasn't the smartest thing he'd done that day.

The sun hid behind hazy winter clouds, keeping the air stagnant and crisp, but dry. He'd walked his way right into the afternoon.

Probably time to head back.

Circling through the neighborhood back to his office took another half hour. He passed the gym and looked inside. Plenty of people on machines. At the back, two guys sparred in the fighting ring while a crowd watched. Tate winced. They reminded him of a few vicious fights he'd seen. Not something he'd do for recreation.

He preferred lifting weights in his extra bedroom.

And walking.

He let himself in the front door, disarming the alarm system. He passed through the reception area to his desk. Two missed calls, both from Conroy. No voicemail. Nothing from Savannah. Just a text from Elexa that her mom still hadn't woken up and she was headed to Hope Mansion to write a history paper.

Tate didn't return the police chief's calls. Not yet. He didn't know how much Conroy knew about what was happening. What did the chief even want to talk about?

The private investigator who'd trained him, signing off on his hours for the licensing board, had been careful with information. He held it close, and then used it when it served his purpose. As leverage, mostly. Tate was trying to do the same with Conroy and his, "need to know."

Too bad Tate could find nothing on Savannah. Even if he was prepared to hold it over her in the event she decided to pursue a murder charge. Which he wasn't sure he'd be able to do.

Tate snatched up the phone and made the call he should've made earlier.

"Special Agent Cullings."

Tate said, "We need to talk."

"Talk, like the time you needed another guy for your basketball league, or the time your car was totaled, and you didn't have cash to pay your deductible?"

"Neither." Tate leaned back in his chair. "More like the time you married my receptionist and took her with you to Denver."

"Uh-oh."

He said, "Making sure my nephews were born two states away so I'd have to video chat just to see them."

"You don't seem to have a problem visiting whenever the mood strikes you."

Tate had been there over to see them at Thanksgiving and Christmas, so he figured that was probably true. His sister had been the best, and only, receptionist he'd ever had. Now she was making a career out of having as many kids as possible. Considering the boys and how active they were, not going back to work was probably a good idea.

Tate said, "That's because I need to keep Millie sweet every year for when I need help with my taxes."

His brother-in-law and former partner was FBI Special Agent Eric Cullings. The guy chuckled. "You'll need more than sweet if you think I'll be able to convince her that the boys will be fine with me while she does your taxes for hours. That I'll not lose my mind before she gets done."

"I know. I'm working on saving for next year already." And he wasn't talking about his tax bill.

"I like Hawaii."

Tate said, "Keep dreaming."

"What do you want?"

"I need to talk to Hammer."

His FBI code name—The Hammer—was down to the huge fists he had, though Tate had no intention of finding out what it felt like to be on the receiving end of one of his legendary punches. He'd leave that to the guys Hammer faced in the FBI's boxing tournament.

Eric was quiet for a second, then said, "Face to face, or is a call good?"

"Either, but face to face would be better." He'd be able to see the guy's body language that way. Which meant it would be easier to gauge if he was telling the truth or lying. "Got him on surveillance, wearing my sweater, leaving a murder scene."

It sounded like Eric spit out his coffee. "He *what?*"

"Not his face. I only know it was him since he's the one who took my sweater. Probably for exactly this reason," Tate said. "Given it implicates me, and not him, in a murder. Which he probably had planned all along."

"You think he murdered someone?"

"I'm gonna ask him. I'll find out."

His brother-in-law blew out a long breath. "No. No way my undercover killed someone. I don't care who it was."

"Kenny Aggerton."

"Ed Summers's uncle? The accountant?"

"You see my point?" Tate said, "You think he's the kind of guy to do something like that?"

Eric sighed. "When I asked you to keep an eye on him, this was what I meant. So you cover him. I don't care what you've got to do, but report what you know back to me as you learn it. You cover him. No matter what, he is left alone to do his job."

"He's getting somewhere?"

Tate hadn't been read in on the operation, though he got the gist of what it was, given where the undercover had gone and the circles he showed up in now. Tate also hadn't been contracted to help, even though Eric had used him before. Which was how the FBI agent met Tate's sister in the first place.

What felt like a million years ago, they'd worked together. Before that, they'd been at Quantico together. But Tate hadn't been an agent even five years before he quit.

A year later, Eric showed up in Last Chance County with a case—and left with Tate's sister. It was a wonder they were even still friends.

Eric said, "You know I can't give you specifics of Hammer's Op. But after the Chief of Police arrested Ed Summers, we had to scramble."

Conroy didn't even know the half of what was happening in his town. He had no idea there was an undercover fed among the persons of interest files he had. Tate was the one who'd tipped off Hammer—and Eric—that Conroy was planning a raid. He'd been absent at the party where the arrests were made, and had laid low since.

It was a slippery slope, considering all he'd been part of. But if Conroy did pick him up now—as part of that ongoing case and all the pieces of the puzzle—they would have to deal with it.

"Thankfully Hammer had what he needed by then to move up the food chain."

"For real?" Tate said, "I knew he found whoever supplied Ed with the drugs. We're one step up on the food chain?"

"We?"

"You know what I mean."

Tate didn't need a recap of that same old, "I'm a fed and you're not even a cop" speech. The one Tate's sister so enjoyed. She even had her own version of it now.

Both of them thought he should have become a legit lawman. Only Millie understood why he was a private investigator now. And why that was all he'd ever be.

Eric said, "We're in the thick of it. Hammer will get what we need, and you'll keep him off Conroy's radar."

"We?"

Eric chuckled. "Touché."

Tate's cell buzzed. A text from Maggie at Hope Mansion that Elexa was all tucked in for the night. Apparently Elexa had been worried about her mother, so Maggie prayed with the teen.

"What's going on with you?"

Tate didn't want to get into the weeds of his ex-wife's poor choice in husbands and risk another lecture he'd heard before. Instead he said, "If I send you a picture can you run it?"

"Am I your secretary now?"

"You took mine, so I'm thinking yeah." Tate wasn't going to let this go.

He sat at his computer, pulled up the doorbell camera footage from when Savannah had shown up, and took a screen shot. He attached the image to an email and sent it to his brother-in-law.

Eric was quiet for a minute. Tate thought he could hear keys clicking. Then he finally said, "Any particular reason you're interested in this—ah."

"What?"

"I have to guess, she's more than just a local cop?"

"I plead the fifth."

"You know that doesn't work with me." Eric said, "Who is this girl to you?"

"She's investigating Aggerton's murder."

"No. That's not it."

"Can you just run her? Humor me. See what pops." He gritted his teeth. If he snapped at Eric, his brother-in-law would realize something was up.

Of course, nothing was up. He just wanted to know Savannah's history. There had to be a reason she was so guarded. Why she'd moved here and now lived so far under the radar he knew basically nothing about who she'd been.

Tate wouldn't be who he was if he didn't employ his unique methods to keep safe the people he cared about.

"She's hot."

Tate frowned. "Says the man married to my sister."

"And exactly your type." Like that was supposed to make his comment better.

Tate said, "Would you focus? This is important."

"Yeah?"

Eric was the first guy he'd approved of for his sister, and even that was tenuous. He wasn't going to trust the guy any further than he could prove Eric was on the same level as Millie.

Tate sighed. "Just put some feelers out. I wanna know if there's something to know."

"I'll be sure and word it exactly like that."

Tate said, "Shut up." And hung up. Two seconds later he got a text.

Love you, too.

It was followed by a series of emojis that included a kissy face, a pineapple, and a ghost. Whatever that was supposed to mean. He figured his nephews had gotten ahold of the phone somehow.

Tate packed up for the day, took his laptop upstairs, and settled in for the night. The security for his apartment above the storefront office was a separate system, so he armed the downstairs. He pulled a dinner out of the freezer, slid it from the box, and punctured the plastic with a fork. He stuck it in the microwave and jabbed at the buttons.

How long it would take Eric to get Hammer to return a call, Tate didn't know. It was difficult with an undercover. There were methods for the FBI to make contact with him. Sometimes those methods took a day or two. Once it was a week. Hammer would have to find a safe place to get his clean phone, not to mention time to make the call.

Tate wanted to know what the man had to say about Aggerton's death.

He also couldn't wait to find out more about Savannah. Not because he wanted her to owe him for keeping her secret, thereby ensuring she stayed safe—though his old mentor certainly would have played it like that. Tate just wanted to get to know her better. To know where she was coming from, so he could better protect her from having to face all those things he'd seen in his line of work. He knew she had also seen seen her fair share of trauma on the job. He just didn't want her showing up as another victim.

A crime stat.

Hospitalized, like Claire.

Killed, like his parents had been.

No, that was the last thing he wanted for a woman trying to live a quiet life. Savannah had her secrets. Maybe she deserved to keep them. But if he was able to help, then he would do what he could.

Tate's phone buzzed. He assumed it was a text. When the buzzing continued, he figured a phone call. Probably about the warranty for the car he didn't have.

But it wasn't.

His security system app flashed on the screen of his phone. A call had been made to the police department, and the security company wanted him to confirm he was all right—that he wasn't responding under duress.

That only meant one thing. The sensors had tripped. Someone was breaking in downstairs.

Tate grabbed a gun and went to meet the intruder.

When he opened the door at the bottom of the stairs the first thing he saw was the knife.

6

Savannah put the car in park. "Front door is open."

Through the speakers Kaylee said, "Security company said his system was triggered."

"And I was closest?" She wanted to get inside ASAP, but needed an answer. There may have also been the tiniest bit of reluctance. Mostly at the thought of finding Tate in a way that was beyond her professional—and legal—help.

"If you want me to call someone—"

"I'll let you know if I need backup." Savannah shoved the door open, disconnecting the Bluetooth connection from her phone. Kaylee would have to hang up on her end—the phone was still in the cup holder. Savannah pulled her weapon and sprinted to the front door of Tate's downstairs office.

He'd indicated he lived in the floor above. She'd figured he had some kind of fortified cabin in the woods, not right in the middle of town. So she could admit to being interested what it looked like up there.

The call had come in at the diner, only minutes from here. She'd relocated there after she'd spent three hours interviewing Kenny Aggerton's wife, and not just because Bernice had been uncooperative with answering the first few questions.

Bernice's cruise, the one she'd purchased *prior* to her husband's death for one passenger traveling alone, was not more important than finding his killer. A police investigation trumped the woman's vacation plans. Much to her consternation.

If she'd seemed even remotely upset about his passing, Savannah might have had a modicum of compassion on her.

"Hudson?"

She called his name again, louder.

Listened.

A thud. Savannah headed for the noise, reaching the hall that branched off the front reception area. Away from the office, toward a short corridor. Door on one side, an EXIT sign at the end.

In the middle of the two doors, two men struggled.

Tate cried out and reared back. He shifted and she saw the gun in his waistband.

She lifted her own gun and aimed it at the man over his shoulder. "Police!"

Tate took a quick step back to the wall, moving farther out of the line of fire. Most people would at least look up at her warning. This guy turned away. She caught a glimpse of a wool mask over his face, round slits at the eyes and mouth.

He wore a huge, dark blue ski jacket over jeans and scuffed black shoes.

"Hands up!"

Knife in one hand. A blood-stained knife.

He ran.

She started toward him, steady, measured steps that ate up the space between them. When he hit the bar on the door, Savannah broke into a run. Seconds that felt like minutes stretched on as adrenaline flooded her body.

"Tate?" She had to know if he was all right.

He held his arm to his chest. "Go after him."

She did, but only because he wasn't in imminent danger of bleeding to death. Not because he'd ordered her to.

Savannah hit the bar on the EXIT door and was rushed at by a wall of cold air. She hadn't put her coat on.

Gun pointed, she twisted one way and then the other looking for this guy. Anger surged in her. Aggerton's killer had been here. He'd targeted Tate.

She saw a dark figure racing away and gave chase. But the guy was fast. Much faster than her, in fact. Like serious cross-country runner fast.

And he was getting away.

She forced her legs to move more quickly than they wanted, pounding the sidewalk after him. Aggerton's killer.

A car passed, right in front of her. Savannah was forced to slow, which gave the guy even more of a lead.

She let out a cry of frustration.

Two buildings later, she heard the roar of an engine. When she reached the next street she saw a dark-colored compact driving away from her.

Savannah stomped back to Tate's office like she was trying to get snow off her shoes. Frustration burned hot in her stomach. When she couldn't get back in through the same exit door, she rounded the building to the front and stepped inside.

"Tate?"

"Savannah?" He didn't waste time saying, "I'm in the bathroom!"

She headed for the hall, where the door swung open. He held a handful of paper towels against his arm.

"You okay?"

"Came at me with a bloody knife." His teeth flashed in the dim light of the hall. He looked about as frustrated as she felt. "I'm guessing the one he used to kill Kenny Aggerton."

She nodded, glanced around, and noted his camera high on the wall. "Surveillance?"

"It's off. Because I'm here." He said, "Did you lose him?"

"Whoever he is, he's fast."

Savannah blew out a breath. They'd seen the killer. The

murder weapon had been here. Both the knife and the person wielding it, right in front of them.

He could have died. She could have walked into an entirely different scene.

Images flashed in her mind. Tate, laying on the floor like Kenny Aggerton. Torso speckled with knife wounds.

She moved to the reception area, mostly so she could have a minute to get herself together. When he followed she said, "Come and sit down." She waved at the reception chair.

Tate slumped into it.

She had him peel away the paper towels. The slice was four inches and seeping blood. "You should see the doc."

"I'll send Dean a picture. He can tell me if it needs stitches."

"You need stitches."

He shook his head and quickly winced. "It's not deep, and it was the flat of the blade."

"And you didn't shoot him?"

"I try to avoid it. Even if I'm being sliced up by a murderer, killing someone is almost never the right answer. It should only be a last resort."

She blinked, not really sure what to say about that. So many people were inclined to shoot first and ask questions later.

She grabbed him a water from the refrigerator in his office and walked back, twisting the cap as she went. "Here. Take a drink, and then tell me what happened from the beginning."

"Thanks."

His voice rumbled through her, not completely washing away the fear she felt that he'd been so close to being killed tonight. But it helped. He was here. He was mostly whole.

"Tell me."

"The security system tripped, which means a sensor was interrupted because someone had opened a door or window."

"But the video wasn't on?"

"I didn't have time to get out my gun before he swung at me." Tate winced. "I can't believe he cut me."

She hissed out a breath through clenched teeth. "You should've shot him."

"It really is sweet that you care."

"Shut up."

He chuckled. Okay, she could admit she'd probably be offended if he had said that to her. Even though he apparently didn't care, she still said, "Sorry."

Then she turned and perched on the edge of the desk at a right angle to him. She could feel his gaze on her. She shut her eyes and tried to process the fact Kenny Aggerton's killer had come here. "To kill you?" Or to plant the knife.

"That's what I think," he said.

He'd tried to *kill* Tate.

Savannah squeezed her eyes shut, at first trying to recall features she'd need to recount later. When they hunted this guy down.

Then all she saw were her father's eyes.

"You okay?"

She lowered her head, bracing her hands on her knees while she breathed. Long, slow breaths.

"I didn't realize you'd react like that."

She sniffed and lifted her head. "What do you mean? I always react like this."

She had to push away thoughts of her dad.

Any other day. Or any other person. Lots of other scenarios, and she'd have been fine. Right? But she wasn't. Peace and joy were supposed to be part of her life, but they weren't. What was the point of going to church if it didn't make her life better?

He stood, then sat beside her on the edge of the desk. "It's okay to not be okay."

"I'm fine." She was pretty sure she'd said that out loud. Hadn't she? He'd better not ask her to tell him what this was about. Better that he just thought she was freaking out because he'd been cut by a murderer.

That was true—and far simpler than the depth of the actual truth.

"You're allowed to have 'off' days."

She said, "That would be Sundays."

"I mean days when you're off your game."

"I know what you meant," she said. "But when I'm 'off' like that, I miss things. People who should be in jail go free, and people who should be safe end up as collateral damage."

She gritted her teeth, forced again to push away thoughts of her father. Not something she wanted to remember.

There was no room for being lax. Or not performing to the very extent of her abilities every day she worked. Allowing that had cost people their lives, or the quality of their lives—hers included. Bad guys had gotten away with stealing, intimidation, and causing pain. So much pain.

She sniffed.

"That sounds like a lot of pressure to be under."

She shrugged, striving to lighten the mood. "It's why they pay me the big bucks."

"Do they?"

"I asked Conroy for a raise when he became chief. He hasn't gotten back to me yet." They were so far off topic now. Despite the fact he was sitting so close, and she wanted to have that sweet conversation with him that he seemed open to, Savannah did have work to do. She should get back to it.

Besides, he'd almost *died*. She hopped off the desk and turned to face him. "I need you to ID this guy so I can catch him."

"I have no idea who it was," he said. "You saw the mask."

"Clothing. Height. Weight. Build. Did he say anything?"

"I have legal pads. I'll write you out a statement."

"Good." She nodded.

"That's it? You shove it aside, and the moment is over. You're all about the job, and whatever is wrong with you just isn't there anymore?"

"Nothing's wrong with me."

He just stared at her.

"You probably don't feel good. If you give me that statement, I'll let you get some rest."

"Nope." He shook his head, winced, and said, "I don't buy it."

She folded her arms across her chest. If he called her a chicken, she would probably punch him. Knife wound or not.

He sighed.

"When you write your statement, you can also write out your alibi for last night. I still need something from you if I'm going to officially rule out you as that guy wearing your sweater."

"It wasn't me."

"And you can prove that beyond a doubt?"

He pressed his lips into a thin line, then said, "I'm working on that."

"Give me all your phone records while you're at it. And access to your work computer."

"No chance."

"Just checking." She patted his shoulder. "Your head is fine."

His lips curled up on one side. "Told you."

"And your arm?"

"Savannah, I'm good."

"Okay." She waved a hand. "Whatever. I was just asking."

He took hold of the hand. Savannah's whole body stilled. What was he doing standing, moving closer to her? He even leaned in. Speaking close to her face.

Not too close. This was…nice.

"You care about me."

She made a pfft sound that was far too loud. "No, I don't." And then she kept talking like an imbecile. "You're just another victim. And a suspect in my case." That was all there was to it. Nothing more.

"You do this with all suspects?"

"We're not doing anything. So there's nothing to not do."
She stepped back and tugged her hand from his. "Write your
statement. I want to look at your back door."

She strode away from him. *Coward.* She could do with some
bravery added to the peace and love she was supposed to be
feeling. None of it came. She didn't feel any different now than
she had a minute ago. Just Savannah.

And goodness, but wasn't that just the entire problem.

Savannah, who acted a whole lot like that woman she was
trying *not* to be. Not anymore, anyways. This woman was
supposed to be the new and improved one. *Yeah, right.*

She blew out a breath and twisted the handle to the back
door.

The killer had come here with the murder weapon.
Assuming Tate wouldn't be here, since it was so late in the
evening? No way could the guy know that when he'd broken in.
Obvious to anyone who knew what they were looking for. He
might as well have kicked the door in for all it hid of his intention to get inside, regardless of the lock being engaged.

First the sweater—hoodie—now this? Tate was being
targeted. Whether he was involved in Aggerton's life, or death,
he would be part of her investigation in some fashion. Either as
the suspect, or as a key witness who helped her break the case
and find the killer.

Had the intruder been planning to leave the knife somewhere inside Tate's office? Could be this was a simple frame job.
A way to cause her confusion by implicating him.

Could be.

Savannah heard raised voices from the reception area but
couldn't make out what was being said. She tugged her gun
from its holster just in case and tiptoed back to the hall.

"...coming here." That was Tate.

A man's voice boomed. "You know why. Don't deny it." He
called Tate a foul name. "You took my wife and daughter
from me."

7

———

Robert Gaynes was an inch shorter than Tate, and at least thirty pounds lighter. His frame was packed tight, though, since he worked out incessantly—something Tate figured he did to compensate for his small eyes and hook nose.

What he didn't have in physical stature, he made up for with a grudge against the world the size of Alaska. Tate figured he'd have inadequacy issues, too, if he had Rob's same occupation working on the city council housing committee.

"Claire isn't here, Rob." Tate widened his stance. He wanted to fold his arms but didn't, keeping his fists free to use at a moment's notice. Thankfully there wasn't a gun within reach, as he'd just stowed his in the desk drawer. He'd have been tempted to shoot the guy, and then Savannah would have no choice but to arrest him.

Tate had to fight to keep his composure. Punching Rob would be immensely satisfying, but that was what this guy had done with Claire. Why perpetuate the cycle? Especially with someone who had no problem with what he'd done.

Tate said, "She's unconscious in the hospital. From what *you* did to her."

There was no remorse in his eyes. No shame and not an

ounce of guilt either. Rob also didn't seem surprised that Tate knew about it. Since he wasn't surprised to hear she'd been hurt, did that mean he probably had something to do with it? He could have found out from a number of sources, but Tate decided then that his guilt was plain to see.

Rob opened his mouth. Probably to fire back a smart remark.

Tate said, "Don't bother."

He wasn't in the mood for an argument. His arm stung. He'd come face to face with a killer and been sliced up. Throw in Rob catching him off guard and the way the gash on his arm throbbed incessantly. Now he was just irritated.

Savannah was still here. Her reaction to him getting hurt, and what it meant, was something he needed to seriously process—when his mind could actually do that. Later. After pain meds, and a nap in his recliner.

Truth was, Dean had told him in their last text exchange that Tate should be taking a visit to see the doctor. Tate likely needed to, and not just because the former Navy SEAL knew what he was talking about when it came to injuries. Tate needed his cut secured with butterfly tabs and then bandaged. Sure, it wasn't that deep. But it also didn't feel good.

Rob said, "I shouldn't bother asking you why my daughter took all her stuff and never came home last night?" The little man—that was how Tate liked to think of him—was gearing up for a fight.

Tate shrugged one shoulder. "Did you file a missing person's report for your *step*daughter?"

"She's a teenager. She probably ran away."

He'd been her stepfather for years, but hadn't ever adopted her. Not that Elexa would have agreed. She didn't like him now any more than she did the day he walked into her mom's—their —life. Half the conversations Tate had with her were about the despicable things he'd said, or done.

He'd lost count of the amount of times he'd tried to

persuade Claire to press charges. But Rob had, so far, left Elexa alone. Thankfully. No doubt when that changed he'd be able to convince Claire, but Tate didn't want it to reach that place. Not ever. And for what? Some false sense of what her life was supposed to be, denying the mess it really was.

Tate couldn't know what went on in Claire's head, and he'd given up the right to have a say in how she led her life. But she wasn't safe—to the extent she was now unconscious in the hospital.

Still needing to wake up.

And when she did wake, he would try to appeal to her again. Happiness was never worth the price of being hurt. Even if it was pretend happiness.

Tate said, "Maybe you should check with the hospital. Then you can find out how your wife is doing, and at the same time, see if Elexa has visited." He folded his arms then, just to keep his fists from starting a fight with Rob.

He wanted this scumbag to face what he'd done. Instead, Rob shrugged. "They'll take care of her."

"That's supposed to be your job. As her husband."

"Like you'd know," Rob fired back. "The way you treated her. She told me all about how you *hurt her and then left her.*" He said the last few words with a high-pitched voice, then broke into laughter.

Tate took a breath. Then he said, "Yeah, I hurt her. Neither of us would deny that. But I can't say I recall taking my fists to her or slapping her. Not even one time. Not ever." He shifted half a step closer. Far enough he could bump Rob with his arms and send the guy back a step—or onto his butt. "Not like you, *Councilman.*"

"Like you can prove that."

"I hope she wakes up and presses charges. Then files for divorce."

If she woke up. There was a chance Claire never would, and he'd have to support Elexa through the burial of her mother. He would be right there with her. Trying, right alongside Elexa, to figure out a life without her in it. Not a chance he'd let her go through that alone. They didn't spend much time together. Not with Rob in her life. But Tate still cared about Elexa, and she knew it. Counted on him.

Not always a healthy situation, but he was never going to let her just swing in the breeze, unprotected from the person who was supposed to be keeping her safe.

Rob roared. He launched himself at Tate.

Before they connected, he heard, "Councilman Gaynes. How nice to see you."

Savannah. He'd been wondering when she would emerge from the back hall. He'd have to remember to commend her on her excellent timing. He shifted back and to the side, so that Rob stumbled two steps with nothing to grasp. Tate wasn't going to give him the satisfaction of being another one of his punching bags. Someone to take his frustration out on.

"Detective." Rob straightened, clearing his throat and touching his hair. The back of his knuckles were split and bruised. Abrasions from a fight.

Tate said, "How'd you get those?"

He didn't figure he'd admit to beating his wife, but wanted to try to trip him up in front of a cop anyway. No way to avoid the question.

If Savannah hadn't been here, and Tate had been fighting fit, he'd be playing things much differently.

Rob looked at his hands. "I fell."

Tate bit down on his molars. How many times had he heard Claire say that before he finally got her to admit what Rob had done? "And your wife, in the hospital? How'd she get there?"

"How would I know?" He shot Tate a defiant look. "You're the one who's seen her. Maybe you put her there."

"Elexa called me. She said you were planning on having dinner with Claire so the two of you could talk."

"Fine." Rob huffed. "I'm filing for divorce. I wanted to tell her so she could prepare, but instead she lost it and came at me in a rage."

"I've never even seen her lose her temper." Tate studied Rob's face. There was something in his eyes that told Tate this was more than simply covering his own behind. He was hiding something else.

Savannah said, "Councilman Gaynes, perhaps we should head to the police station. Make this conversation official, instead of a collection of unsubstantiated claims being bandied back and forth."

When that was so fun? Tate glanced at her. He had to wonder what she thought was going on.

Rob said, "That won't be necessary. My wife is missing, so I figured I'd ask the man who's been sleeping with her for years where she might be."

"Years?"

"Certainly most of our marriage."

Bile filled Tate's mouth. "And you can prove this, I guess?"

That would be hard to do considering it wasn't true. Savannah had to know that.

"You're a private investigator, so I'm certain you know how to cover your tracks. But I know what's true."

Tate said nothing. Or he'd wind up getting arrested instead of Rob, which was likely what the guy hoped for.

"I'll be paying a visit to the hospital, Councilman." Savannah said, "Just as soon as your wife wakes up. I'd like to get to the bottom of whatever this is."

"Good idea," Tate said. "You might also want to find out if there's any love lost between Kenny Aggerton and our esteemed councilman."

While they were here, he might as well make the valid point that Rob probably had as much of a grudge against the dead man as anyone else. Certainly more than Tate might have.

"Are you accusing me of murdering him?" Something

sparked in Rob's eyes. "Where were *you* when Aggerton was murdered?"

Tate said, "None of your business."

"No?" Rob smirked. "Word from the police department is that you're a person of interest in the case. Their number one suspect, even."

"Is that right?" Tate wouldn't give him the satisfaction of seeing him frustrated when the truth was Savannah was just doing her job.

"After all," Rob said, "why else would the police be here?"

"This office was broken into," Savannah said. "That's why I'm here. Not because I'm questioning Mr. Hudson about his involvement in any of my other open cases."

That was a nice touch, referring to him like that. Though Rob might've seen them around together, or heard they'd worked side by side to help Mia and Conroy. Or, maybe he had no idea she and Tate knew each other at all, outside of this call and her showing up here to investigate a break-in.

Who knew how far Rob had his finger in what went on in this town? Far enough he managed to keep his marital strife to himself so no one other than Tate suspected a thing.

Too bad Elexa couldn't prove what she believed—that Rob had been the one who hurt her mom. This time, at least. Otherwise Tate would convince her to press charges on her mom's behalf. Maybe she could give a statement about some of the other things he'd done…

Tate needed to talk to her about that.

Rob sneered. "He's not at the top of your suspect list for no reason. Sooner or later I'll find out."

Savannah said, "I'm happy to confirm with my chief, but it's my understanding that police investigations aren't your purview over at city hall as head of Infrastructure and Transportation. But if there's a pothole on my street, I'll give you a call."

Tate pressed his lips together, but Rob probably saw the smirk that wanted out. Still, a niggle of worry entered the picture. Not for him. Tate had no problem going up against Rob. The guy could use his position in local government to cause problems for him, sure. But did Tate care about that?

A muscle shifted in Rob's jaw, his eyes shifting around like he had to plan what to say next. Or what to do.

What Tate really cared about was when innocents got caught in the crossfire. Or when people close to him were hurt as a result of collateral damage. The thought of it threatened to mentally break him.

Savannah needed to tread carefully, or she'd wind up on Rob's list of people he had a grudge against. Tate was pretty sure his own name was underlined and highlighted—at the top. She had to be careful, or her honest attempt at a new life would blow up in her face, and her good intentions wouldn't survive what this town did to her.

Tate said, "Time to go, Rob. You said your peace. Now leave."

"I'm barely getting started."

He wanted to play it like that? Tate said, "Me too. And if I get what I want, not only will Claire and Elexa never again cross the threshold of your house, but you'll never see them again for as long as you live. Unless it's in a courtroom."

Rob laughed. "We'll see about that."

Savannah said, "Did you just threaten your wife and stepdaughter in front of a police detective?"

He turned his venomous stare on her. "One who consorts with the suspects she's investigating." Rob's smile turned smug. "We'll see how well it goes when everyone finds out you overlooked evidence that clearly showed Tate as the killer."

8

———

Mia was at her desk when Savannah got to the police department first thing the next morning.

"Hey." Savannah dumped her backpack on the floor at her desk.

Mia leaned back in her chair and stretched. "Ready to take another stab at Aggerton's wife?"

"In a minute." Savannah sat. As she did, she blew out a long breath. All she'd done all night was think about Tate. And Rob. But mostly Tate.

"We can't hold her much longer before we either have to formally arrest her or cut her loose." Mia said, "Is Tate okay?"

Conroy headed their way from his office. Savannah nodded and glanced at him. "Just a cut on his arm." She gave them a description of the guy who had attacked him.

"I guess he's no longer your number one suspect in this murder."

Conroy had a point. Savannah nodded, half with relief and half upset at the reminder of Rob Gaynes's parting comment. She said, "I saw the killer with my own eyes."

And he'd gotten away.

She stood. "We should talk to the wife again."

They'd had one conversation with Bernice Aggerton already. Long enough they'd realized they weren't going to get anything but belligerence out of her, and then she'd called her lawyer. Bernice and her lawyer had been in conference when she responded to the call about Tate's office being broken into. Savannah had been at dinner, waiting them out.

Today was a new day. Right?

Conroy said, "Sit back down, detective."

She planted her butt back in the seat. "The lawyer won't be happy we kept her in jail overnight, but I think we should be able to get something out of her."

Conroy nodded. "True. Only there's more to be said, so you'll make them wait some more."

She shrugged, ready for him to just spit out whatever it was.

"How did Tate seem?"

What kind of question was that? "Annoyed." Savannah said, "What's your read on Councilman Gaynes?"

"Now there's a question." Conroy pulled up a chair and sat.

Mia offered her opinion. "He's older than us—in college while I was still in middle school, I think. Don't much remember him."

Conroy nodded. "He didn't come back home right away. When he did, he got straight into politics. If you can call city council 'politics.'" He shrugged. "Married Claire, gave her daughter a father. That's what I've known of him since I started working here. He began climbing the ranks in this town before I graduated college."

Rob wasn't "old" though, he was just a good ten or fifteen years older than Conroy and Mia. Older than Savannah—more like around Tate's age. Mid-forties. Yeah, she was aware of the number of years between Tate's age and hers. However, since a relationship wasn't in their future, it didn't exactly matter. Did it?

Savannah told them about his visit, and what she'd learned about the nature of Rob and Claire's relationship, that it was no surprise she'd been admitted to the hospital. Still unconscious.

"Kaylee!" Conroy's voice echoed across the bull pen.

Mia said, "She isn't in yet."

He got his phone out. "I'll send her an email."

"For what?" Mia glanced at Savannah, but she didn't have an answer for her.

"So I get word the moment Claire Gaynes wakes up."

Savannah said, "Are you going to convince her to press charges?"

"I'm gonna try."

She nodded. "If you can persuade her daughter to as well, you'll have a better shot at Claire." When she woke up. *If* she woke up. If she didn't, the charges would look a lot different. But they would also be harder to prove.

Conroy stilled. "You know about Elexa?"

"I've seen her around." She tried to sound nonchalant. Neither of them bought it.

Mia leaned forward on her chair, elbows on her desk. "And..?"

Traitor. They'd talked. She was only being like this because Conroy was here and she was using the chief's presence to force Savannah to dish up something good.

As if.

Savannah shrugged. "And what? He cares about her."

Conroy and Mia glanced at each other, wearing looks on their faces that resembled some secret "engaged people" language that Savannah obviously wasn't privy to. Conroy said, "And you've...talked to him about her?"

Savannah resisted the urge to roll her eyes. She stood. "Let's go, Tathers. We've got a woman to interview."

Conroy stood, blocking her path.

Savannah looked up at him. "What?"

"I just want you to make sure you're being careful. That's all."

She recalled what Rob Gaynes had said. About her purposely overlooking evidence that pointed to a certain private investigator with a reputation for being wild. She had yet to see that, but she'd heard plenty. The idea that she'd turned the other way because of her feelings for him wasn't something that sat well with her.

Someone looking like Tate had been caught on surveillance. He needed to get back to her about who he thought it might be, or she'd have to assume it really was him. Evading the truth was going to get him nowhere. Now, on top of that, she had to wonder if the killer had come by his office with the plan to discard the bloody knife. Where someone would find it.

Someone like her.

Savannah lifted her chin. "Why would I need to be careful? There's nothing between Tate and I. Either I'll arrest him for killing Aggerton, or I won't. Which do you think is more likely, considering I chased the killer from his office last night? How I feel about Tate doesn't factor in."

She squeezed around him before he could object. No matter what happened in this case, she was going to keep her emotions in check. Accusations had been thrown around. The mountain of evidence she'd been working her way through—until she responded to the break-in at Tate's—barely had a dent in it.

Mia met her in the hall.

Savannah joked, "At this rate, we'll probably be unpacking this case until your wedding date."

Mia's eyes flared.

"Oh, no."

Mia grinned. "Why would that be bad?"

Savannah folded her arms. "Spill. When are you getting married?"

The only time Mia's business face, which was still on point from her time as a federal agent, slipped? When she talked about Conroy.

"Mia."

"Fine. He asked me last weekend." She tugged a necklace from the collar of her shirt. Hanging from it was a simple silver ring with a diamond setting. "We're getting married in the fall."

"That's not enough time!" She realized too late that she'd screeched.

"You think we're still going to be working on this case?"

"Goodness, no. But there are things to do. You have to have time to plan."

Mia said, "The beach at my dad's house. Red and orange leaves everywhere. A small amount of people, and my dad and Conroy are going to grill chicken for lunch. Salad, lemonade. Tiny cupcakes. What's to plan?"

Savannah opened her mouth, realized she didn't have anything to say, and then closed it again.

"Will you be my bridesmaid?"

"What?" The word came out breathy, and barely audible.

Mia frowned. "Unless you don't want to."

Why on earth would she think that? Savannah had lived here two years and Mia was the first real friend she'd made. No way would she pass up the chance to support this woman's marriage to the best boss Savannah had ever had.

Mia turned to the interview room. "We should—"

"Savannah Wilcox isn't my real name." The words tripped over each other on the way out of her mouth.

Mia glanced back. "It isn't?"

Savannah shook her head. Maybe it was time someone in her life knew the truth. There was no doubt she could trust Conroy or Mia. Maybe if she told them both the truth she wouldn't feel so alone.

Her friend and partner was about to ask another question when the door to the interrogation room opened. A suited man with a thinning, brown comb over stuck his head out. "Can we please get on with this? My client has waited long enough."

They shared a look. Then Mia said, "Very well."

She sat first. Savannah didn't, choosing instead to lean against the wall.

"Yeah." Bernice Aggerton glared at her. "You stay over there. Don't come any closer to me."

The lawyer cleared his throat, smoothing a clammy hand down his tie. "Mrs. Aggerton will be writing out a statement, detailing the subpar methods employed by this department to encourage her to come here in good faith and talk about her husband. She will also be passing along an invoice for the amount of money she lost after being forced to cancel her vacation at such a late date."

"Yeah, the day before."

"Bernice."

She shut her mouth.

Savannah said, "Make sure she writes down all about how she used her purse like a baton and swung it at me."

The woman could embellish all she wanted, but Savannah would simply respond with completely justified assault charges.

The lawyer glanced at Bernice, then said, "Let's get on with the questions."

"Good idea." Mia leaned back in her chair. "Mrs. Aggerton, how—"

"You can call me Bernice." She flashed her Hollywood teeth at Mia.

"Okay, Bernice. How much—"

"Because, hon." Bernice leaned forward, like it was just her and Mia in the room. "Just between us girls, I was gonna divorce him anyway. That's how I come to have that cruise all booked up, you know? Just me. I was gonna celebrate."

"You filed for divorce?"

"Well, no. But I was gonna get to that. Soon as I got back, like."

"Right." Mia said, "How much do you know about your husband's business, his clients?"

Bernice wrinkled her nose. "Patti...she works at the nail

salon." She wiggled her fingers so they could see her white tipped pink nails. A couple had sparkly stones glued on. "She told me he did her books." She shrugged. "News to me."

Mia said, "Do you think he was well liked around town?"

"Sho' nuff. We had parties all the time, and we were invited places all the time, too. The theater in Upton. The casino they opened on that Res. All kinds of fancy places."

"Anyone from one of those fancy places seem like they had a grudge? Maybe they argued with your husband, or made threats?"

"I see all kinds of things, you know?" She glanced at her lawyer. He nodded. Bernice said, "I couldn't say for sure there was an argument from one of our events that I remember."

Savannah would put money on that being very careful wording. She figured either Bernice was busy at the slot machines while her husband chatted with his cronies, or she'd simply been too drunk at the time. If Savannah's sense was right, she may literally not remember anything at all.

Mia said, "What about specific clients? Is there anyone you know of personally who worked with your husband?"

Asking about Aggerton's nephew, Ed Summers, would be a good place to start. Summers was in jail, but whatever blood was between the two men had turned bad recently. Could be Ed had ordered a hit from jail. They knew Aggerton had held on to evidence that could be used to convict Summers. Serving the warrant and obtaining the evidence had been how Conroy managed to bring him down.

Savannah figured they'd get more from his computer files than anything Bernice would willingly give them. This had been a waste of time. A power play, trying to see who got the upper hand. Because Bernice was the kind of woman who always had to come out on top. And Savannah had fallen right into that trap.

Bernice shrugged. "I don't know who hired him. Why would

I? He didn't let me in on his business. Not like that Tate Hudson, letting his sister work for him."

Savannah bit the inside of her lip.

Bernice smirked—probably supposed to be a smile. Always on top. "That's what I need to tell you. So you know what happened."

"Tell us what?" Mia's tone coaxed her. "Whatever you say could help us bring in your husband's killer."

"He came over. A couple of weeks ago."

Savannah figured Bernice was trying to look distressed. It wasn't all that convincing. What would be a whole lot more convincing were Aggerton's files. She should leave Mia to do this, and would, just as soon as Bernice finished up her story.

The real work was waiting.

She said, "Late one night. I heard them in my study arguing. Then a door slammed, and I looked out my TV room window. I saw him outside, getting into his truck with another guy."

Savannah bit out one word. "Who?"

"Tate Hudson. I'm sure he's the one who killed my husband."

9

Hot coffee poured in a steady stream into his mug. "Thanks, Hollis."

"No prob, Tate." Hollis managed the diner after her father had been injured and couldn't run the show anymore. But she still preferred to wait on customers. Her full figure was covered with a salmon-colored waitress uniform. Her hair was light brown and caramel, her eyebrows thick brown.

For a while, a few weeks back, he'd tried to get her to tell him what was wrong. She hadn't taken the bait. Tate didn't plan on letting it go, though. Hollis knew who he was. If she needed help then she would come to him, or she'd call on one of the cops who frequented this place for the waffles.

"You want your usual?"

Tate said, "No potatoes. Extra hot sauce."

"Ah, the 'Steve.' A dramatic variation on the 'Saturday Tate Special.'"

He halted his cup, halfway to his mouth. "Say what?"

She grinned. "Nothin'." Her smile faltered. She blinked, then shuffled out of the way when a hulk of a man passed between her and his table.

No, not a hulk.

A Hammer.

He slid into the booth across from Tate, one glance at Hollis. "Coffee, please."

She blinked and took him in like bees to honey. "Sure, uh, hon." She winked and popped a hip, then whirled around and nearly collided with a customer.

Tate took in the man across from him.

Blue, button down shirt. Glasses. A brown, leather band on the watch he wore. Tate leaned over to see under the table. Tan khakis and shined brown loafers. All he needed to complete the look was a bible and a 'John 3:16' pamphlet.

He sat back upright. "I already know Jesus, but thank you."

"Do you really?" His companion grinned, a wolfish smile that was completely at odds with his slicked and shined appearance.

"I know enough."

He went to church on occasion, and not just when he had to tail someone for a job. Even church people were investigated. Tate had listened. He understood all about sin and salvation. He just didn't want to change everything about himself. Conroy's words to him the last time they'd spoken still rang in his head, though. That he should give it a chance.

Tate felt worse about Savannah though. She was doubting him, and he didn't like that feeling at all. Leave it to Rob to basically tell her that he'd killed Aggerton. Afterwards, she'd made a bunch of excuses and run out of there.

He wanted to talk to her. Try to explain himself.

Hollis poured his coffee. "Cream?"

"Just sugar."

"You like it sweet." She smiled.

Tate cleared his throat.

She blinked, then asked his companion, "Breakfast?"

He said, "Saturday Tate."

"Coming right up."

Tate frowned, not quite sure what had just happened. "Wait, what?"

Hammer just sat there looking like he'd won a prize. Then he shifted, pulled a wallet from his back pocket, and slid out a driver's license. Tate read the name aloud. "Phil Tilley? Really?"

"Eric gave it to me. Write it down, check it out. He said it's almost foolproof." He grinned, apparently excited about his new —clean—identity. "Call me Phil."

Tate's brother-in-law probably bust a gut laughing about that name. The only concession was that Phil probably seriously enjoyed having a break from the swill he waded through all day as The Hammer.

Tate said, "Is Phil the one who was on the surveillance footage outside the CPA office during the time Aggerton was murdered?" His eyes swept over him again. Hammer did not dress like this. At least not normally. He'd worked for Ed Summers, had two eyebrow piercings, and a spider web tattoo on the side of his neck.

This guy's tattoo was nowhere to be found, and he looked like he was ready for his first day on the job as a sales guy. Or a missionary.

Since Ed had been arrested, causing Hammer to go under the radar, he wasn't sure what he'd been up to.

Phil's face twisted. "Kenny Aggerton? That's what this is about?"

"Did you kill him?"

He made a pfft sound. "I wouldn't waste my time."

"So you're busy? You still have that sweater you grabbed from my car?"

"That's what this is about?"

"Can you just answer the question?"

Hollis set their plates down. Tate had to sit back.

She glared at him—probably for yelling at Phil—and then wandered off. She glanced over her shoulder and glared at him again. For good measure, of course.

What? All of a sudden, he was the bad guy. Did she think Tate would lead Phil astray with his wild ways? She had no idea who this guy was.

When she was out of earshot he said, "Walk me through what you've been up to."

"Last I checked you weren't FBI, which means I don't have to tell you anything."

"Humor me."

Phil squirted tomato sauce over his hash browns in a criss-cross pattern until it was virtually unrecognizable. "Ed got me Aggerton. He was the key to the supplier."

The local money guy. "You know where the drugs are coming from?"

"Not yet. I got the local guy, but this stuff is coming in over the border. I don't know where yet, or who. Or how."

Not much of anything, then.

"Aggerton was my route up the chain."

"Now he's dead," Tate took a bite of spicy sausage. "Maybe because you talked to him." He shrugged, offering it as a question.

Phil studied him. "Anything's possible."

Tate said, "I think they're gonna try and pin it on me. I also think I have a related player, but I don't got a way to tie him to your business."

Tate explained a bit about his ex-wife's current husband.

Could be he just had a giant grudge against Rob because of how he treated Claire. Could be Councilman Gaynes was a spouse abuser, but otherwise a law-abiding citizen. Maybe.

Phil considered this new angle. "It's a mess, that's for sure. More complicated than my grandma's cross stitch. Bunch of yokel players who think they're big time when the real money isn't here. It's in the major hubs."

"Small town kings."

Phil shrugged. "I've seen it before. These guys at least aren't the crazy type. They just think they're tough. It's the guys above them in the food chain that worry me. I haven't been able to get anything on who they are, or where they come from."

Tate blew out a breath. He'd been hoping for more than this. Then he'd have had his brother-in-law read Conroy in on the undercover FBI operation going on in Last Chance County.

"But I have an idea," Phil said. "And I need your help with it."

"Okay."

"You have no idea what it is."

Tate shrugged. "Does it matter?"

"No."

"Does it involve something I'm not going to like doing?"

Phil narrowed his eyes. He took a moment to study Tate. "No."

"Good." Tate ate another bite of his breakfast. The "Steve" apparently. A variation on the "Saturday Tate." Whatever that meant. He had no idea. "So when are we doing this?"

"Tonight."

"Plenty of time for you to tell me what you and Aggerton talked about minutes before he died."

Phil said, "You can read all about it in my report."

"When you're done with this Op. In what, two years?"

He made a face and took a sip of coffee. After he'd swallowed, Phil said, "My plan was to get Aggerton to roll over on his bosses. Then, I'd flip for the international contingent. Go all the way up the chain and dismantle the entire operation. Aggerton was dragging his feet."

Tate nodded. Not surprising.

"He was also murmuring about things getting too hot."

"Did he know who you really are...even just an inkling?"

"No." Phil said, "But there's a rumor going around that someone sold out Ed Summers. A lot of finger pointing going on, everyone looking at everyone else to see if they can figure out who the weak link is."

"Could be that Aggerton knew who it is. Or figured it out."

Tate knew Meena Tathers, Mia's sister, had provided the location of Aggerton's books—the ones that had been confiscated by police. They were the basis of the case against Summers.

Tate considered the man across the table from him. Sure, the guy was an FBI agent. But undercover work took a certain kind of person. Could be that "Phil" had decided killing Aggerton was the way to protect the integrity of his operation. The means being justified by the end result everyone at the FBI was watching and waiting for.

Phil nodded. "Maybe whoever killed him did it to shut him up." His gaze narrowed. "Yeah, no. It wasn't me."

Tate shrugged. "I don't know you, man. I know my brother-in-law, though. If he vouches for you, then I'm good."

Tate would be calling Eric as soon as he left to make sure Phil was solid. And that whatever Op he had planned was above board. Not that everything Phil did had to be run through his handler, but Eric had to be aware. At least of the gist of things.

"He'll vouch." Phil said, "He really married your sister?"

"Came here, asked for help with a case. She was my receptionist at the time. The rest is history."

Phil chuckled. "No way I'd let a feeb touch my sister. I know too much."

The guy had sisters? Tate didn't have time to find out, or the headspace to care all that much. But it still said a lot about a man how he treated his sisters. And how he felt about the bureau he worked for.

"Got a picture of this guy you think is connected?"

Tate pulled out his phone. He went on the city's website and pulled up the file photo for Rob Gaynes, then showed it to Phil.

"Huh."

"What does 'huh' mean?"

"I seen that guy around."

Tate waited, but Phil didn't say more. "If he's involved in…"

Someone walked past the table. "…what you're doing. I need to know that. It's important."

"Guess we'll find out when we go to work." He finished his breakfast. "So the cops are looking at you?"

"No thanks to you—wearing my hoodie." It was important to Tate that he point that out.

Phil cocked his head. "All part of the service. Except where a killer avoided surveilance while I was spotted." The fed meshed his lips together.

Tate said, "If I don't figure out who had a beef with Aggerton enough to cut him up, I'm gonna be in hot water with the cops. And I try to stay on their good sides."

"Knife?"

Tate nodded.

"Nasty way to go."

Tate pulled up the sleeve of his sweater. "I know." He lifted the bandaged part of his forearm. "Same knife that killed Aggerton." Or so he was assuming. Maybe he was wrong.

Phil shook his head. "They are after you."

"No kidding."

"Help me with my Op, and I'll help you figure out who killed Aggerton. Could be the same people trying to keep their ID's from me, killing him so their names don't get out."

"Deal." Which meant Aggerton knew more about the drug trade in Last Chance County than Tate had ever realized.

"Phil is here to help."

Hollis took his plate. Another wink. Thankfully, that last comment was all she heard. When she moved away, Phil watched her go.

"Don't get too helpful there. You need your head in the game."

Phil took one last look. The hulking man apparently had a soft spot for the diner owner. Then he turned back to Tate. "You gonna tell the cops Aggerton fronted you the startup money for your business?"

"Now that I know it's dirty? No way." Tate shook his head. "I paid back that debt in full, plus interest."

Now that Aggerton was dead, there was no way he'd be able to come back to try to collect more. Not the way he'd attempted to do a few times over the years. He'd even had to have Eric walk into Aggerton's home, flash his badge and tell Kenny to quit pressuring Tate.

He wasn't proud of some of the things he'd done. But Tate stood by the man he was, even if that man had to call in favors every so often to keep a hold on his honor.

Just so long as Savannah never found out.

10

————

"So you're springing her loose?"

Savannah sank into one of the chairs in front of Conroy's desk. Mia sat in the one beside her. She was pretty sure she saw the chief wink at her partner but chose to strategically ignore it. They were engaged now, so she knew it wouldn't be the last time she saw him do that. Might as well get used to it.

She said, "Mrs. Aggerton saw Tate arguing with her husband and so decided he must have been the one who'd killed him. Except that she didn't really see them arguing. And she only came up with this story after her lawyer went into conference with her."

Conroy leaned back in his chair. "So this might be a conspiracy, where a group of people are working together to make it look like Tate did it?"

"When you put it like that, it does sound far fetched." Savannah said, "It only works if I've got a grudge against Tate, and I don't want to look at anyone else for this. Plus the fact that I literally chased the killer from his office."

At least, she was assuming that man was the killer.

"So who could this guy be?"

Savannah didn't have any idea—yet—who it was, and she

had no other clear suspects. Before she could admit that to her boss, Mia said, "We're not done looking through Aggerton's personal files, but we're most of the way there."

Savannah tried not to look surprised. She stared Conroy down. "Once we're done, we'll let you know if there's anything of note."

Fact was, she hadn't liked the idea of Tate being her main suspect anyway. Maybe she'd ignored pertinent information—or at least stayed in denial. Maybe she needed to step away and face the truth. Admit he was clearly involved.

But then she would also have to face her own shortcomings, the ones she'd always known were there, and just do her job.

The first test? Fail.

Savannah couldn't let that happen again. She couldn't allow her feelings for Tate to override what was plainly obvious to everyone else.

Savannah said, "I'd argue Tate doesn't seem to care about Aggerton either way. Not enough to fly into a rage and stab him multiple times with a knife."

"Does the reason matter?"

"If I had possession of clothes he wore that night, covered in Aggerton's blood, then maybe," she said. "But otherwise, I'm still putting it together. As it stands, I don't think he's involved other than as another potential victim, or the one they're trying to pin it on."

Mia shifted toward her. "Have you worked a lot of murders?"

Savannah shrugged one shoulder. "I haven't counted, and there haven't been so many since I moved here. Before two years ago? Yeah. There were a fair amount. Each one is different, but eventually I solved them all."

"All of them?" Conroy said, "I knew you were good. But *no* cold cases?"

She shook her head in answer to Conroy's question. "Most get solved in the first few weeks, but one took three years. I got there, though." She said, "I really don't like unanswered questions."

The cases would keep her up at night, along with everything else swirling around in her brain. She much preferred to work instead of sleep. Especially in the middle of a case. As much as she'd not been bothered at the scene itself, the images had stayed with her. Now when she closed her eyes she could see Aggerton, covered in blood. Once in a while, it would turn to a nightmare. He could even blink, his eyes white. The worst ones were where he reached for her.

Conroy nodded. "We all saw Tate in the house with Ed Summers. His loyalty isn't like ours, firmly rooted in this department. He doesn't work all day every day to safeguard the people in this town and enforce the law."

Savannah wasn't sure that was completely true. She actually thought Tate did protect people. In his own way.

The chief continued, "The attack at his office could be completely unrelated. Who knows if the knife he got cut with was even the same one used to kill Aggerton?"

"He's right." Mia spoke softly.

"I'm not in denial."

Maybe she had been, but going forward she planned very much to *not* be in denial.

Savannah said, "If he's the killer, then I will arrest him. But I need enough evidence to erase any question. The wife's testimony is suspect. All the rumors floating around town are just hearsay, and the video doesn't even show his face. Unless we find his DNA on the body, or the knife with his fingerprints on the handle, then who can say? There's a lot more work to do on this case, guys."

"We know," Mia said. "We just want to know that *you* know."

Savannah shot her a look. "You don't need to tell me how to do my job."

Mia nodded, conceding the point. She'd been a federal

agent up until a few weeks ago. Now she was a lieutenant on probation, and Savannah was the one who got to sign off on whether or not Mia could do this job going forward. And that was in addition to the giant question mark over Mia's future in law enforcement because of her hearing loss.

Savannah said, "What about the books that were found in Aggerton's office, the ones that were admitted as evidence in the case against Ed Summers?"

Summers was Aggerton's nephew, but there was no love lost between them. Summers had recently made Conroy and Mia's lives a living nightmare. To top it all off, he'd killed Mia's older sister in a car accident in high school. Saying they weren't friends was putting it nicely.

She said, "Could be Summers had him killed from prison. Maybe he didn't want Aggerton to talk."

Conroy said, "The state police did come by and talk to Aggerton about his nephew. They reported to me that he shut them down, didn't want to talk about anything having to do with Summers, or the account books found in his office."

"And charges against him?" Surely there was something, considering the money laundering and being an accessory to all kinds of things.

"Pending."

She said, "Can I look at the books?"

"You think something in Ed's books will indicate a motive for murder?"

Savannah shrugged one shoulder, reminding herself again that Mia had been an ATF agent and not a homicide detective. "It could give us a broader perspective on his associates."

Of which Tate was not. At least not recently. She'd searched for him first in Aggerton's files. There had been no mention of him in the records, which went back seven years.

So why would Tate hold a grudge long enough to finally snap, then bring a knife to their meeting and murder the man in a fit of rage? Didn't make sense to her.

Especially considering she'd seen the knife in the possession of a completely different person.

"Risky. If you're trying to rule out Tate." Conroy said, "Since Tate surely had business with Summers, his name could be in there."

"What business?"

Conroy shrugged. "Aggerton has financed a lot of local companies. Got them their start. I'm only guessing, but I figure Tate as well. Though, that would've been years ago."

Savannah bit the inside of her lip.

"I'm sure it's just lending but given the fact Aggerton's money was dirty—who knows?" Conroy picked up the phone on his desk. "Anyway, I'll find out where the books are now."

Savannah blinked.

Tate could have borrowed money from Aggerton to start his PI business?

"You okay?"

She glanced at Mia, but didn't answer.

Conroy said, "I figure the books are either at the courthouse in the hands of the district attorney—or someone on his staff— or they're in eviden—Yeah, this is Chief Barnes…"

Savannah glanced at Mia while Conroy talked. "I can go get it, wherever it is."

Conroy said, "Thank you," and hung up the phone. "They'll call back and let us know."

She grabbed her coffee and refilled it. A chance to give herself a minute for her brain to process everything. When Savannah settled back at her desk, she pulled up the flash drive.

Given what had been copied and edited, along with the comments in the margin, she could tell Mia had gone through it. Savannah decided to look again at the hate mail folder. Her brain just kept going back to Tate, though. No matter what information she went through, Savannah couldn't stop thinking about him.

She had to face the fact she didn't know Tate Hudson. After

all, there was a young woman in town who called him, "Dad." There was a relationship there. One she was not exactly privy to.

He had a life. She'd had one, and it had almost destroyed her. Everyone had a past. It was always complicated.

So she knew Tate's would be no different.

She didn't know him enough to say he wouldn't do something like kill Aggerton. Though, if she was trying not to be in denial about the whole thing, she'd have to admit to herself that he was the kind of man who might kill if the occasion warranted it. Not a stabbing though. Tate wouldn't be about the mess. He'd figure out how to make Aggerton disappear, and no one would ever figure out what had happened to him.

Mostly because that was exactly what she'd have done.

Mia said, "All this seems clean."

"Too clean?"

Mia shrugged.

"The financial records were like that. Which was why it was key for us to get that second set of account books for Ed." It had made the whole case. "So if Aggerton did that much for his nephew, a guy he didn't seem to like all that much except for his money, why wouldn't he do that for his own accounts? Wash what could be found and keep the real stuff secret."

"Did we ever find out if the receptionist knew anything?"

Savannah pulled open the file of her notes. "The officers who knocked on her door for a follow-up interview got no answer. Both times they went."

"Want me to look into that?"

"Yes, thank you."

Mia needed to be careful in any situation. Noise above a certain decibel level would destroy her hearing on a permanent level. Savannah wanted to tell her to be cautious, but her partner already knew that.

"On it." She grabbed her weapon from her drawer and headed for Conroy's office.

Savannah went back to the folder of hate mail. At least it would give her another guide for her next round of interviews.

Aggerton had investments all over town. In fact, he'd had his finger in so many businesses in town that they numbered far more than those that hadn't been at least partially funded by him. He also prepared tax returns for nearly everyone in town—except those who worked at the police department, or Tate.

Savannah tapped her pen on the edge of her desk. There must be people around town seriously grateful he was dead and their debt had been wiped clear—assuming no one took up where Aggerton left off.

Mia waved as she left. Savannah read an email. Hatred dripped from the words—which included a detailed description of what the sender intended to do to Aggerton. It wasn't a stabbing though. The address was nondescript.

Savannah sent a note to Ted on their internal messaging system and asked him to take a look at it.

The next was from Patrick Dearnum—Robert Gaynes's assistant. Vague threats, veiled in disappointment and distrust. Basically, the city council was no longer going to outsource certain accounts to Aggerton's business. It was pretty pompous sounding; someone stuck up on their high horse, refusing to give a reason that would justify the end to their association.

Her desk phone rang, the extension for Conroy's phone.

"Yeah, Chief?"

"Summers's account books are ready for you at evidence lockup."

The basement of the courthouse, next door to city hall. Only a block of walking. Savannah didn't do "cold," so she'd drive over there.

"Copy that." She hung up and wrote herself a note to look into Patrick Dearnum and find out what went on between the city council and Aggerton.

Could be there was bad blood. Above board, or no, she was going to find out where they stood and why.

Savannah locked her computer profile and waved to Kaylee on the way out. She waited a couple of minutes for the car to warm up before pulling out, all the vents pumping warm air. It wasn't even fifty degrees. She might have lived here for two years now, but she planned on *never* growing accustomed to the weather. Talk about freezing.

She needed a vacation somewhere warm.

The desk sergeant in evidence lockup seemed like the only one in the courthouse this late at night. And he wasn't happy about it. Not even with a ball game on the radio.

Savannah signed for the account books, and they were turned over to her, sealed in an evidence bag. "Thanks."

He didn't smile.

She headed back out. Another couple of hours at her desk, and she'd call it. Head home for some sleep. She was dedicated, but she knew what happened if she burned out.

Savannah beeped the locks on her car. She heard a shuffle right behind her. Before she could turn, a heavy body slammed into her.

Savannah's forehead hit the driver's side window and everything went black.

11

———————

Tate was deciding whether or not to honk his horn when he saw Phil round the corner of the house. No, this wasn't Phil. The Hammer was back. His bald head covered by a beanie, he had on a heavy, dark-colored jacket, jeans, and boots.

He pulled the door open and climbed into the passenger seat. "Hey."

Tate stared at the spider web tattoo, visible above the collar of the jacket. "How'd you cover that earlier? Assuming you didn't just draw it back on."

Hammer said, "Basically it's makeup. Got it off the web. Cover up that actors use to disguise tattoos for a performance. Works pretty good."

Tate pulled out. "And you don't mind the back and forth?"

"For the chance to be…not me, but someone good? Yeah, I don't mind. Being this guy—" He grasped the edges of the jacket for a second—"It gets old pretty fast."

"And no one's recognized you?"

"The Hammer and Phil Tilley do not frequent the same places."

That was good procedure. Tate said, "Where to?"

"House on Candlewood. But we need to come at it from the back, so we're going to circle around."

"Copy that." He said, "What is this place?"

"Stash house."

"Anyone there tonight?"

"It's been clear for the last few nights. I put a camera in the yard, and no one's come or gone, so we should be good to take a look around inside."

"Looking for what?"

"Evidence I can run with. Something to take to Eric, get him to approve a raid on the mid-level guys, get them to flip over on their suppliers."

He could hear the fatigue in Hammer's voice. Despite his new lease on life as Phil—which might have been Eric offering him some respite in the middle of what was proving to be a long operation—The Hammer seemed to be tiring of the job.

"How long have you been on this?"

"Eleven months," Hammer said. "Took me a while to get to Summers as the point man. After he was taken down, thought they were going to pull me back. Instead I get new orders to go through Aggerton to the next level. Take down the whole organization."

"Rough."

"Yeah."

Tate said, "I did a few assignments like that with the FBI, back in the day. Mostly Texas, Colorado. Guy like me would stick out in LA or Miami."

The Hammer snorted.

Tate followed his directions and they parked under a heavy tree, then made their way through two backyards—thankfully not guarded by dogs—to the back door of the house Hammer was interested in. A stash house where drugs would be hidden as they transferred hands from supplier to dealer, or from the dealers to their runners. Somewhere along the line the product was cut, often multiple times. Concentration diminished as everyone in the chain sought to maximize profit.

Money grew as addicts needed more and more to get their hit.

Tate drew his gun from the shoulder holster he wore under his jacket and checked it one more time. Sure, not as easily accessible as it would be if it were simply on his hip—up and able to fire in less than a second. But he sacrificed that second or two for the way his gun was stowed inconspicuously—less obvious to an attentive bystander. But tonight it would be in his hand. Given the people Hammer was up against, Tate wasn't going to take any chances on either of their safety.

"Ready?"

Hammer nodded.

Tate tried the handle on the back door. Unlocked. Gun loose by his side, Tate stepped in. A rancid smell came from the kitchen. No one had cleaned since the residents moved out, and whoever was last here had left food, dishes, and paper goods strewn across the counter.

He'd done that early on as an adult but then quickly realized that wasn't the way to impress anyone who came over—not to mention how sick he'd gotten because of the filth. Cleaning up his act, literally, was also how he'd finally gotten his sister off his back for being a slob.

They walked through the kitchen and living areas, then headed for the bedrooms. Closets. The bathroom. There was no furniture that he could see, and the fridge and oven had both been unplugged. Was there even any power in the house?

He found a broken plastic hanger.

"Clear."

Hammer nodded. "Wish I had a K9 drug dog." He slid his gun into a holster at the small of his back. "Let's check the floor and the vents. Look for anything that might've been left behind."

Tate nodded. He went into the second bedroom while

Hammer took the master. He didn't mind backing up the under-cover agent. Spending an hour or two with someone who wasn't a criminal, doing something that, at least to an extent, felt like actual police work was invigorating.

He wandered around, checked the vents in the floor. Looked for boards that were loose. Whatever carpet there was had been removed at some point.

In the kitchen, Tate leaned up on the toes of his boots and looked at the top of the refrigerator. "Bingo."

Hammer came in a second later. "Yeah?"

Tate grabbed it and showed Hammer. "A phone." One of the old, flip kinds. Probably a burner. He flipped it open and powered it up. "Left it here, switched off. Basically a perfect place to hide something, on top of the fridge where you know no one looks."

Hammer looked over his shoulder, a smirk on his face. Then he said, "Eric should be able to pull all the recent calls and texts off it."

"I can, if you want me to take a look." Tate said, "No sense sending it in if there's nothing on it."

Hammer nodded. "Sounds good. But shouldn't you be working to prove you didn't kill Aggerton?"

When he hadn't done it, and there was no evidence that pointed to him? Seemed like a waste of his time compared with taking down a drug dealer. "I have time to help you as well."

Hammer didn't seem like he agreed with that assessment. Tate ignored his tone. He didn't kill Aggerton, so who would be able to prove that he had? There couldn't be any evidence, unless it had been planted.

The Hammer could have planted evidence the night Aggerton was killed. But if he had, then Savannah would've found it already. Tate would have been hauled into the police department to answer questions he had no response for.

Tate handed it over. "See if anything jumps out. I'll do one more walkthrough, make sure we didn't miss anything."

Mostly he figured the phone was discarded for a reason. They might be able to get something from it. Or not. It wasn't Tate's case, so he didn't have a vested interest in it being solved. He'd rather be at the hospital, with Claire awake, trying to talk some sense into her about Rob.

After he'd exhausted all the necessary searching, he went back to the kitchen. "Definitely nothing else."

Hammer looked up. "Bunch of threats. Demands. Instructions. Whoever owned this phone, they were low level. Seems like several people thought they could make him do whatever they wanted."

"Any idea who they are or who the owner was?"

"Just one name. Not the phone's owner, but someone else. West."

"Heard it before?"

"No," Hammer said. "It's a new one."

"Hope it plays out into something."

"Me too."

A car pulled into the drive. Headlights swept across the front window, lighting the kitchen entrance.

"Time's up."

"I need to see who it is." Hammer moved to the door of the hall and looked out. "Two guys. Muscle, but not brains."

Tate would've questioned how Hammer knew that, but he could do the same himself. It was all in the swagger. How a person carried themselves spoke volumes about who they thought they were before they even opened their mouth and dispelled all doubt.

Hammer muttered something under his breath. "One went around back. The other is headed for the front door."

"Rush them and run, or hide?"

"Closet. Let's find out why they're—" Hammer said nothing else. He just moved.

Tate got the message, moving to the pantry where he closed the folding door on himself and held his breath. Mushed between the shelves and the door panels, he couldn't move much. But he could see through a gap.

Enough to see one of the men enter through the back door, the same way he and Hammer had come in.

"You in?"

His friend called out in reply. "Yep!"

Both shut doors. The man in the kitchen held a gun and moved out to the hall. "Let's find it."

"You don't have to tell me twice," the other sounded like he was tired and in a bad mood. Probably hangry as well. "If we don't get that phone back, he'll take it out on us and I'm not looking forward to that."

The other made a noncommittal noise. Probably figuring he'd run before that happened, make his associate face the music for him while he got as far away as possible.

After a few minutes of boots on the floorboards, banging doors, and yelling, Tate figured wherever Hammer had hidden was a good spot. They hadn't found him.

One of the men returned to the kitchen. "It's not here."

"Maybe he never dumped it. Now he's dead, and we'll never find it."

Tate bit down on his molars. The second that one of them decided to check the pantry, he was going to have to be ready to fight.

"West is gonna be pissed if we don't find it."

The other man shoved him. "I know, idiot. You said that already. Just keep looking."

They moved out of the kitchen. Tate pushed at the hinged section of the door, folding it enough so that he could slip through when it was time. Then he'd duck outside. Hang around, hide in a better spot while making sure Hammer got out all right.

Phil needed to make another trip to the diner so Hollis could give him that look. He'd smile at her, and she would swoon.

Tate watched it happen all the time. Some people just fell for each other that way, while it had always been much more complicated for him.

And why did that make him think of Savannah?

"They're here."

Tate froze, halfway out the pantry. More guys? He moved to the hall, saw both their backs turned and headed down the hall. Bedroom, or bathroom? He found Hammer halfway out the bedroom window.

He lifted his gun, realized it was Tate, and said, "Come on."

"More are here."

"I know." He dropped onto the grass outside.

Tate stuck a leg over the window ledge after him.

"Hey!" A man stood in the doorway. He lifted a gun.

Too late. Tate had nowhere to go.

He made a split second decision, based entirely on gut. Which turned out to have a healthy dose of, "one of us should get out of here."

Out the window, Tate signaled to his companion. *Get out of here.* He didn't need Hammer, with the phone he'd confiscated, to get captured either. That wasn't going to be good for either of them.

He heard a low, "Sure?"

Tate made the signal again.

"Get back in here!" The gunman's yell echoed in the empty room.

He heard Hammer leave, a shuffle of boots headed away from him. Tate swung his leg over, and he was back inside the room.

"Lookie what I found."

His friends showed up. The two manhandled Tate until he was facing the wall, and then patted him down. They took his gun, wallet, keys, and phone.

Most of it they tossed aside.

When they spun him around, he said, "How you fellas doin' tonight?"

"Shut up." Gun guy shoved the barrel in his face. "And tell me what you're doin' here."

"Hard to tell you, if I shut up. Don't you think?"

The guy punched him with the hand holding the gun. Hard metal slammed into his ribs. Tate went down on one knee.

"Get him up."

They hauled him to his feet to face the gunman.

"You okay, old man?"

Tate blew out a breath. It was a pretty fair jab. Too bad he'd been sliced yesterday, or he'd probably be more on his game right now. Maybe he *was* getting to be too old for this.

"Now tell me why you're here."

To hear something they'd probably kill him for overhearing.

Tate figured this phone had something to do with Aggerton's death, and might even belong to him since he was the only person he knew who'd died recently. Hopefully his mind was firing correctly. He'd assumed Aggerton was low level, but maybe not.

Did all this really have to do with an undercover operation?

And why was Tate getting dragged into it every time he turned around?

12

———

S avannah moaned. She lifted a hand to touch her forehead and found an explosion of fire. Under her, the ground was hard. Her entire body ached.

Her phone was vibrating in her back pocket, underneath her.

She tried to blink. Felt for her gun—still there. That was a relief, at least as much of a relief as she could experience right now. *Still can't see.*

She blinked and realized she *could* see, but it was dark outside. She turned to look at a street light. Not blind. Her whole body shuddered. Hot. Cold. Pain. Warm numbness. It was like it couldn't decide how to feel.

Her phone was still ringing.

She shifted enough to slide it out. Focusing on the screen hurt a lot. She was pretty sure there was blood all down her face, and her nose might be broken.

"Hello?" She sounded like she had the worst cold in the world.

"Savannah?" It was Mia. "You okay?"

"No." Sounded more like, "Bo."

"You didn't come back, and it's been ages. We were getting

worried." Mia said. "Ted ran a trace on your phone, so I'm on my way to the courthouse. You're still outside?"

She tried to sit up. It took a second and a lot of groaning, but she planted her hand and managed to finally sit up.

The world spun like a kid's spinning top, and she leaned back against her car door.

"…can you hear me? Savannah?"

"Yep." She hissed out a breath and groaned.

"I see you." The call ended.

Savannah let her hand holding the phone drop to her lap and closed her eyes. Her upper lip was wet, and when she swallowed, her mouth tasted metallic. Like blood. She knew what that meant.

After a couple of seconds she heard shoes on the sidewalk. Running toward her. Sounded like more than one pair.

She turned her head to see who was coming and saw Conroy first, Mia right behind him.

Her partner said, "I'll call Dean."

Conroy came over and crouched. He shined a white flashlight beam at her face. Savannah hissed and turned away from it. He touched her chin. "Let me see."

Savannah said nothing.

"He's on his way." Mia stepped to her other side. "Ouch, that looks bad."

Conroy touched his thumbs to either side of her nose. She knew exactly what he was looking at.

"Don't." Didn't matter how gentle he was being.

He said, "Dean can reset it when he gets here. I've seen it done, but I haven't done it myself."

Just the idea of it made Savannah groan. Tears spilled down her cheeks.

"I'll check the glove box for napkins." Mia's voice trailed away as she rounded the hood of Savannah's car.

"What happened?"

She didn't want Conroy's voice to be soft, but it was.

Savannah looked around for the evidence bag she'd been carrying. All she saw on the ground was her phone with its now shattered screen. "Took the books."

"Huh?"

She had to be clear. Otherwise she'd have to say this more than once. Savannah took a breath and blew it out slowly. "Shoved me against the car. Took Summers's books."

Conroy stood. "I'm going inside to find the guard."

Mia tucked some napkins into Savannah's hands and said, "Dean should be here in a minute."

"He needs to reset her nose first." Conroy turned away.

Savannah wasn't going to sit here and wait for the torture. She shoved off the car and got her feet underneath her. Her foot smarted and she leaned on the car anyway. She pushed to standing, trying to ignore the way her brain didn't seem to know if it wanted to spin or throb. Maybe both. At the same time.

"Easy." Mia reached for her.

Savannah grasped her hand for solidarity, not necessarily for help staying upright. Her friends were here.

"Want me to call Tate?"

Savannah turned to her. Frowning hurt a lot. "Why would I—"

"Never mind. I just…" Mia shook her head. "Never mind."

"Let's go inside."

"Not so fast." The male voice called out with such authority Savannah's legs nearly buckled.

She turned to see Dean striding in her direction. His long legs ate up several feet of sidewalk with each step.

"That looks fun. How's the other guy?" He dumped a duffle bag on the ground beside her phone that she hadn't yet picked up and reached for her face. He touched her chin, turning it to one side, and then the other. "Well?"

"What?"

"The other guy?"

"Oh. He ran off."

"Coward." He dug a pair of rubber gloves from his bag and snapped them on. "I much prefer gunshots, but I guess this will have to do."

He reached for her face.

Mia said, "I *don't* prefer gunshots."

"No, I don't suppose you do." He slid his thumbs down her nose. She knew it was coming and grabbed the sides of his shirt at his waist. "Good. Steady, yeah?"

Savannah pressed her lips together.

"A regular southern belle."

She started to gasp. He snapped the bridge of her nose back into place. Savannah cried out, mostly out of frustration. How did he..?

"Ow. That *really* hurt."

He ignored her, digging around in his bag. He grabbed a packet that looked like a cold pack and, flicking it back and forth between his fingers, snapped whatever was inside the packaging. He reached for her again, but she backed off. He held out the package to Savannah and glanced at Mia, "I figure you probably prefer explosions. Right? Flames and burning police cars." He said it like the whole thing was a running joke.

Savannah took the package. It was cold, and growing colder, even in the first few seconds she held it.

He got out a couple of bandages and taped them across the bridge. "Hold that to your nose, and don't let go until I tell you."

"That hurt." Savannah was seriously pouting. She said, "We are not friends. Are you even a medical professional?"

"I'm fast. Does it matter?" When she said nothing, he grinned. "In the Navy they used to call me Frankenstein."

She nearly dropped the ice pack.

"As in, the doctor." He winked, bent for his duffel, and then was gone.

"That…"

Mia was laughing.

Savannah finished, "Wasn't funny. At all."

"Come on, partner. Let's go find the Chief. I'm a little worried he's in there reading the security guards the riot act for not seeing what happened to you." Mia wound her arm in Savannah's so it looked like they were walking as girlfriends, not cop partners, and not like Savannah needed help.

Which, considering the fact her head now pounded and she had to hold an ice pack against her nose, meant she probably did.

"Here." Mia led her to the waiting chairs in the foyer. "You take a load off, I'll go find everyone. And maybe some water."

"That would be good."

Savannah had to sit there, alone in the semidark, for five minutes. Just five, but it felt more like half an hour. She watched the clock tick every long, agonizing second.

Conroy strode back from the hall, followed by Mia and a security guard. The desk guy. "There's one guard on duty for the whole building. Can you believe that?" He shifted her hand holding the ice pack in order to take a peek, and winced. "Put that back on."

She wanted to fire back a comment, but her brain wasn't catching up.

"Cameras caught it, though."

She raised her free hand. "I don't want to see. Maybe later."

"Yeah, no." Conroy pulled out his phone. "I have to make a couple of calls. I want to know where Tate is."

"Why…" He was already gone.

"That sweater—hoodie—again." Mia groaned. "The guy running from Aggerton's office? He was the one that did this to you."

Tate had done this? No. It hadn't been him before, so it couldn't be him now. She couldn't think straight. The person with his sweater had shoved her.

The security guard stuck his hands in his pockets. "You probably need to be seen by a doctor." He looked around. "Uh, you want me to call one?"

Mia frowned at him. "What I want you to do is figure out who could have assaulted a police detective outside a building you're supposed to be patrolling. I can take care of my partner."

"Outside? Not my purview."

"Lucky for you." Mia's expression seemed to indicate she thought that was suspicious. As though the guy had purposely ignored what had happened outside. Maybe he was even paid off to look the other way and not call the cops when she was knocked out and had the books stolen.

That could be why he'd ignored her when she came in to get the books. He'd only shoved the clipboard and then the evidence bag at her, asking to see her badge.

Had he been paid off?

Mia turned to her. "Shall we?"

"Yep."

They found Conroy outside, pacing. "Call me." He ended the call he'd been on and spun around. "I left Tate a voicemail. No idea where he is. But the DA picked up. He has notes and copies of the books, and he said he needs to talk to us anyway."

"Let's go then."

Mia and Conroy both looked at her.

"One stop, one conversation. Then the hospital." When neither of them moved she added, "Dean already put my nose back in place. What else is there to do?"

Conroy sighed. "Let's go."

They loaded up in his car and drove across town. With the passing of each street, the houses sat farther and farther back from the curb. Longer and longer driveways. Then L-shaped houses. Detached, double-height, three-car garages. Welcoming lights that lined driveways.

They pulled up to a wrought iron gate, and Conroy pressed the bottom button on a keypad. He told the speaker his name, and who was with him.

A second later the gate rolled open.

"Huh."

"Yeah, right?" Mia and Savannah shared a smile. Then Mia said, "Conroy's been here before, but I never have."

The door opened like a great yawn. In the entryway stood a suited man, pencil thin with gelled hair. "The district attorney is expecting you."

He led them to a study, where an older gentleman sat behind a desk. "Conroy."

"Yes, sir. This is Lieutenant Tathers and Detective Wilcox."

She could have kissed him for leaving off her first name. The last thing Savannah needed was attention from the local district attorney. She'd had enough of a relationship with one in her previous life. As it was, she stumbled only to fall into a chair. Probably should have stayed standing, considering the smeared blood on the front of her shirt.

The assistant guy reached for her and winced. *Sorry to muss the expensive furniture.*

She shot him a death glare that seemed to work. Maybe not, though. She figured she didn't look too good.

He turned to his boss. "Sir?"

"Coffee please, Fenris."

Savannah resisted the urge to find that satisfying. She should be a better person than to relish in the fact someone else had to take an order.

"Rough night?"

She turned to the district attorney, too fast. Her head throbbed and she winced. "You could say that."

"Makes two of us."

Conroy said, "Sir?"

"Chief Barnes, I'm afraid someone is trying to kill me."

13

His back was against the wall. Metaphorically, if not literally. There was nowhere for Tate to go.

The boot connected with his ribs again. He was pretty sure that one cracked something.

Tate said, "All *right.*" That was more than enough.

"So you'll talk?"

Tate gritted his teeth. He took a second and just breathed, trying to clear his head of the pain that made his whole body feel like lead. Or one giant bruise.

He had to breathe a thank you to Whoever was up there listening. That he hadn't been kicked or hit in the head was no small thing. And it was a relief they hadn't settled for kicking and punching him in the gut, either, because he'd have raised his arms to defend himself, and then been tagged in his stitches for sure. Ouchie.

"Talk." The gunman pulled his leg back.

Tate raised one hand. "Okay. Give me a second." He pulled himself to sitting and said again, enunciating each syllable, "Just give me a second."

The gunman shifted his hand, pointing the barrel of his Glock at Tate's face. He didn't like being faced with a gun that was so much like one he owned. This one had the safe action system, unlike the regular safety that could be disengaged with the thumb, like most handguns. Anything that made you think in order to operate it—instead of just a point-and-shoot with no consideration—was always his preference.

While holding a deadly weapon, the worst thing a person could do was act on instinct without thinking. Contrary to popular belief.

"In a *second*, your brains will be all over this wall."

"Okay." Tate was repeating himself now. "I came here alone."

"I know who you are, Mr. Private Investigator. You on a job?"

"That's confidential." Tate decided to just go for it. "And I'll only talk to your boss." He gave the guy a second. "I want to see West."

The gunman hesitated. One of his buddies snickered. How many were here?

Tate lifted his chin.

The amused guy said, "Maybe we should give him what he wants," with a smile on his face. As though Tate would regret making that request.

He knew what would likely happen when he went up against the big boss. West had managed to keep his name secret for a long time. Tate had never even heard of him and didn't have a clue who the guy was. But apparently he was worthy of fear and respect.

These guys might think their boss warranted caution, but playing it safe had never gotten him anywhere. Certainly not results, at least. The cops had their ways of doing things, and he had his.

"Take me to him."

The gunman chuckled. Before he could speak, red and blue lights flashed outside.

"Cops!"

Three of them scattered like rats through the house. The gunman moved in as though he had all the time in the world. He pointed the gun right at Tate's forehead, pressed the cold metal against his skin. "Until next time."

Using the gun, he shoved Tate's head back. The back of Tate's head ground against the wall, and then the gunman was gone. Climbing out the window without a look back.

"Last Chance Police Department!"

Boots on the wood floor, down the hall. Moving at a steady pace.

"Clear."

"Anyone here?"

Tate didn't move. He wasn't even sure if he could, so that was probably for the best. Probably he looked pretty nonthreatening.

"Hands!"

Tate lifted his fingers on both hands, shifting only slightly to raise his palms. Not that he even had the strength left to raise his elbows.

"Tate?"

He blinked and focused on the officer, trying to rally some strength. "Basuto?"

The sergeant crouched in front of him, stowing his gun as he took in Tate. "That looks nasty."

Behind him another officer said, "Sarge?"

"It's Tate. Radio in it's all clear, and we'll get him taken care of. He's pretty messed up. Looks like he had the snot kicked out of him."

"Copy that." The younger officer stepped back into the hall. Donaldson was his name.

Frees was just scary looking, and a former marine. Allen was on a desk since he'd been shot a few weeks back. There were other officers, but Tate hadn't met them much. He and Basuto had worked a couple of cases together.

"What happened?"

Tate said, "I was about to ask you the same thing."

"Got an anonymous tip. Caller said an off-duty cop was being attacked inside this house."

He said nothing.

"And then it turns out to be you. Can you walk?"

Basuto helped him up. Not without a lot of groaning and gritting of teeth, which the sergeant seemed to think was funny. "Let's go, old man. You need a hospital."

Tate didn't laugh, though any other time he'd have been amused by the jab.

"How many?"

"Twelve, at least. Maybe twenty. It's all kind of blurry."

Basuto chuckled. "The truth?"

"Four. Get me mug shots, I'll ID them."

"Priors?"

Tate said, "Probably."

Having photos on file with the police department would only be the case if the men had been arrested prior to meeting Tate tonight. He wondered if Hammer's photo would be among them, and then it occurred to him that the undercover fed must have been the one to call in the anonymous tip. He'd had to leave Tate to those men, and so he'd done what he could to keep Tate alive.

It hadn't gotten either of them a result for the operation, and certainly no closer to West. Well, except the phone Hammer now had. But his anonymous phone call had probably saved Tate's life.

West. A name they now knew. Which meant the operation hadn't been a total loss.

Basuto walked him outside. Donaldson winced. The other two officers he didn't know couldn't care less and were walking up ahead. Donaldson said, "Should I call the chief and fill him in?"

"He's probably home for the night, right?" Tate didn't want Conroy to be bothered. Since Tate had stood on the opposite side of the fence, making sure Hammer's cover hadn't been blown, Conroy had reason to distrust him. If Tate could read him in about the FBI Op, things would be different. But he couldn't, so they weren't.

Sergeant Basuto said, "He was still in when the call went out that Detective Wilcox had been attacked."

Tate spun around to him. Too fast. Everything got dizzy.

Basuto continued, "They were supposed to go straight to the hospital, but made a stop off."

Tate wanted to ask where they were, since he thought Basuto might know but wasn't saying. Only he thought that if he opened his mouth, he would throw up. He managed to say, "Savannah?"

Now everyone would know he had feelings for her, or at least cared. Tate brushed off the worry about their opinions.

Basuto said, "She was collecting evidence from the court-house. The chief said she was slammed against her car so hard she broke her nose."

"Let's go."

They drove him to the hospital, and Tate got seen to. Pokes, prods. X-rays. He let them check everything, since he didn't plan on coming back soon to see the doctor about anything else.

Mostly he got funny looks, but he didn't feel that he owed anyone an explanation about what happened. He figured the fact he'd been brought here, checked in by the police, and then left in the doctor's care was answer enough.

He sent half a million texts to Savannah, but she didn't answer. Then he started with Conroy. Eventually he got back one message.

On our way.

He figured that meant Conroy was bringing Savannah in, so he called the number he had for Hammer before they got there. No answer. Tate sent an email to his brother-in-law—a report, essentially.

"Somewhere to be?"

Tate looked up from tying his shoe to find the doc standing there, eyebrows raised.

Tate lowered his foot from the bedcovers. Not how his mom had taught him, or how his sister raised him after her death. Shoes didn't belong on the furniture. He didn't answer, just asked a question of his own. "Cracked or just bruised?"

The doctor said, "Your ribs are just bruised."

Tate nodded. "Not steel-toed boots, then." Getting kicked with those was a surefire way to break a few bones.

The doctor frowned.

"Sign me out, doc."

"Mr. Hudson—"

"I don't like hospitals during the day, and during the night even less so. People walking around talking. Phones. Machines. You can never get rest, so instead of feeling better, you wind up feeling worse the next day. I'd rather be at home."

The doctor's gaze softened in a knowing way. Whatever. Tate didn't care what his words said about him, or his prior experiences with hospitals.

"Sign me out, doc."

"Copy that." The doctor tapped the screen of his iPad and said, "Give me two minutes. I'll send a nurse in with your prescription."

He disappeared, and Tate moved to the doorway. A nurse frowned at him, but he ignored her, watching the double doors to the waiting area. The nurse picked up the phone, then hit a button that opened the doors.

Savannah walked through first, flanked by Conroy and Mia.

Tate gaped. "What happened to your face?"

She winced.

Okay, so maybe he'd yelled. But seriously. What *on earth*? She turned and spoke to Mia and Conroy. Her boss eyed Tate, but nodded. Then Savannah continued alone, her gaze on him.

Tate spoke more quietly this time. "You okay?"

She came close enough to say, "I could ask the same about you." Her gaze skittered across his face.

"Just a couple of bruised ribs." He motioned to her face, and the abrasion on the bridge of her nose. She still had blood on her clothes, but it had been wiped from her face. "Broken?"

"Dean set it for me."

Tate rubbed his own nose. "He's good at that. Just not super friendly about it."

She smiled.

"Detective Wilcox?" The nurse had a tablet of her own and a collection of papers in one hand.

"Yes." Savannah turned to her.

"If you'll come this way?" The nurse waved her forward. Then she handed him the papers. "This is your exit ticket." She motioned for him to go in the opposite direction.

He took the papers, but didn't move. "Thank you, ma'am."

Savannah said, "You're leaving?"

He had been planning to. Now, with her looking at him like that, he felt the need to rethink it. "I'll go check on Claire. Elexa said she's been improving, and the doctors are really positive. I'll come back after. Okay?"

"Oh. Yes, okay."

She wandered off with the nurse, leaving him to wonder about these flashes of vulnerability he continued to see in her. Tate was pretty sure she didn't show them to anyone else. But he didn't know that for sure, did he?

Tate moved to the doors where Conroy and Mia had stood watching the entire exchange between him and Savannah. "Is she okay?"

Mia said nothing. Conroy offered an answer. "Knocked out for a few minutes, nose broken. The evidence she was transporting was stolen, and she was left lying on the street."

Tate saw a flash of gritted teeth. The chief was not happy.

"Not like you're responsible," Tate reminded him. "Savannah's a big girl."

"So she has to swing out there, left to fend for herself?"

"I'm not saying she should have to, I'm saying she can handle herself. She's the first one who would tell you that."

Conroy was not appeased.

"Heard the name 'West' before?"

"In what context?"

"The local drug trade." Tate let him draw his own conclusions about that.

Mia said, "Does this have anything to do with you looking like you got the snot kicked out of you?"

"I was on a job, helping a friend." That was all he was going to say about it. "Heard the name West. Got a lead that Aggerton's death might have something to do with drugs in Last Chance."

The skin around Conroy's eyes flexed.

Before he could say anything, noise erupted out in the waiting area. Conroy hit the release button and pushed out.

"Sir, if you could just calm down." The female staff member was dressed in slacks and a wool sweater.

Rob shoved her up against the front counter. "You don't tell me what to do. I want to see my wife."

14

———

Savannah heard the yelling and turned back.

"Let's get you situated. The doctor will—"

She broke off, ran back to the door and hit the button on the wall. It slid open achingly slow. As soon as there was enough space for her to move through the door, Savannah turned sideways and slipped out. Her face hurt. It felt like the worst sinus infection in the world. Like she needed to blow her nose, but she knew doing so would only make it worse. Make the most painful thing ever even more painful.

The hospital staff lady stared at Rob, fear on her face.

Tate stepped between the two of them and shoved Rob back.

"Easy." Conroy got between them. "I'm already arresting him. Don't make it so I have to take you in as well."

Mia saw Savannah coming. "Conroy."

He turned. "Go see the doctor, Detective Wilcox."

"I thought you might need help."

One hand still planted on Rob's chest, Conroy said, "I got this. So go." He glanced at Tate. "You, too."

Rob pushed his hand away. "Yeah Hudson, you too."

Tate shifted toward him.

Savannah said, "Tate!"

She wasn't even sure it would work. Would he allow her to draw his attention from the man who had beaten and hospitalized his ex-wife? She wanted to arrest Rob as much as Conroy probably did, and now would, for this. But until Claire woke up and made a statement about what had happened to her, there were no witnesses. No proof that Rob had hurt her.

Tate glanced at her.

Rob chuckled.

"Yeah," Conroy said. "So funny." He grasped Rob's wrist and snapped on cuffs, then secured the other. "You're under arrest for assault. We'll start with the hospital staffer, and see where things progress from there."

No one moved.

Conroy glanced back. "Tate?"

"Basuto is bringing me mug shots so I can make ID's."

The chief nodded, then left. Savannah watched Tate stare after them as Conroy walked Rob outside. Mia squeezed Savannah's arm. She didn't need her partner to say anything. Savannah nodded to her. Mia crossed to the staff lady and spoke with her. Taking her statement.

Savannah said, "Tate?"

He turned to her then, a dark look on his face. "Did you see that?"

She nodded, though she'd only seen part of it. That was enough. Tate seriously needed to sit down, and she was about to fall over. Her face *hurt*. "Come on."

"Detective Wilcox," the nurse was at the door. She sounded impatient. "The doctor is waiting for you."

She didn't take her attention from Tate. "Come with me?"

He studied her face. Then nodded. She held out her hand and held her breath. He took it, lacing his warm fingers through hers.

Savannah said, "Mug shots?"

He didn't speak. They reached the door.

"Back so soon?" The nurse smiled at him.

He didn't smile back.

Savannah tugged on his hand. "Mug shots?"

"Of the guys who jumped me."

There was more to it than that, she was sure. Before she went any farther, Savannah stopped and requested he tell her what happened. All of it—being on a solo operation, hearing guys come in and say "West," only to be discovered before he could slip out. Finally, Basuto's arrival.

She blew out a breath. "They could've killed you if that neighbor, or whoever the anonymous caller was, didn't act fast enough."

He shrugged, a sharp movement that induced a wince.

"Might want to curtail that activity for a while."

"Shrugging? Like you, and blowing your nose?"

She grinned at him. He didn't seem amused. Actually, it seemed like he didn't like the look of her right now. She felt the pang in her chest of hurt feelings.

"Speaking of which—" The doctor pointed a tanned finger at the bed. "—park it up there, Detective." Savannah studied him. A doctor who seemed well rested with sunglass tan marks to prove it.

"Let me guess, Hawaii?"

Surprise washed over the doctor's face. "How did you know?"

"Police detective. Comes with the territory. Could've been Florida, though. The Hawaii part was a guess."

The doctor chuckled.

Savannah hauled herself up on the bed as the doctor came close. Tate let go of her hand but leaned against the wall and watched. She could tell he was far from here, though. Deep in his thoughts. She had enough regret over the past to know what that looked like.

The doctor felt around her face with his gloved hands. "Who set this for you?"

"Dean Cartwright."

He leaned back. "Oh. Well. You can put ice on it, but Dean did a good job. So…do you want a prescription for Ibuprofen?"

"No."

He pulled the gloves off. "That's all she wrote, then."

Tate pushed off the wall. "That's it?"

"Nothing to X-ray. It was well taken care of." The doctor shrugged. "I might have to persuade Dean to take on a job as a concierge doctor with all the fixed-up patients he's sending me."

Tate said nothing.

She didn't want to disappoint the doctor with a reality check. Savannah might not know Dean all that well, but she figured he wasn't interested in being a medical professional. All his skills had been learned in the military. He was doing the things that translated into civilian life, while making his own way with everything else. At least, that was what Ted had told her about his older brother. The kid was actually pretty worried about Dean.

The doctor said, "Any concerns?"

"About my nose?" Savannah said, "No."

"You have a problem—anything at all—you know where to find me."

"Thanks."

He nodded and wandered out. Tate closed in.

She looked up at him. "What now?"

"Are you really all right?"

"My face feels like it's going to explode. You?"

He said, "I can't breathe all the way. Other than that, I'm fine."

She had to smile. It was that, or groan. Neither of them were fighting fit. "Seems like we both had an eventful night."

"I'm sorry you got hurt and I wasn't there to help."

How could he have known she would run into trouble

retrieving the books? "Nothing you could've done." She said, "What if I felt guilty that I didn't stop those boots from making impact with your ribs? Not that you'd have needed my help stopping anything, since it seems you have a guardian angel."

"I'd have needed you anyway."

What did that mean? "Now I *do* feel guilty."

He shook his head. "Not my intention. Even though I could have used help—someone to watch my back—I wouldn't have wanted you there."

"Because I'm a cop?"

"I don't like knowing you're in situations where you have to handle yourself like a trained pro. You got hurt tonight. Nothing you could've done to fight back, just total surprise. I do wish I'd been there. Like I wish you'd been with me."

Savannah sighed. "Maybe it's the pain, but I don't know what you're talking about." It sounded like he was speaking in circles. Was that circular logic, or whatever it was called?

Tate twisted and sat on the bed, facing her. "I'm talking about partners."

"I already have one."

He shot her a look.

"Fine. The lieutenant is on probation, and I'm not going to call her in if I don't think I need backup. I was picking up evidence from the courthouse."

"Never know when something like that will happen."

"So I'm supposed to have backup whenever I go out?"

Tate shrugged. She saw the flare of pain in his eyes. He said, "In an ideal world, yeah. But that isn't what happens."

"You don't have backup."

"Exactly," he said. "I work solo a lot."

"So do I." And yet, they clearly both cared that the other one swung out there unprotected a lot. No backup, no one to call for help when it was needed. "We should make a pact."

"What kind?"

"You need help, you call me. If I get in a situation, I'll do the same. Of course, when I need official 'cop' help, that's who I'll call. Some things need to be above board, and I won't jeopardize that. But if I don't want to be alone, or I think it might get dicey, then I'll tell you. And you do the same."

"A courtesy call."

She shrugged.

"Concierge protective detail."

Savannah grinned.

His gaze dropped to her lips. She watched as he leaned in. Anticipation came in like a rush as she realized what was coming.

"Okay, then." The nurse whipped back the curtain. "I—No!"

Tate leaned back. Savannah saw the woman over his shoulder rush over and whack Tate with a stack of papers. "No kissing! She has a broken nose!"

Tate flushed red.

Savannah started to laugh, groaned and tried to touch her face.

"Hand down!" The nurse blew out a breath. "Sorry." She straightened the papers and held them out. "You're good to go, and this is your prescription."

Tate scratched at his jaw. She took the discharge paperwork and said, "Thanks."

The nurse said, "Do you have a ride home? I wouldn't recommend driving."

Tate said, "We can split a rideshare?"

"Works for me." The nurse left.

"I'd like to check on Claire first, though. Is that okay?"

Savannah didn't want to nod. She hopped off the bed. "Ready when you are."

They walked together down the hallway, and Savannah waited to see if he would take her hand again. He didn't.

But he had almost just kissed her. That had to mean something, right? At least it was a nice thought, although frustrating. Certainly nicer than thinking about whoever had slammed her against the car.

"There had to have been something in those books that implicated whoever killed Aggerton."

Tate glanced at her. "So they stole them before it could be made public? Trial's coming up."

"The DA has notes, though. He has copies. And with someone trying to kill him as well, it can't just be about covering up the fact they killed Aggerton. Or getting Summers released because of lack of evidence."

It had to be more than that.

"Someone's trying to kill the DA?"

She nodded. "We met with him before we came here. He's being threatened. And get this, there was even poison in his drink. He's been getting sick."

"Poison?"

"Yeah, like Aggerton."

He tipped his head to the side. "I thought Aggerton was stabbed?"

Savannah opened her mouth to explain. Then she realized that while he might be attractive, and attracted to her, Tate was not a cop. He wasn't working this case with her as a consultant. She should talk this out with Mia, not Tate.

The other option was to have Conroy bring the PI on as a consultant, but the chief would never go for it. Especially when he realized she had feelings for Tate—assuming he didn't already know. He was way too much of a wild card, regardless of his skills and experience as an investigator.

"Poison?"

She shook her head. "Never mind. Forget I said it."

He frowned, and they stepped onto the elevator. After the doors slid shut he said, "Ever heard the name 'West'?"

Savannah thought about it.

"I have a confidential informant. He's the only one who's ever mentioned that name to me. He said it like he was scared, and in awe. Never told me why, though. Was a while back... probably six months." She shrugged. "Haven't even seen him since. I figure he dropped off the wagon, so I don't know how credible the information was."

They rode the elevator upstairs, to the second floor where Claire was being monitored.

"Might want to look into the guy. This 'West' person, whoever he is?" Tate said as the elevator doors slid open. He stepped off first. "I think he's pulling strings."

"First I've heard of it."

Was she really missing something? Savannah worked all the major crimes in Last Chance. The town wasn't big, and that was a pretty loose description. Still, if someone in town were pulling strings, even running things like some kind of organized crime boss, surely she'd have heard about it. At least, more than just two mentions of his name.

A nurse ran from one room and nearly ran right into her. "Sorry."

She reacted to the near collision, pain rolling through her head. Savannah reached for her nose. A reflex. Probably not a good idea.

Tate touched her elbow. His attention was on the hall up ahead of them.

"What is..."

She realized she could hear beeping. Two more nurses, or orderlies, ran into the same room. "Is that her room?"

Tate nodded, his face gray.

"Hey, what are you guys..."

Savannah turned. The young woman who'd been outside her house the night she'd collided with Tate stood behind them.

"Elexa." His voice was a low rumble.

The girl's face fell. She shoved between Tate and Savannah

and raced for the room, but stopped just short of the open doorway. Elexa stared inside.

Savannah followed and stopped behind her. Tate right beside her. She touched the girl's shoulder, but her hand was shrugged off.

Inside the room, the doctor who'd treated her stepped back. "Time of death, ten sixteen p.m."

15

———

ime of death. Tate took a step back. Elexa gasped. He swung around and caught her before she fell to the floor.

"Mom." She moaned the word.

Tate sank to the floor, holding the teen tight in his arms while she sobbed. Tears ran down his face as well. Tears for his ex-wife, or simply because Lex cried and there was no reason to hold his tears back. Didn't really matter which it was.

Tate squeezed his eyes shut. He didn't know how long they sat like that before a nurse crouched beside him and touched Lex's back.

"Honey."

She shifted to look at the nurse. No, not a nurse. This woman wore regular clothes and had an ID badge. She was a grief counselor.

"I'm so sorry." The woman seemed compassionate enough, but Tate figured she dealt with this frequently. Enough to be numb to it by now. She handed Elexa a wad of tissues, then glanced at Tate. "Let's go somewhere more comfortable than the floor, yeah?" She kept her voice soft.

Lex nodded. Tate helped her to her feet, and the counselor held her elbow.

"I'll catch up."

Lex glanced back at him, tears on her face.

"Go."

She went with the counselor. Past where Savannah stood watching. Tate backed up to the wall and leaned against it, bent over with his hands on his knees.

She moved closer. "You okay?"

Tate straightened. He pressed his fingers to the inside corners of his eyes and nodded.

"I need to speak with the doctor." She'd already turned away by the time he looked up, two long strides catching her up to the doctor. He watched her hold her hand out. "Detective Wilcox."

The doctor working the second floor tonight shook it. "You knew Mrs. Gaynes?"

"Can you tell me about the manner of her death?"

He folded his arms, phone in one hand. His tie was purple, his shirt high-quality white. Black slacks and brand name sneakers. Different doctor than the one who'd treated him and Savannah, but there were a number of doctors serving the people of Last Chance in this facility. Tate knew a couple by name, ignoring the implication of what that meant. He was a frequent flyer, that was for sure, but not just to tend to his own injuries. He came in quite a bit to sign in a client of his or a victim he'd come in contact with.

This doctor he didn't know. Although it was clear from his stance he wasn't all that impressed with Savannah's line of questioning.

Tate scraped at his cheeks with the flat of his palms, brushing away the remnants of his grief. But it didn't get rid of the pit in his stomach—the sour knot that sat there—the one that rose up to choke a person until they dissolved into a ball of emotion.

Not super manly, but his sister had always told him that holding it in would make things worse. Considering what he and

Millie had been through, losing their parents the way they had, she'd been forced to walk him through his grief. His older sister had taught him so much. Mostly about sticking close to the people you cared about.

Tate pulled out his phone and sent his sister a text.

LOVE YOU.

She'd taught him it was right to still care about his ex-wife, even after the divorce. In this way, Claire had known she could always count on him. He'd also been a part of Elexa's life in a way that was supportive, but not confusing, ultimately giving her the freedom to choose. The space to realize she didn't like her stepdad and she wanted someone else—Tate—to fill that spot in her life.

Savannah glanced at him, then returned to her conversation. "So there was nothing to indicate this might happen?"

Tate closed in on the two of them. She seemed worried about him, that was good. Right? He'd almost kissed her earlier. She'd seemed receptive to him doing that. If they hadn't been interrupted, things might have turned out entirely differently.

But she was back to professional Savannah now. Though it was clear she cared, the detective was at work.

Her questions gave him pause. Did she think something nefarious had happened here?

The doctor said, "The medical examiner will have to make an official ruling."

"But you're qualified to have an opinion."

"Of course, however, that means you might not like the answer."

Tate said, "Which is?"

The doctor said, "Sometimes complications arise. The unforeseen can happen, and despite the advances of modern medicine, patients can still succumb to their injuries. Or the ravages of disease."

Savannah didn't back down. "I'd like to speak with the

nurses on duty, to ascertain if anyone unauthorized entered or exited this room in the time prior to the patient's death."

The doctor lifted his brows.

"Please."

"Where's your warrant? I know you people like to throw your authority around, but there are regulations that ensure we respect patient privacy." He wandered to the nurse's station muttering to himself.

"You think it might be foul play?"

Savannah turned to him and went to scrunch up her nose, kind of a shrug. "Ouch. Murder, or malpractice."

Tate said, "Maybe he's right, and she just had a blood clot break loose and reach her brain or something."

"You really think that?"

"Not everything is something you need to investigate."

She stepped closer. "Do you want me to drop this? Because I'm going with my gut here, but if you don't think I should pursue it then I won't. I'll leave it alone."

For him? She would. He saw it in her eyes. Savannah would drop the entire thing if he asked her to. She had enough on her plate without shouldering a whole other case. Then again, what if her gut was spot on?

"Check surveillance. If no one was in or out," he said, "then that answers the lingering question."

"What question would that be?"

"What Rob was playing at in the lobby." Tate said, "He was here right before she died. Could be it was planned as a distraction. Conroy and Mia were here, along with you. If someone was planning on killing her, he could have orchestrated that disturbance to throw everyone off."

"Or he had reason to believe his wife was in danger," she said. "He came here to check on her, played it wrong, and wound up getting arrested."

"Then he should've told someone."

When he'd been marched away by Conroy, Rob could have said he believed Claire was in danger. But he hadn't. Because he had too much pride, or because he hadn't known? The third option was his theory that Rob had been leaving an open window for a killer to get into her room. End her life, and make it look like an accident.

Had she been murdered like Aggerton?

"If Claire was killed," he said, "then does that mean her death is linked to Aggerton's death?"

"It could be."

Tate blew out a breath. "I don't know how we'd find out for sure."

Savannah stepped closer to him, touching the outside of his biceps. "Let me do this. If there's something to know, I'll tell you. Otherwise, can you not worry about it?"

He liked that she didn't tell him not to worry. No, she asked if he was able to not worry. Tate said, "I'd like to know. And I'll trust you to get me that answer."

His ribs hurt, among other things. Her face looked like she'd gone a few rounds with someone bigger.

Tate pulled her in and hugged her, needing the comfort more than she did. Probably.

Savannah returned his squeeze. "I'll let you know."

He nodded, dismissed as she went back to work. Tate needed to also get back to work, after he checked in with Lex. He doubted the girl would want to go back to her stepfather's house. She was fine at Maggie's right now, staying in the same house as Savannah. Tate could get the detective to check in on her, as men weren't allowed past the front parlor.

"You okay?"

He nodded to the nurse. "Where did the counselor take Elexa?"

"The kitchen would be my guess. It's pretty quiet in there this time of night." She hesitated. "One second."

She retrieved a grocery bag from behind her counter. "I'll

leave these with you for now. There's some paperwork involved."

"I'm not Claire's husband. You'll have to talk to him about the legal stuff." He lifted the bag. "This, I'll pass to her daughter."

"I'm not sure—"

"Elexa will take care of Claire's personal belongings. You talk to Mr. Gaynes about the legal stuff."

Tate didn't wait around to get dragged into her objections. He dug out Claire's phone and took a look. She'd gotten a handful of texts and calls since being admitted to the hospital the night she was brought in.

Was it really Rob who had hurt her? If Tate could prove it, then it would give him a solid alibi for another crime that had happened the same night. Not that that conclusion would be good for Rob, but then he'd be off the hook for Aggerton's death.

If he was honest with himself, Tate would be happy to see Rob found guilty of both—and everything—just because he thought the guy was a scumbag.

But he needed proof. Nothing could be set in stone without evidence. He'd had entirely too much cop training to live his life any other way.

So far he had nothing that tied Rob to Aggerton, and it was just hearsay that tied Aggerton to this "West" person—assuming that the phone they'd found in the house actually belonged to the dead man. It was highly likely Claire's husband had nothing to do with the CPA's death, simply because there was no reason to believe otherwise.

Tate walked in the direction the nurse pointed and found Lex with her hands around a paper cup. The counselor sat across from her.

She looked up and saw the phone in his hand. "Give it to me. I'll unlock it for you."

The counselor's expression changed. Tate wasn't sure what to make of it. He glanced between them. "Everything okay?"

"Elexa is working through the grief in perfectly understandable ways that are not out of the ordinary."

Lex shot him a look, but he could see the grief in her eyes.

"Especially when the future can be so uncertain."

Lex twisted back in her seat to face the counselor. "I'm not getting put in foster care."

"I'm afraid that for a minor, things can be out of your hands. You might feel powerless, but there are adults you can trust to take care of you if you don't wish to return to your stepfather."

It was looking like it would turn out for the better that Rob had never bothered to adopt her.

"You're right." Lex said, "There are adults I can trust, and I know that because I'm looking at him." She pointed right at Tate.

"That's sweet, Lex. But you and I aren't related."

She shot up out of the chair. "So adopt me."

"That's not a decision we're going to make right now."

"But you will make that decision." She stood in front of him, eyes desperate. "Just not right now."

"You know I'm not going to let you slip away."

She sniffed, straightening in front of him. "I do. I know that." She nodded. "But it's still nice to hear it."

He gave her a hug. "Don't squeeze too hard. I have bruised ribs."

Lex huffed. The hug didn't last long, and then she pulled back. "Give me the phone. I want you to have it so you can see how he treated her."

Tate waited. She handed it back and he looked at the slew of text messages Claire had missed after she was rendered unconscious from the attack. The thread with Rob was buried under new messages, including a string from a local number she hadn't added to her contacts.

I KNOW YOU WERE SLEEPING WITH MY HUSBAND.

There were more, some more graphic than others and many laced with profanity. Tate frowned, reading the string Claire hadn't replied to. Someone accusing Claire of sleeping with their spouse? Had she really been having an affair?

I'LL KILL YOU.

"Did he murder her?"

Tate looked up.

"If Rob hurt her, and she died, then it's murder. Right?"

"Detective Wilcox is looking into it. I'm sure she'll keep you updated, no matter what happens." He gave her shoulder a squeeze. "You just worry about you."

Regardless of how she felt right now, grief would come like a wave and she would experience many different degrees. He thought about his own grief over his parent's deaths.

"It doesn't get easier, Lex. But you will learn how to live with it."

16

———

Savannah gripped the phone and stood in the hall outside the security guard's office waiting for him to show up.

Convoy sighed, the sound audible over the phone connection.

"I know," Savannah said. "Could've been anything...a complication...a mistake in her treatment." She didn't want to say malpractice, but that was a reality. Even doctors were human. If she couldn't give them the space to be fallible, then how could she ask anyone to give her the same grace?

"Or murder."

She was glad he said that. Savannah didn't want to say it out loud where hospital staff could hear. "I'm about to find out."

"You do that." He sounded tired. "I took a chance on you, Savannah. Figure this out. I want reports on my desk. I want recommendations I can take to Ilkins that will make us all rest easy."

Nolan hadn't said much before he'd had his assistant pretty much kick them out of the house. Despite her obvious injury, their story, and what the DA himself was facing, he hadn't wanted to admit he needed help.

He only wanted to pass it off as an annoyance when it was

clear to all of them that he was scared. Hang ups. Nolan Ilkins was being watched, but he had no idea who might be behind it. Then there was the issue of his drink being poisoned.

Whoever had targeted Aggerton was now targeting the DA.

Aggerton had done the DA's taxes for years now, but Savannah couldn't be sure that was enough of a connection, unless the work meant Aggerton had known too much about people and then abused his access to it. Maybe he'd been blackmailing someone, and they'd struck back at him—with a knife. Could be that he'd pushed a victim too far. Now they were scrambling to cover up what they'd done.

"Wilcox."

She started. "Yes, chief?" A nurse turned to glance at her, but she waved the woman's concern away and said to Conroy, "What is it?"

"You didn't respond. I thought the call got dropped."

"Just running down some theories in my head."

"I know you're tired. You've been working around the clock on this, but I want answers. This murder needs to be solved."

"Yes, sir." Savannah hung up before he could make any more demands. It was a chicken move, but he was right. She was tired. Her face hurt. She needed ice and more pain meds.

Still, Tate was with Elexa. Consoling her. There was no way Savannah was having a harder time doing her job while injured than either of them were doing right now handling the shock and grief. Though Tate was injured, he wasn't above helping a teen who had just lost her mother. To say she was impressed was a giant understatement.

She needed the autopsy on Claire Gaynes to be done quickly, but in the meantime there was still plenty to do on the Aggerton case.

Savannah leaned against the wall. The nurse wandered back with a cold pack and handed it over to her. "Put this on your face. Hurts just looking at you."

Savannah said, "Thanks."

She shut her eyes, the cold pressed to her face. Just enough to feel it, but not so it hurt more than it already did. *Ugh.* She'd never handled pain well. It tended to make her grumpy, like when she'd kind of lost it with the DA earlier tonight. He needed their help. Why did he not want to admit that? Seemed dumb to be so stubborn.

At least she hadn't told him that to his face.

I took a chance on you, Savannah. Why did Conroy have to go and throw that in her face? She'd been the only detective in Last Chance. Now she had Lieutenant Tathers for a partner. She was trying not to let it feel like they were ganging up on her, outranking and challenging her.

Any other time she'd have seen it as an occasion to excel. A reason to work twice as hard and prove to everyone else what she knew to be true about herself. This case? A day when she'd been attacked on the street? She'd lain there for only minutes, unconscious. But the fact she was left like that made her feel vulnerable.

Savannah shuddered. It would take time for her to work through that. Time, and arresting the person who'd had the brazenness to sneak up behind her, knock her unconscious and steal her evidence.

The same person who had killed Aggerton.

Which meant the answer was in those books that the DA had given them copies of. Not the entire thing, since he'd only copied pages relevant to his case, but he'd also passed along his notes, and it wasn't just a small portion of the books.

The answer was there, in her email inbox, waiting for her to get back to it first thing tomorrow. After she tried to sleep, which of course would do nothing but lead to a fitful night of tossing and turning.

But the fact it was just regular police work settled her more than anything. Despite all she'd been through, and all that was going on now, Savannah was a detective. Always had been, and always would be. That identity was what grounded her.

"Detective Wilcox?"

She lowered the ice pack, and the security guard winced. Like she had time for his opinion of how she looked? "I need to see the surveillance footage for the second floor." She gave him the room number Claire had been in, and the approximate time.

He tugged on keys tethered by a cord to his belt. "Let's take a look-see."

The computer took forever to wake up. Savannah grabbed a chair from the far side of the security office. It was unmanned at this time of night, while the other night security guard did his rounds of the hospital.

She sank into the chair and tried not to tap her foot, waiting for him to peck on the keyboard with two fingers and navigated through to the screen she needed.

Finally he played the footage while she watched the screen, fully expecting to see the same sweater she'd now seen twice— once outside Aggerton's office, and then again on the footage of her being shoved against her car.

But this guy had a green jacket on over a black, zippered sweater, the hood up. He looked both directions before slipping into Claire Gaynes' room. "Wind that back." The display at the bottom put this just minutes before her death.

The security guard slipped the bar left.

Savannah turned to him. "Play it."

He turned and huffed at the screen.

Something about the man bothered her. Savannah kept her mouth shut while she watched, long enough she could confirm it. Bingo. The walk. "She's trying to hide it, but that's not a man." Savannah watched her enter the room, her back to the camera the entire time. "Any way we can see from the other direction?"

The security guard shook his head. "Only camera in that hall is this one."

"How about when she comes out again?"

They kept watching. The woman came out, midturn. With her back to the camera, she walked in the opposite direction she'd come from.

The security guard said, "Could be she passed a camera in the stairwell, or the lobby."

"Keep watching. I want a copy of every angle you can get on this lady. We need to know who she is."

On screen, the staff around Mrs. Gaynes' room suddenly jumped up and ran in. Savannah turned away.

"I'll send it over."

She pulled the door open. "Thanks." As she strode down the hall, she sent a text to Mia.

It was a woman.

Mia's reply came quickly.

Means whoever killed Aggerton and took the books isn't the same person who killed Claire.

Savannah dialed her number so she could just cut to the chase instead of wasting time with a long text conversation.

When Mia picked up, Savannah said, "It could be a cooperative effort."

"But Rob Gaynes has an alibi. He was beating his wife when Aggerton was killed."

"Right." Savannah bit her lip. "We know he didn't kill his wife tonight, because he was in the lobby. But it could be he was the distraction so that woman could come in and do the deed."

"How do we know she didn't kill Aggerton as well?"

"It wasn't a woman at Tate's office. That was a guy in a ski mask. But it still could be someone connected to him." Savannah thought about it. "Like I said, a cooperative effort."

"Because you want to somehow protect Tate, in a way, by taking down the person who is the biggest threat to him."

And his family.

Mia hadn't said it, but Savannah heard the words as well as if she had. "This isn't about Tate, or how I feel about Gaynes. You should know me better than that by now."

Mia said nothing.

"He was on the suspect list, wasn't he?" She pointed out. "That means we believe he—Tate or Rob— could've killed Aggerton."

"But not Claire. And he didn't hurt you."

She made a good point. Savannah walked into the elevator, "So actually, we can rule Tate out as well if we're following that logic. Because the person who killed Aggerton also hurt me, and it was *not* Tate. He was nowhere near the courthouse at the time."

"So he says."

Savannah glanced at the ceiling for a second. "You're the most cynical person I've ever met. I thought you liked Tate. He told me he was planning on asking you to be his receptionist."

Mia snorted. "Me? Sit behind a desk?"

"Might be in your future, if things don't go to plan."

"That's why I'm enjoying field work while I can."

Savannah allowed her true feelings to show on her face. She was alone in the elevator. If Mia wanted to tempt fate, and risk permanent hearing damage, what was it to her? Mia was the one who would be relegated to paperwork and desk duty if she got into a situation where the decibel level around her rose too high. Given the scar tissue from the gun going off so close to her ear, she couldn't even handle being outside on the fourth of July. Let alone get into a shootout with someone.

Mia said, "But going through these files is also *super* fun."

Savannah snorted that time. "Mmm. I can tell. Though, it's probably better than getting your face smashed against a car window."

"Eek."

"I'd feel better if we can figure out who this guy is before he gets to someone else. So far, we have no idea who he is. Now there's a woman in the mix."

Savannah had a certain gut instinct that the person who'd stabbed Aggerton was tied in some way to Rob Gaynes. Why else drag Tate into this, like it was easy to try and implicate a man like him in a murder?

Savannah said, "Gaynes's assistant sent hate mail to Aggerton, right?"

"You talked to him already."

Savannah said, "Seemed pretty kowtowed. Like he lived to do Gaynes's bidding, probably as scared of him as Claire was." She hadn't gotten the sense from Patrick Dearnum that he was a killer, under that "assistant" veneer he and Fenris had. And what was it with these assistants and their ridiculous names?

The elevator doors opened, and she stepped back out onto the floor where Claire's body was being wheeled out of her room under a sheet.

"Kowtowed enough to murder for him?"

"Guess we should have another chat," Savannah said. "See where the chips fall." It wouldn't solve the mystery of the woman who had visited Claire, but it might help with this case.

"I'll take a look at the surveillance from Aggerton's office and the one from outside the courthouse again. See if there's a way to tell if it's Patrick Dearnum."

It was a long shot, but considering Conroy's expectation that she'd be able to solve this case, Savannah was more than happy to explore every avenue.

Mia said, "Are you on your way back to the office?"

"In a bit. Not yet. I'll let you know."

"I won't be here much longer, I'll probably end up picking this back up in the morning."

"Copy that."

An orderly rolled past her with Claire's body lain out on the bed under the sheet. Savannah stared as they moved to the elevator. She hung up, her hand falling to her side.

Was that what the DA in New Orleans had looked like? Rolled away on a stretcher after he was gunned down and left on the street, no longer good for anything but a body bag.

For a long time she'd thought that was how she would end

up. Every minute of every day she'd walked around knowing that was coming. The end—the roll of that zipper over her face. The clack of the metal teeth meeting each other.

And then, nothing.

All her effort would be wasted. It would be the ultimate failure to not be able to keep herself alive. Savannah had been slammed against that car, powerless to stop it. She could have died.

Aggerton's killer, still out there.

Her business in New Orleans, buried. Swept away. No one left to tell the truth of what had happened. It would die with her. Locked away in her memories.

"Van?"

She twisted around, half expecting to see her past in front of her. But it was Tate.

"You okay?"

She wanted to answer no, that she wasn't all right, but beside him was Elexa. The girl stood there with a dry face but puffy eyes, a tissue balled in one hand.

Savannah just said, "It's been a long day."

"If you're not doing anything—" Tate motioned to the girl. "Can you take Lex home? Maggie is expecting her."

17

———

Tate shut the car off but didn't get out. He'd parked down the street a little ways, facing the police department.

He rubbed his face, then remembered he shouldn't move even that much and continued to stare through the windshield. His ribs hurt every time he breathed. More now than earlier, before he'd hugged Lex and she'd squeezed him entirely too hard. But he hadn't objected.

Sending her home with Savannah had been a good idea, even if it was spur of the moment. Who knew where she would live now that her mom was gone. Rob wasn't her adoptive father, just her stepdad. Would he fight for custody of her? The girl was sixteen, nearing the age when a lot of kids tended to—sadly—age out of the foster system, left to live life on their own. Whatever happened to her now would alter her view of the future. Most likely for worse.

A responsible young woman with a safe place to live and other women to guide her wasn't a bad idea at all. Any judge would see it as a positive arrangement—better than one under the thumb of a man who had beat his wife. Her mom.

Or with a private investigator.

He sat on the street watching the police department until the night shift guys came in for lunch. Conroy was in there. Tate knew he hadn't gone home.

He should go in. Get the chief to let him talk to Rob Gaynes.

Though, they both knew how that conversation would end up. With Rob getting a taste of his own medicine. He'd show Rob the pain Claire felt, and then Conroy would be forced to break it up. Then Tate would be in a world of trouble.

His passenger door opened. Tate had his gun up and pointed at the man before his backside hit the seat.

"Easy." Hammer lifted both hands.

"Phil?"

"Not right now."

Tate said, "Would you even tell me your real name?"

"Why does it matter? I'm not that guy right now, and I probably won't be until this investigation is over."

"Isn't that how you get lost in the persona—no better than the criminals you're trying to take down?" In his experience, even playing the thug included a certain amount of risk of forgetting who you are and whose side you are on—and that was with a clean ID. For Hammer, he'd think it was a legitimate concern.

"Better than remembering at the wrong time who your mama raised you to be and screwing the pooch on the whole operation."

Tate shrugged. The front door to the police station opened, and a uniformed cop walked out to his vehicle. "How'd you find me?"

"Eric has GPS on your phone."

Of course he did. Maybe he should send that to Detective Wilcox. Proof Tate was nowhere near Aggerton's office at his time of death. Too bad their knowledge of what the FBI had access to would expose everything. Who Tate was and what he got up to as a private investigator, including working contracts with the FBI.

"Sorry about those guys." Hammer shook his head. "You tell them who you are?"

"They knew," Tate said. "Can't pretend to be someone else in a town where everyone already knows who I am."

"Do they really?"

"Lived here most of my life." His words faded to nothing in the quiet car.

Hammer also said nothing. They both knew a little something about presenting a front to the people around them. Showing a face that wasn't exactly a lie—make it at least resemble the truth—and keeping the rest buried deep.

Did Savannah see the truth? Maybe she was so busy hiding what she didn't want people to really see about herself that she didn't see that he did the same thing. And that it would take some time to see the truth.

Or that the connection they had was based on the fact that like attracted like. They'd been drawn to each other because they were so similar.

Both showed the world one thing, and banked on it being enough to get things done. If they had any hope at all of staying sane, then it *had* to work like that.

"Heard about that lady." Hammer said, "I'm sorry for your loss."

Tate gritted his back teeth. "Don't need sympathy."

"You cared about her. Enough to marry her."

"Not enough to stay that way."

"Doesn't mean the feelings are gone. You care about the kid, you cared about the woman." Hammer shifted in his seat and the leather of his jacket creaked. "That's why you're sitting out here trying to figure a way to get in there and ream the husband for what he did to her, at the same time pretty darn glad you can't get in there, because you'd probably end up doing three to five for attempted murder."

"I'm not sitting here figuring out how to kill him."

"Just maybe punch him a few times."

Tate pressed his lips together. "I don't need whatever reverse psychology crap this is supposed to be. Just tell me where you're at with West."

He could use the distraction. Later, when it fully hit him that Elexa was alone now, he'd have to process it. Right now it was easier to think about something else that didn't have a whole host of emotions tethered to it.

He couldn't think clearly about Claire. Not when he'd gone from being beaten by those guys, to the hospital, to that almost-a-kiss with Savannah, to Claire being dead. A second after she'd lost her life, he'd had to provide Elexa a place to feel what she was feeling.

None of it was about his feelings, or needing time to process them while a whirlwind swirled around him.

Hammer said, "Eric got into the phone since you were busy with those guys. The FBI has only completed a preliminary look at the information on it, but they believe it belonged to Kenny Aggerton. His second phone—a burner he used to communicate with men who work for West."

"But not the man himself."

Hammer shook his head. "Nope, but Kenny was more in the business than even I realized, and it seemed he had some blackmail going on the side."

Wilcox needed to know that if she was looking into his death. The phone could provide relevant evidence.

Only problem was, if the FBI turned it over—even anonymously—it could jeopardize the entire case with Hammer right in the middle of it. Not to mention endanger his life.

Tate said, "Blackmail? Like, someone wanted to kill him?"

"Eric will let you know."

Why did Tate need to know? "He should tell Savannah."

"You're the one who needs to prove it wasn't you that did the murder."

"Except it was you in that video. You're the one who was there."

Hammer's big chest shifted as he chuckled, though it was barely audible. "Earlier. I was there earlier. Not when he was being killed."

"Can you prove that? Maybe I should tell Wilcox it was you in that sweater."

"Please." Hammer huffed. "Prove it."

Tate sighed. Eric never would have sent Hammer to him if the guy wasn't above board, but these undercover guys were always loose cannons. *Hello, pot. I'm kettle.* Who knew what this guy would be prepared to do in the name of closing their case? He figured that list probably didn't encompass murder, but truthfully what he knew about this guy wasn't much.

Tate decided to get the conversation on a more productive track. "Any indication a connection can be found linking Aggerton and Claire Gaynes?"

"I'll have Eric look. Think the deaths are connected?"

He wouldn't have said it was possible. But there were just far too many unanswered questions. "There was no medical indication that she wouldn't eventually make a full recovery. Would've taken a long time, but she'd have gotten there. But...dying?" Tate shook his head.

He'd been in the hall, standing there with Savannah. Distracted by her. Taken with her, thinking about going in for a kiss. And she seemed willing to share that kiss. How he wanted another shot. And how he appreciated that she went with him to find out how his ex-wife was doing. How many other women would have been confident enough to do that?

Lex had been right in front of him and he'd caught her. He'd felt every ounce of her shock and her grief, absorbing it all into himself like a lead weight that sat in his stomach. She'd been devastated.

"Murder?"

If it was, Wilcox would have another death to look into. Like she needed another case. Though, he had to admit he wasn't so much worried about that than about his preference that it not be murder.

Tate said, "I'd offer Conroy my services to help investigate, but he'd say I'm too close to this." Too close to Savannah was probably more like it.

"Could argue you're not too close to figure out who killed Aggerton," Hammer said. "Maybe you're just the right person to figure it out."

"When I was their first suspect?"

"Not for long. Killer was at your office." Hammer shot him a look. "Means you have more reason than anyone to find out the truth, and why you're the one being targeted."

"Can't prove I didn't do it, though. Just that it's unlikely." He couldn't manufacture an alibi he didn't have.

"Story of my life."

Tate had to smile at that. But the feeling was short lived. Grief over Claire's death came back, cresting over him like a wave. It slammed down and rushed over him, draining to his feet and pooling on the floor of the car. Like nothing he'd ever experienced before.

His view of the police department shimmered. Tate scratched at the late day stubble on his jaw and tried to push away the emotions, knowing that would only make it worse, but determined nonetheless.

"I'll leave you to this." Hammer reached for the handle. "Eric will call if there's anything else, yeah?"

Tate nodded, not trusting himself to speak without giving away the emotion that would no doubt drip from his voice.

"Don't do anything I wouldn't do." Hammer slammed the door shut. Tate was pretty sure he heard the guy chuckle.

Tate shifted to tug his phone from the front pocket of his jeans and sent his brother-in-law a text.

Nice guy, that mutual friend of ours.

The reply came a few moments later.

HE WAS WORRIED WHEN HE LEFT YOU IN THAT HOUSE.

Tate answered back.

I DON'T GO DOWN EASILY.

He locked the phone and slipped it into the cup holder, then turned the car back on. He drove toward his office and his apartment above. When he turned down the street, though, he kept going. Place was dark. Not that he'd have expected otherwise.

Without putting too much thought into it, Tate headed for Hope Mansion. He wanted to check in with Maggie. Make sure Lex had settled in all right. He imagined the whole house would rally around the girl just as soon as they found out she'd lost her mom tonight.

He pulled into the parking lot. A security flood light came on. In response, a curtain in one of the downstairs bedrooms shifted. Someone looking to see who had shown up.

A few seconds later, his phone buzzed with an incoming call.

The screen said, *Wilcox.*

He swiped to answer. "Not asleep?"

"Thinking about it, but no. I was gonna go back to work, then I realized what time it was."

Tate looked at the dash. 2:04 a.m. "Oh."

"Want some company?"

"It's cold out."

"So leave the heater running." She hung up.

A couple of minutes later, Savannah slipped outside, tugging a long, wool sweater over her shoulders. Hair up, but loose, in a messy bun. She had sneakers on her feet and what looked like sweats.

She climbed into the car, and he saw the letters down the side of her leg. Louisiana State.

"Pretty big give away."

"Huh?"

He pointed to the lettering.

"Oh." She shot him a wry smile, her face free of makeup. The bandage on her nose was bright in the dark interior of the car. "I also have an Ohio State sweater and a Boise State blanket. And a Navy T-shirt."

"Equal opportunity."

"Of course." She settled back into the seat. "Lex… She's not okay. But, you know."

"Do I?"

"Yeah." She shifted to face him, sitting nearly sideways. "Because you probably feel the same way."

"Claire wasn't my mother. And I'm not a teenage girl with no parents left."

"She's going to have a rough road, no doubt about that. She's got a jerk for a stepdad, but on the flip side there's a private investigator who'll look after her. And a whole lot of friends who care enough to not ever let her fall through the cracks." She paused. "You know that, right? There are people who care about Elexa. You don't have to take care of her by yourself."

"Okay."

She set her hand on his. "And it's okay to be sad."

"Who says I'm not?" But he turned his hand over and wound his fingers through hers. "Thanks."

"I'm not doing anything."

Right. She really believed that? A lump rose in his throat. His eyes stung, and his nose started to itch. Tate knew it was coming. Hadn't been long enough to not recognize the signs when the past crept back up and took him by surprise.

"I lost my parents, too. Both of them. When I was twelve."

He almost didn't believe he'd actually said it. Until she gasped. "Tate."

That was what did it. Savannah's pity. He abruptly pulled his hand from hers and started the car. He stared straight ahead. "You should get to bed. It's late."

"Ta—"

She tried again to ask him, but he didn't want to talk about it. "It doesn't matter anymore." Before she could say anything else, he turned to her. "Just go, Savannah."

18

———

Savannah was still steaming about it when she got to work the next morning. Early, since she'd barely slept. She was tired, grumpy, and wearing too much makeup to try and cover up how badly she felt.

Kaylee looked over when she pushed in the front door. "Wow."

Savannah pulled up short. "What's that supposed to mean?" She shot her a look.

"*You* wear this much makeup."

"Actually, more. But that's not the point." Her round figure shifted as she chuckled. "Besides, I make it look good."

Savannah sighed. "Just let me in."

Kaylee hit the release. "Don't wash it off. You'll look worse."

Savannah trudged to her desk and dumped her stuff, stowing her weapon in its holster in her top drawer. She logged into her computer.

"What happened anyway?"

Savannah didn't turn to her. She looked around the room. Mia wasn't in yet. Sergeant Basuto, either. Conroy sat behind his desk, reading what looked like a report. Door shut. An officer sat at the open desk on the other end of the room, typing. He didn't look over.

Satisfied no one would overhear, she turned back to Kaylee. "Tate blew me off."

"I heard his ex-wife passed away last night."

She nodded.

"Probably grieving."

"I know he is," Savannah said. "But he was about to open up to me, and then he shut me right back down. Told me to get out of the car."

Five minutes later, when she'd looked out the window again, he was gone.

"Man like that, lot of story to tell." Kaylee shot her a knowing look. "Kind of like someone else I know. Wondering where to start. Then when you get to telling it, the story could literally go on for days before it's done."

Savannah had to concede the point. She'd held off telling anyone about her past. Then, when she'd found out that the New Orleans district attorney had been gunned down, there'd been no one to talk with about it.

Which meant she regretted keeping her own counsel.

Tate had tried to talk to her. She hadn't done anything to make him change his mind about that—at least, she didn't think she had—so it was on him why he'd rescinded.

Now she knew she wasn't the only one with damage. She might actually understand the depth of what he'd gone through. Losing his parents. An experience like that shocked a person to the core. Only people who had felt pain deeply like that could empathize adequately with the deep pain of others. And even that wasn't perfect.

But she wanted to believe she could at least be there for him. Listen. Keep his confidence. He knew he could trust her not to blab his personal business all over town, right? Surely he did.

Savannah pulled up the information she had on Tate from the case. Digging a little further, she discovered he had a sister who was married. The parents were both listed as deceased—along with the report for a traffic accident that linked to a closed case. Drunk driver. The mom was killed on impact. Tate's father had survived the initial crash and died a few days later in the hospital.

From what she managed to piece together from reading between the lines, Tate Hudson and his sister had gone to live with an aunt for about six months before they popped up in family court, where the sister—barely eighteen at the time—got full custody of him.

Savannah ran her name. When the information loaded, her eyes widened.

She snapped up the phone and made a call. It was early, but if this person was anything like her, then he'd already be at his desk.

When the reception person answered, Savannah said, "Special Agent Cullings, please. This is about his brother-in-law."

Kaylee turned, eyebrows raised.

Savannah ignored her.

"This is Cullings."

She told him who she was.

"Let me ask you something." The agent's words were measured. "Are you still considering Tate as a suspect for Kenny Aggerton's murder?"

Savannah said, "The case is ongoing. That's not what this is about."

Eric Cullings chuckled.

Savannah didn't even know where to start. Or why she'd called this guy. "Are you really married to his sister?"

"Asking him for help on that case was the best decision I ever made." He paused. "Is that why you called, to get the scoop? Or maybe you want to ask me for proof Tate was nowhere near Kenny Aggerton's office the night he died."

"And how do you even know what I'm working on, anyway?" Savannah leaned back in her chair. This was going to be akin to sparring. "Keeping your nose to the ground, I see."

"Part of my job. Not all of it. And I make it my business to know my kids' uncle is safe."

"So you'll vouch for him?"

"I'd bet my job on it."

Wow. That was a solid recommendation, even for family. Eric Cullings was prepared to risk a great deal backing Tate. His sister had taken care of him on her own, with probably little help. She'd made her own way. Tate had grown up into a solid but wild guy who'd quit the FBI and now skirted both sides of the law. Working cases whatever way he saw fit and making up rules as he went—so long as he could maintain his integrity in the process.

"From what I know of him," she said. "It's unlikely he'd take that for granted."

He had an FBI agent who vouched for him. They were clearly a close family. Something she'd never had, and didn't care to try and resurrect from the ashes. What was done was done, and she'd moved on.

"I know he wouldn't," Cullings said. "We were partners."

"When Tate was an FBI agent?"

He was quiet for a moment. "He doesn't really talk about it. But he didn't quit because he wasn't good at it."

"Okay."

"Just so *you* know, he was the best partner I've ever had."

That only gave her more questions. Just as Tate probably had about her and her past before Last Chance.

As a cop, she was a professional. In her personal life, things had been markedly different. She'd seen what she'd wanted to see, until the DA in New Orleans had opened her eyes to what lengths people would go to get what they wanted. Too late she'd also realized the corruption that had been rampant in city hall, stretched into the upper ranks of the police department.

It had been all about the investigation, which had served to put a damper on her personal entanglement with the DA. That, and the fact he'd been married. How nice of him to keep that minor detail to himself. Even years later, she had trouble trusting people at their word. Still struggled with the shame of being involved with a married man.

Not to mention the way it had torn through her family.

Now the DA was dead, and she was living in hiding where those city council members who had gone to jail, and the ones who'd skated out from under conviction, couldn't find her. The DA should've known she wasn't the only one in danger. He should have known he would be, too. After all, he'd prosecuted the case—even if it had been a bunch of watered-down charges kept all hush hush so the media didn't find out why so many city employees had been let go all of a sudden.

When it finally came out, he'd hung her out to dry with no care for her safety, or that she had to leave town and change her name. All he'd cared about was the promotion he got from prosecuting a major case. A reference was the most he'd been willing to give her at the time, and she'd had to barter for that. He'd owed her. Savannah had made sure he paid for it—by sending a file to a local newspaper.

Her own brand of justice.

Maybe she and Tate weren't so different after all.

Eric said, "Do you want my take on the shooting of that District Attorney in New Orleans?"

Savannah blinked, realizing she'd been lost in her thoughts. Her jaw tightened. "Excuse me?"

"Tate sent me your picture from his security cam. I ran it."

"Has…" How did she even ask when Kaylee was still listening? "Do you know?"

"No one knows who you are, or where you are. No one except me." Cullings used a soft voice his wife probably liked a lot. This was a man who cared about a woman in danger, and he wasn't going to sit around doing nothing when she needed protection.

"Okay." Her voice was breathy. "Tate?"

"I haven't told him yet."

Savannah fought for control, then said, "What did you find out—about the DA, I mean?"

"Talked to the investigating detective." Eric's voice was soft still. "Asked in reference to a case I'm working that is above his pay grade, but one that might actually be connected."

"A solid Tate Hudson move." He'd essentially lied, but he'd done it for the right reason. Who had taught who? "Makes me wonder if that alibi will even be legit, considering you seem to have no problem bending the truth."

"Touché." He chuckled, but it evaporated quickly. "It was pretty brutal. Couple seconds, and he was done. Clean and clear it was a retaliatory shoot. Not afraid who they hit, obviously since a couple of bystanders got tagged. Minor injuries. But the New Orleans DA caught three shots to the chest."

"Who was he having dinner with?"

"Some woman, no one knows what her name is. They're trying to ID her from surveillance and his phone records."

Savannah pressed her lips together.

"If you have any ideas about that, you could tell me and I'll pass it back. Anonymously, of course."

"Of course," she said. "But it's been two years. I don't even know the DA anymore. That life isn't mine, considering I basically set fire to every bridge I had and walked away. Anything else?"

"No."

"Tate really asked you to look into me?"

"Yes."

She had to absorb the fact Cullings knew who she really was. No, that wasn't true. Savannah Wilcox was who she really was. That other woman, who'd been too naïve but still a good police detective, wasn't her. Not anymore. She'd died the night Savannah left town.

"He cares about you."

Savannah said, "Okay." Not sure what else to say.

"That means something. To him, and to me."

"I should get back to work."

Cullings said, "Put me through to Conroy's line. I need to run something by the chief."

Savannah frowned but put him through. What did Special Agent Cullings want to talk to her boss about, anyway? Conroy already knew about the case she'd been involved in. She'd given him the highlights.

Despite the reference from the DA, she'd figured she owed him the truth. No way would she have made a hire like that without the story. Especially when it meant putting your life in someone else's hands.

Conroy picked up the phone at his desk and she replaced her handset. He glanced at her, then spoke into the phone to the FBI agent.

She turned to her computer and pulled up the file—a list of local people named in the books, that the DA had compiled. Those that bought or sold the things he supplied around town. Not just drugs, but other stuff as well. Favors. Business. The DA had gone through all of it.

She scanned the list.

People with something to lose a few months from now when the evidence came out during Summers's trial. Really, she had to consider that any one of these names could be linked to Aggerton's death. With the motive of trying to keep something quiet. Or cleaning up a mess, like whoever killed the DA in New Orleans.

Savannah ran a quick search for, "West," but came up empty. He wasn't mentioned here.

The person behind this was also targeting the DA here, if the DA's paranoia was real. She didn't want to see similarities in the two cases. Not now, not ever. Kind of like not wanting to see similarities between the woman she had been in Louisiana and the woman she was now.

She continued down the list, finding a few names she knew, others she didn't. One stuck out to her.

Robert Gaynes.

The DA's name wasn't on the list. Which only meant he likely had no reason to want Aggerton silenced, but that was not surprising.

The person threatening him was the same one behind the murder. She needed him to talk to her.

Savannah wrote herself a note to call him right at nine o'clock, the time most people got to work. If she could sit him down and explain the severity of the case, then maybe he would open up. Worth a try, even if her tactics didn't work with Tate. She'd only just stuck the note to the bottom of her computer monitor when Bill, the dispatcher, raced out of his soundproof office and stood in front of her.

"The DA's assistant just called in. Showed up at his house this morning and found the guy stabbed to death."

Savannah dropped her pen on the desk.

Bill's bushy, white brows folded together. "You've got another body."

19

———

Tate gripped the steering wheel, his cell connected to the stereo by Bluetooth. "You did what?"

Eric's voice came through the car's speakers, "Well, are you there yet?"

"I just turned onto the street. And you didn't answer my question."

Tate lifted his foot off the gas. The car slowed as he took in the scene. Up ahead, two black and white police cars, lights flashing, were parked on the road. An ambulance was parked in the driveway. There was no medical examiner van. Any dead body would be transported by EMTs to the hospital and sent to the basement facility run by the doctor who was contracted for autopsies.

"And?"

Tate pulled over to the curb. If this had nothing to do with Hammer's undercover operation, then what did it have to do with? "Bro, you could've told me what I'm doing here. I thought I would be helping Phil again." Not that he'd been especially looking forward to it. "What's going on?"

"Conroy got a call while I was on the phone. The district attorney is dead."

Tate had never met the man, but that didn't mean he didn't feel something. "Too much of that lately."

Eric was quiet for a second. "Ok, but before I tell you, I want you to know you don't have to do this."

"Why don't you tell me what *this* is, and I'll let you know what I decide?"

"Fine," Eric said. "I bargained with Conroy to get you access to the investigation into Aggerton's death. He needs your skills, whether he wants to admit it or not."

"My guess, not."

"It can't hurt, at least. Besides," Eric pointed out, "then we'll have access to what the police knows."

Tate figured there was a chance it very much *could* hurt. "Because of Aggerton's connection with West, there's also a potential connection to Phil's Op."

"Exactly."

Tate sighed. "When were you planning on letting me in on this?"

Not to mention, what Savannah would say when she found out she was supposed to work with him. Or the shiver of fear he'd felt about going home alone. Not super heroic, but he could be the target of a murderer—and the repercussion of telling West's guys that he wanted to speak with the man.

Eric started, but Tate cut him off. "And how did Conroy say yes, anyway. Last time I checked, *I* was their prime suspect."

"No one thinks you killed Aggerton. Conroy just needed Savannah to prove it." Eric said, "She knows it was the guy who broke into your office. On account of—duh—he was holding the murder weapon."

Tate said nothing. None of that could be proven.

"Plus I sent Conroy your GPS location. At the time of the murder, you were at home. Like you said."

At the time. "And I couldn't have left my phone at home?"

"Not since you were texting at the time of the murder."

Tate wasn't so sure that was unequivocal. Still, Eric had

gotten him in here, and Tate would do what he did best. Dig for the truth. "Did you tell him I work for you sometimes?"

Conroy knew Tate had been an FBI agent back in the day, but likely not what he did for them now. Or, occasionally did.

"He's a police chief, I'm an FBI agent. Those conversations are 'need to know'."

Tate said, "Bye Eric. Thanks for nothing."

"By—"

His brother-in-law never got the whole word out. Tate hit the button on his phone and disconnected the call. Then he left his phone in the car so he couldn't be found or bothered by it, pocketed his keys, and strode to the front drive of the district attorney's house.

The cop at the tape looked up. "Name?"

"Seamus Aloysius Pumpernickel."

The kid, an officer whose nameplate said "Donaldson," blinked. Then he looked down at his paper and wrote while he said, "H-U-D-S-O-N. One 'S' or two in Aloysius?"

Tate laughed. Apparently the kid knew who he was— enough to know his last name, anyway. "Tell your chief I'm here."

The kid grabbed his radio, a grin on his face. "Uh, Chief? There's a Mr. Pumpernickel here for you."

Conroy strode outside a second later, peeling rubber gloves off his hands. "Funny. Real funny." His face said otherwise.

"Kind of like this entire situation."

"Yeah, like the tit for tat of how I'm supposed to give you full access to an investigation that involves you, in return for what I believe your brother referred to as 'ongoing cooperation.' Whatever that means."

Tate said, "Brother-in-law."

"Ah, Millie." Understanding washed over his face. "I was so blindsided with your connection to a fed I missed that part. She left and married that guy."

Tate nodded.

"So you decided you'd ask my girlfriend to be your receptionist, instead."

Tate tried to look innocent. "Where'd you hear that?"

"You want in on this or not?"

That was the question. "Is Savannah in there?"

Conroy frowned. In another life, they'd probably be best friends. The nature of their jobs didn't put them exactly on opposite sides of the law, just in different camps. Ones constantly attempting to do an end-run around each other and come out in front. This whole thing was going to be awkward to say the least.

Conroy didn't move, and he didn't answer the question. He said, "Tell me what that is. Between you."

After how he'd shut her down last night? He wasn't even sure he knew what it was. He had so much swirling around in his brain he hadn't made sense of it. Claire was dead. He'd seen Lex this morning, and Maggie was going to stay with her today. They'd have Lex help around the Mansion with the cleaning to keep her occupied. He had an invitation to visit later and have dinner with her.

"Tate. Savannah?"

"She and I are…I don't know what. We're still figuring it out." That was the most honest answer he could come up with.

A muscle in Conroy's jaw shifted.

The man was younger than Tate by a few years at least, but he was Savannah's boss. And even though he was younger than Savannah as well, he acted more like an older brother. Go figure. Conroy acted like that with Cassie who was his actual sister. It was good that Savannah had someone in her life who cared about her like that, since she had no family nearby. Did she have family anywhere?

When he boiled it down, Tate and Conroy both cared about her.

Conroy said, "Let's go take a look."

He followed the chief of police inside, noting the smell

before anything else. Then the sound of crying. Not the kind Elexa had done in his arms last night. No, this sounded like a ten-year-old girl denied a trip to the mall.

A slender man in a suit and shiny shoes, his hair gelled but now mussed, lifted his hands. "I don't know. I told you that."

Sergeant Basuto stood with him, pencil in one hand and notepad in the other. "Sir—"

"No." The slender man waved. "This is…it's just too much to—" He gaped. "What is he doing here?"

"Fenris." Conroy stopped. "What's the problem?"

Tate hung back.

"He…"

Fear washed over the man's face. With a name like Fenris—first or last, Tate didn't know—he wasn't exactly sure what to expect. But the guy seemed to be scared…of him. "Dude. I don't know you. Whatever you've heard about me, it isn't true."

So many rumors about Tate were flying around town. Maybe he'd heard Tate was suspected of Aggerton's murder.

Basuto ushered him away.

Conroy said, "What was that?"

"How am I supposed to know?"

"Is the same thing going to happen at every turn during this investigation?"

"I hope not." Tate sighed. "I did nothing to that guy, and I can't control hearsay or people's opinions."

A muscle in Conroy's jaw flexed. Tate followed him to the study where the smell originated. The police department's computer technician, Dean's younger brother Ted, sat at the desk, working on the computer.

"Over here." Conroy waved Tate to the far wall, mostly made up of windows that showed a view of the DA's expansive property. In this part of town, the lots were four to six acres. Tate had no interest in mowing that much lawn.

As he neared the windows he saw Savannah, crouched and bent over a man's torso. Blood had pooled around the body.

The DA had been stabbed multiple times. Thinking about it like that, all clinical as a statement of facts, helped. The smell did not.

She stood and turned. The bruising on her face had been covered with a shimmery layer of makeup that lightened her cheeks but didn't totally disguise the purple color. Or how tired she looked. "The doc is on his way to take a look."

"Copy that. I'll leave you to it." Conroy left.

Savannah's top lip, under her nose, glistened. She noted his gaze and said, "Peppermint, for the smell."

Tate waved in the direction Conroy had gone. "He seemed disappointed, right? Or was that just me."

At the computer, Ted looked over. "He was probably hoping you'd lose your cookies, so that he could complain about you contaminating his crime scene."

Savannah spun to the computer tech. "His?"

Ted said, "You know what I mean."

She said nothing.

The computer tech pulled a flash drive from the tower under the desk and stood. "Any-hoo, I'm done so…bye." He wrinkled his nose and skedaddled out the door into the hall.

"Seems like someone else's going to toss their cookies."

Savannah smiled for a second. "You okay this morning?"

He didn't really want to talk about it, but said, "Better. Lex, too."

"I know." She turned back to study the body. "She and I had coffee earlier."

"Oh." That was a good thing, right? He figured Lex could use as many supportive, solid women he could send her way. "So, what have we got going on here, aside from the obvious fact that Nolan Ilkins, District Attorney, is very dead?"

She crouched. "Because you're on the case now?"

"Eric." He muttered his brother-in-law's name like a curse word.

"The FBI seems to think you have something to contribute."

Or it was just that Eric had a case, and he wanted an insider to know if the police's investigation was at all relevant.

Still, he said, "I'd like to believe that's true."

He was the kind of person who would work to make it so. And not just because he'd blown her off last night. In the dark, his fear and the past had gotten the better of him. Now, in the light of morning, things looked a whole lot different.

Savannah had gone back to her cop persona.

He could do the same, pulling on the cloak of his private investigator license. "Stabbed. Same as Aggerton?"

"Yep."

He scanned the body with his gaze, looking for anything of note. "No one heard or saw anything?"

"Nope."

"Surveillance?" They'd caught a shot of the guy before.

"Hoping to squash anything involving a black sweater that, at one point, belonged to you?"

He pressed his lips together. "I'm not here to save my hide. And I won't be touching any evidence, let alone tampering with it."

"Well, that's good to know at least." Her words had an edge to them.

"Besides, we know it wasn't me because we both saw the guy in my hallway." He motioned to his arm, and the stitches from the knife wound.

"Until we catch him, or prove irrefutably it was him, we can't know for sure he's our killer."

"Savannah…" He didn't know what else to say. She was mad, and he deserved it. Even grief was no justification for being rude. Opening up, and then blowing her off like he did. She was trying to be a professional here. He had to give her that.

"It's okay. Let's just do this."

As though it were a chore to suffer through, after which they would go their separate ways and things would again be normal.

As though *he* was nothing but a chore to complete. Tate blew out a breath, realizing he hadn't had normal since he was twelve. At this point, he wasn't sure if he'd even recognize it.

Instead of bothering her more, he circled the room and looked for anything that jumped out at him. He wouldn't know out of place since he'd never been here before but figured his instincts were pretty good. Savannah bagged a couple of pieces of evidence. Fibers of some kind.

Tate glanced along the bookshelf and saw a couple volumes out of place. He moved over and used his shirt sleeve to shift them. Just enough to see behind.

"Savannah."

She rose, stretching out her back. "Yes?"

When she lifted her arms above her head, he turned away. "There's something here." She moved to him, and he smelled mint along with her perfume. "Wrapped in cloth. Stuffed back there."

"Get the camera." She waved at an open duffel.

He took a handful of pictures, then she reached over with her gloved hand and removed it. When she opened the cloth, they both inhaled.

A bloody knife lay inside.

"Murder weapon."

She winced. "What do you wanna bet it's been wiped clean of prints?"

"Could be DNA, or a partial, right? Or something else."

"There was nothing on Aggerton. According to the tests that have come in so far. This guy was in and out."

He grabbed an evidence bag, and she dropped the knife inside, sealing the bag and making a notation on the outside.

Then she said, "Kind of like this. The housekeeper left after she cleaned up for breakfast. The assistant was late. Maybe twenty minutes between the two. He came in, stabbed the vic, and then left."

"And dumped the knife," Tate said. "Like he tried to do

when he tagged me." He figured probably they'd find his blood on the knife as well. More evidence against him? It could certainly be read that way.

"What does the FBI have to say about that?"

Before he could ask what kind of a question that was, Conroy appeared at the door. "Murder weapon?"

She lifted the bag. "Looks like it."

"Good work." Conroy nodded. "I left a voicemail for Mrs. Ilkins. Not sure where she's at until she calls back and I can go see her."

"What about the assistant?" Tate said, "Does he have any idea where she is?"

"Basuto will ask."

Tate headed for the door. "I need to make a call."

Conroy stepped aside, and Tate strode out. Down the hall to the back patio where he let himself out. Being inside where there was a dead guy on the floor made him itchy. A dead guy, and then another person blocking the door was even worse. Too many people. Cops or not, didn't matter. They made him itchy and claustrophobic.

Tate rolled his shoulders and tried to slough off the feeling of being boxed in. The need to not have this pinned on him was visceral. Not only had he not committed that murder, he also didn't figure he'd last a day cooped up like that. Locked away.

He glanced at the trees, then stared at the sky. The mountains beyond the town.

Eric might think he'd done Tate a favor dragging him into the middle of this.

But it was far from a good thing.

20

———

"I guess he's not as immune as I thought."

She moved to Conroy's side and followed his gaze to where Tate stood outside, looking up at the snowcapped mountains.

There weren't any of those where she'd grown up. She loved them now, and wouldn't ever take the view for granted. Seeing this side of Tate touched her in a way she needed to keep to herself. Certainly her boss didn't need to know what the consultant meant to her. How these tiny displays of vulnerability affected her.

Conroy turned.

Savannah said, "His ex-wife died last night. He cared about her." As though that wasn't obvious, so she needed to explain it to him.

"Claire Gaynes," Conroy said. "Knew her, back when she was Claire Baxter." He made a face she couldn't quite decipher.

Baxter was Elexa's last name.

"When I got home from college, they were headed to divorce court. Can't say I was surprised. What I remember from high school was…" He winced. "She got what she wanted, laid waste to guys. Boys, men. She didn't discriminate. Claire had a reputation."

"And that validates the choice she made to marry a dirt bag after her divorce. One who roughed her up." She shot him a look. "She deserved that?"

"No." He flinched. "Of course not. Robert Gaynes is going to answer for his actions, specifically what he may have done that contributed to his wife's death."

"She wasn't murdered?" What about the woman on the surveillance? It had to mean something that she'd been there moments before Claire had flat lined.

"When the autopsy results are in, we'll find out. Until then, Gaynes had better not leave town."

Savannah pressed her lips together. "You tell him. I don't think he likes me."

"I'll do that. Right after he's arraigned for assault on the hospital employee. I'm headed to the office. What's Mia working on?" Totally innocent, like he wasn't checking up on his girlfriend.

"When I got the call about this, we were preparing to do a couple of interviews. The first two names on the list. One's a bank employee, the other is an elder at the church."

"Associated with Ed Summers's business and Aggerton's hidden financials for his nephew?"

Savannah nodded. "They are names we found in the books."

"This is big, Wilcox. If we have prominent members of the community exposed for illegal dealings, we'll have to play it right or we'll have a firestorm."

Of all people, she never would've imagined Conroy as the kind of cop willing to downplay crime so people in the community could save face. Nope. She wouldn't be a part of that kind of negligence. She'd walk away. Hand in her badge and leave.

Savannah gritted her teeth. "Perhaps those prominent members of society should not have broken the law."

"We don't know for sure they did."

"If we have evidence, then I'm certainly not going to sit on it. You break the law, I pass everything I have to a judge and put my faith in the system."

He shifted to face her. "Not in the people of this community and their honesty?"

She nearly laughed. "No." What faith she still had was placed in God, and that was enough. Everyone else was human. Frail and fallible. Corruptible.

"Wow." Conroy smoothed down the buttons of his shirt. "Glad I don't have anything to confess to you."

She said nothing. The cop in her had been battered by people and their manipulations, to the point she was often hard when she should be compassionate. The woman she had been died the day she walked away.

"Go easy on Tate, yeah?"

"You think he did something?"

Conroy said, "I suspected there was an FBI operation going on in town, and the call I got this morning confirmed it. I just don't know who or what they're getting into."

And yet, she was the one who'd called Eric first. "What's your read on him and Tate?"

"They were partners. Now they're family." He shrugged. "What's there to read?"

"And now he's shadowing me on this case?" She closed in so she could speak low to her boss. "You think they think that we're dirty?"

He glanced at Tate, still turned away from them, and shrugged. "Maybe Tate is their man inside the police department, passing information back on us."

She flashed gritted teeth at Tate's back.

Conroy chuckled.

"It's hardly funny."

"No, you're right," he said. "It isn't. But I don't think this is about us. You have nothing to worry about. I figure this murder investigation is related to their case. Something about Ed Summers connects to ongoing business Aggerton knew about. Through the course of his prosecution of the case, Ilkins would have exposed it. There's a wider scope now. A conspiracy to cover something up, what with the books being stolen and the DA being killed. Someone is trying to wipe away tracks."

She said, "Of course, we have nothing to worry about. So…"

"Did you hear anything else I said?"

"What about leaving the murder weapon?" She lifted the bag.

Conroy shrugged. "Who knows, unless the person who did it eventually tells us why it was left behind."

She sighed.

"I should get back to the office."

She figured that meant he would swing by and check on Mia's progress on the way, partly as the boss of the probationary lieutenant, and partly as her overprotective boyfriend.

Savannah said, "I'll finish up here. What's going on with Gaynes?"

"Robert Gaynes is due in court this morning for his arraignment. He'll likely be out on bail by lunch, pending a court case about the assault of a hospital staff member."

He was speaking slowly. As though she'd forgotten something elementary.

"Do me a favor?" she said. "Give me a heads up when he's about to leave the courthouse."

"Why?"

She glanced at Tate. "Just a hunch. Let me see where it goes."

Conroy gave her a nod and spun on his heel to head for the front door. Savannah glanced once at Tate, still staring at the mountains. These days it was rare to see anyone stand like that. Thinking. Being quiet—not the way some went about occupying their brains mindlessly on a cell phone. Nothing but unhealthy distractions that rewrote the neural pathways in the brain.

Though, to be fair, the only reason she didn't have social media was because of her own safety. She didn't think it'd be smart to give the people trying to kill her a way to find her.

So, probably she shouldn't get too comfy up on her high horse.

Savannah just wanted to do her job, with none of the politics Conroy had to deal with as the chief. If people in this town were determined to break the law, not to mention cover their tracks with murder, well, that just meant it was up to her to find the truth.

It was what she did. No matter what, Savannah would seek justice for people who couldn't get it for themselves.

The doctor showed up and did his preliminary examination of the body, but not after cracking a joke about starting up a punch card for her.

She didn't laugh.

The DA had been stabbed repeatedly, earlier that morning, in the same manner as Aggerton. But only the doctor could tell if it was the same weapon—or at least one that measured the same. The blood on the knife would tell them more. If the blood of Aggerton and the DA, along with Tate were present, then it would confirm the same knife had been used for all three.

"I'll know more when I—"

She finished for him. "Do the autopsy?"

He blinked. "Yes. How did you…"

"Punch card." She stood and saw Tate in the doorway. "Can you grab Donaldson for me?"

He nodded, disappearing again.

"Talkative one, that guy."

"Tate?"

The doctor nodded. "Patched him up a couple of times. Of course, I also met him a long time ago."

Savannah would rather he hadn't mentioned it than breach

even that much doctor-patient confidentiality. Still, she ran with a hunch and said, "You were working in town when Mr. and Mrs. Hudson were killed?"

"Terrible tragedy. Of course, no one fully comprehends that kind of loss. The ripple effect it can have on an entire town."

She nodded.

"He thought they'd forgotten him." The doctor's eyes glazed over, lost to memory. "He kept telling me they'd be there. That they were coming to get him."

The doctor seemed to realize where he was then and turned back to the body while Savannah just stood there. Tate had expected his parents. They'd never shown up, killed by a drunk driver.

She wanted to cry. That stuff about being all cop with no compassion? It was out the window on this one. Because of Tate. She should tell Conroy she couldn't work this case because of her personal feelings. But it wasn't like he didn't know she had feelings for Tate. There was a level of trust there. Professional respect.

"Detective?"

She turned to Donaldson. "Search of the house is done?"

"Yep. The sergeant said to tell you."

"Help the doc with the body, please."

"Will do."

"Mr. Hudson and I are leaving." She said, "Call if you need anything." That was for either of them, and she got a nod and a flick of Donaldson's fingers.

Tate led the way to the front door, and at the tape they signed out with a different cop who noted on his clipboard who came and went.

A crowd had gathered, including a couple of reporters from a local TV station. Tate lifted his chin at a group of three guys. Muscled. They looked military.

"Know those guys?"

"Sure, don't you?" When she said nothing, he said, "They run the facility up in the hills."

"Ah." Yeah, she knew nothing about that place except that it was some kind of training thing for guys like them. Military—active duty and retired. Or corporations who sent people over for team-building retreats. But it was hardly on her radar. "Can't say I've thought much about it given how busy I've been with cases. I barely even have time to exercise."

"That should get better now with Mia coming on."

She shrugged and beeped the locks on her car.

"Mine is down there." He pointed to his little beater, down the street. She would never get in that car. The engine would probably fall out halfway back to the office. Or the thing would go up in flames.

"Follow me?"

When he nodded, she slid in her car. Savannah drove to the center of town, passing by the grocery store. Conroy hadn't texted yet, so she pulled through a coffee place and ordered a sandwich with coffee. The chicken salad on a croissant was to die for. She got it at least three times a week.

Savannah drove to city hall but parked across the street. Good view of the front door.

She got out and carried her sandwich across the street to a bench where she sat down. Tate parked as well, came over and sat beside her, eyeing her but saying nothing as he opened the white bag that matched hers.

She had just pulled out her sandwich when Conroy sent her a message that Robert Gaynes had been let go, out on bail. A second later, the man himself trotted out the front door and down the steps.

Tate didn't even speak, or breathe. His sandwich tumbled to the grass as he raced across the street.

At the curb on the far side, a brand-new, dark green SUV waited. Gaynes' assistant got out of the driver's seat.

Savannah followed Tate, jaywalking with her badge out so

she didn't get yelled at. Just a couple horn honks. She rounded the back of the car to find Rob Gaynes shoved up against the passenger door.

"You killed her." Tate's voice roared over the sound of lunch traffic. He grabbed Gaynes's shirt and shoved him against the car again.

Gaynes said, "Prove it," spittle flying in Tate's face.

"I will. Mark that, because I'll do it." He shoved again. "Knew you were nothin' the minute I saw you."

She needed him to walk away now. Before this got to a place he couldn't get free of. "Tate."

Gaynes whipped around to look at her so fast his neck probably cracked. "Detective Wilcox. This man is assaulting me!"

"The way you assaulted that woman at the hospital, you mean?"

He said nothing.

She wanted to say she was capable of being compassionate to a man who'd lost his wife. But did he even care?

She pointed at the broken nose in the center of her face. "You see this? It means you're not likely to get sympathy from me. I'm liable to help him prove what you did." She waved at Tate. "I guess time and an autopsy will tell about that."

It was the first time in her life she'd leveraged her job for personal gain. She should have said she didn't like it, but Savannah wasn't sure that was true.

Maybe Tate's way of doing things wasn't so bad after all.

21

———————

"Get in there."

Tate fought to keep from stumbling as Savannah shoved him through the door of Hollis's diner. He glanced over his shoulder and shot her a look.

"Find a table and sit down. Since you ruined my sandwich, you also owe me six dollars on top of lunch. Which you're gonna pay for."

He'd be mad she was treating him like a child if she didn't look so scared, and if it wasn't cute that she was worried about him. Then again, his emotions were all over the place since yesterday.

Tate pulled his phone out as he walked to an open booth. He sent a quick text to Lex, asking how she was doing. As he slid across the vinyl seat, his phone buzzed.

Fine.

Tate replied that he'd be there later that day. Was that soon enough? She wasn't his child, just the daughter of a woman who'd been part of his life a long time ago. He cared about her, though. Enough to want to make sure she was all right when she had no family in town, just a whole lot of folks prepared to look out for her. Like it or not, they were part of each other's lives in a way he couldn't ignore, no matter that he'd rather run from his grief.

Savannah sat with jerky movements, then swiped a menu from between the napkins and the ketchup and held it up in front of her face.

Hollis wandered over.

Tate flipped the mug over and slid it to the end of the table. "Doin' okay?"

He shrugged. "Nothing strawberry waffles won't fix."

She smiled and her round face flushed. "Detective Wilcox?"

"Eggs benedict. A whole wheat English muffin." She slid her cup over as well. "And extra cream."

Hollis filled her cup. "Coming right up." Before she left, she said, "Will your other friend be joining you today? I haven't seen him since y'all were in before."

Tate shrugged, regardless of the fact he and Phil had been having a text conversation most of the morning, passing information back and forth. "He's been pretty busy lately."

If he said Phil was working a lot, she'd only ask what he did for a living. Tate would have to pile another lie on top of the stack that already existed surrounding the man occasionally known as Phil, but mostly known around Last Chance as a biker and drug transporter by the name of "Hammer."

When he said nothing else, her face flashed with disappointment. Hollis wandered off.

"What friend?"

He glanced at Savannah. "I have friends."

"Like the FBI?"

"That's a family thing." He shrugged, about to give her more details that sounded like something but actually were more of nothing when Mia walked in.

She waved and headed to the counter, where she retrieved a white paper bag with a receipt stapled to the fold. She hefted the bag up, walking towards them and snuggling it in her arms like it was a squirmy baby.

"Anything from the scene?"

Savannah said, "Murder weapon. Tests from evidence we collected from the Aggerton crime scene are starting to come back."

"Okay." Mia nodded. "I'll take a look and let you know, if you're not back at the office by the time I've looked at it."

"How about you?"

"Talked to Anderson Matthews this morning."

Tate knew him. An elder at the church, he was involved in all kinds of ministries as well as the foreman of a construction crew that did business, though not residential.

"And?"

Mia said, "He had a gambling problem. Aggerton loaned him money, but he took a second job and his wife started a side hustle. Said they paid it all off, plus the exorbitant amount of interest. He's been getting help. He hasn't placed a bet in four months."

Savannah said, "So now that it's all out in the open, his life is back on track?"

Hollis came over with silverware wrapped in napkins. Mia glanced at her watch. "I should go. See you at the office."

Savannah said, "Okay."

When it was just the two of them again, Tate said, "Think Matthews did something to Aggerton?"

"Killed him in a fit of rage? Possible, but not probable."

"Because he turned his life around?"

Knowing there were people with problems at the church didn't bother him. Faith didn't make you perfect, and it didn't solve your issues. Just gave you hope. Let you lean on something. God wasn't a ticket to riches, fame, or even the guarantee of a good life. But it could be a whole lot better than being on your own with no one to rely on but yourself.

He should tell Savannah these thoughts he had swirling around—he'd been paying attention recently as the pastor went through whatever book it was they were in. Hebrews was it?

"He paid off the debt. What is there to be angry about, unless Aggerton was after him for even more money?" Savannah studied him. "Not a big believer in people? I'm with you on that. My faith is in God, not in people. They're selfish, and they'll let you down."

Tate nodded. "Few people in this world are actually reliable, and even the reliable ones make mistakes and hurt those they care about."

He didn't want to think about Claire, but there it was again. He hadn't been right for her. She'd hidden too many things from him. Tate didn't deal well with that, considering his business was uncovering things. When he'd confronted her, she had flipped out, and then told him she already had divorce papers being drawn up.

He'd always thought it wasn't about him not caring enough about her. Neither of them had wanted to change and be better. Still, it was more about the fact he'd discovered what she would have rather stayed hidden.

Tate was the way he was. Maybe that would never change. He needed things to be upfront.

"Take you, for example." She raised her brows, as though the point she intended to make were of significance.

"What's that supposed to mean?"

"Just that you play things close to the vest."

"Like you do."

She nodded, conceding his point. Then stared, while her eyes narrowed on him. "Eric said you asked him about me."

"I know I can trust him, without reservation. So I asked him to run your picture."

"And?"

Tate said, "He hasn't given me anything yet."

"Maybe you should badger me with questions until I crack and tell you everything."

Was this some kind of bizarre woman logic, where the

reasoning made no sense to anyone but her? "Why would I do that, if you don't want to tell me?"

"Because maybe you care about me enough to get me to spill all my secrets. Or not."

He frowned. "How am I supposed to know you'd want me to do that?"

"So you aren't arguing that you care?"

"You're a better cop than that. I'm sure you've picked up on the clues." She had to know he cared about her. After all, he'd tried to kiss her. There was something undeniable between them, and she knew it. "We all have secrets. I don't expect you to spill everything to me until you're ready."

He'd shut her down instead of opening up when they were sitting in the car together. But it had been more about not wanting to be overwhelmed by his feelings.

He said, "For a long time, it was easier to just work on other people's problems and ignore my own. Ignore how I felt about my parents, or anything else. Like the FBI."

Whether he intended to change that or not didn't alter the fact Claire was dead. New emotions had come up.

"What happened with you and the FBI?"

He shrugged. "I didn't fit. I worked better on my own, using my own methods. They didn't like the way I did things, and I didn't want Eric to keep having to cover for me."

At one point he'd wondered if it hadn't all been a waste of time, going through the lengthy application process and all that training. But it wasn't. He knew how the FBI worked, and being one of them had helped. Not only had they ingrained skills in him, they'd also helped to steady him.

She finally spoke. "Feel free to fill me in whenever you're ready. About anything."

"But you looked up the accident, right? You know what happened?"

"Facts, maybe. Things that were in a police report. And what the doctor said about you."

He frowned, wondering what that was about.

She continued, "Not what's real. I don't know *you*."

Before he could respond, a man slid onto the booth beside him. "Scoot over, brah."

Hammer, dressed as Phil, shoved him along the bench seat, then lifted Tate's coffee cup and took a swig. He made a face. "Pass the sugar."

Tate just stared at him.

Savannah said, "Friend of yours?"

"Tate and I go way back." He reached across the table, hand outstretched. "Phil Tilley."

She grinned, shaking his hand. "You rhyme."

Phil grinned. "All part of my charm."

Tate said, "That's not technically a rhyme." They both looked at him. Tate swallowed. "Phil is the one on the surveillance video outside Aggerton's office, wearing my sweater."

Phil didn't move. "Dude, seriously?"

Tate shrugged. "Did you kill him?"

"Of course not."

"Then what do you have to be worried about?" Tate asked, even though he knew exactly what concerned Phil. Savannah was a smart police detective. He didn't want to use the analogy of a dog with a bone, but it was apt.

Savannah glanced between them. She didn't waste any time whipping out her phone and navigating to the notes app. "You left Kenny Aggerton's office shortly before he died. What can you tell me?"

Phil said, "Just a chat with the local CPA. Money stuff, you know?" He turned to Tate. "See if I let you borrow *my* sweater."

Savannah said, "How about we assume I don't know about this money stuff. How did Aggerton seem?"

"Agitated. Said his stomach hurt." Phil leaned back in his chair. "He was sweating pretty badly."

"Just health reasons, or something else?"

"He had an appointment right after me, so he kicked me out pretty quickly, but not before turning down my stellar offer to invest in his business. And his future."

Tate figured that meant he'd tried in vain to get Aggerton to roll over on his bosses—namely this West guy. "Maybe whoever came in after you killed him."

Savannah said, "You see who it was, or did he say at all?"

"Didn't see anyone. He didn't say. And the only other thing was a big, dark-colored SUV that rolled past. But I didn't see the driver. They could've just been heading down the street for all I know."

A random car passing by didn't mean much.

"I didn't think anything of it at the time."

Tate figured he also had likely been trying not to draw attention to himself. In going unnoticed, he'd avoided looking at the driver of the SUV.

Savannah said, "Surveillance cameras didn't show anyone going in or out of Aggerton's office after you."

Phil shrugged. "I didn't kill him."

If Aggerton had known who Phil really was, due to his attempts to get him to roll over for the FBI's case, then Tate had to wonder if Phil might also be in danger.

"This is spiraling out of control," he said. "Aggerton wasn't the only death. The DA is dead also, now." He watched as Phil absorbed that. "Someone is trying to cover up the truth by murdering people and stealing evidence. Be careful."

Phil said, "Think Ed Summers would talk?"

Savannah's eyes narrowed. "Interesting idea, but one I already had. He refused to speak with me or the police chief."

Phil worked his mouth to one side, then the other.

Tate said, "Worth a shot, if there's a way to get to him."

"I'm sure I don't want to know what that is." Savannah shot him a wry look, like this was Tate's doing. "So feel free to not tell me how you'd get to Ed Summers in prison. Who, by the way, has been seriously uncooperative since he was arrested. And none of his guys seem to know a thing."

Phil rapped his knuckles on the table. "Worth a try. Later."

He slid out and headed for the door.

Before Savannah could say anything, Hollis appeared. "He's gone already?" She planted one hand on her hip. "What did you say that scared him away, Tate?"

22

———

Savannah settled into the armchair in the sitting room. "Thank you for speaking with us, Mrs. Ilkins. I can imagine this is a difficult time for you."

The DA's wife nodded. Kicra Ilkins was about fifteen pounds underweight, evidently blowing what should've gone to her food budget on her hair and nails. Currently her hands were in a pair of white, terry cloth gloves. She wore tight-fitting, light gray pants, and a white blouse, her blonde hair perfectly wavy and freshly highlighted.

Keira dabbed at her perfect eye makeup with a balled-up tissue and noted Savannah's observation of her hands. "I had a hot wax treatment this morning." She waved her gloved fingers. "I have to wear these all day to keep my skin soft."

Savannah nodded, like she had any clue what the woman was talking about. "When was the last time you saw your husband?"

"I left at five for Krav Maga, like I do every Wednesday." Kiera sniffed delicately, her eyes red, but not puffy in the slightest. "After that, I went to yoga. Then the spa." She smiled. "I was in the mood to treat myself today."

"I'll need the exact time so that I can confirm your whereabouts."

Kiera's eyes widened. "I'm a suspect?"

"It's just a formality. I'm sure you understand I have to dot every i and cross every t."

"Oh, of course." She glanced at Tate, who had remained standing across the room.

Savannah was about as excited to be back here in the DA's house as he seemed. But this was her job, and while he might get to pick and choose what cases he worked on as a private investigator, she had to take them as they came, and this was her case.

Did he regret his brother-in-law shoehorning him into the case? She wasn't sure she had much sympathy for him if that was what he was feeling. She was too busy working to deal with feelings. She mostly tried to sort out her emotions after she closed cases. Not while in the process of the investigation.

Keira leaned forward and whispered, "Does he have to be here?"

She'd been about to ask her how the DA had seemed last night, before bed. Savannah closed her mouth. She glanced at Tate. He seemed to not even be listening to the conversation. She had to wonder if he was lost in thought, the way he had been when he'd gone outside onto the patio earlier.

It had been a rough couple of days for him. If he was a cop, she'd have sent him home. Or told him to get his head back in the game.

But he wasn't.

And his friend Phil, who had borrowed his sweater and was with the first victim right before he died, was currently trying to get in contact with a man in jail.

The guy had looked clean cut enough, which made her think FBI. Why she thought that, she wasn't so sure. There just happened to be a lot of that going around right now. However, there was also something about him she just couldn't put her finger on.

Savannah said, "Mr. Hudson is consulting with the police department on this case."

Keira whispered, "I heard he's the one who killed Aggerton. He's probably just here to destroy the evidence. He probably killed Nolan, too." She gasped, putting her gloved hand dramatically to her chest. "He'll try to frame me for it!"

Tate said, "Are you kidding me?"

Savannah didn't wait for Keira to justify it. "You really think the police department would bring the murderer in to investigate his own victim?"

That was how convinced Savannah was that Tate hadn't done this.

She wanted to strangle the woman or shake some sense into her, but despite the dry eyes, Keira had lost her husband this morning. Tate had lost his ex-wife, and she could see the toll it was taking on him, so she had to consider this woman was likely experiencing similar emotions. If not deeper. People dealt with grief in so many different ways, and you could never judge someone based on their public reaction. It all depended on the type of person, who the deceased had been, and the status of their relationship. That was a lot of variables to sort through.

Keira blinked. Her eyes filled with tears and she started to cry again.

"I'm sorry for your loss." Savannah tried to really feel the words as she spoke them, instead of just saying them by rote. "Mr. Ilkins believed someone intended him harm. Do you have any idea who he might've been referring to?"

She glanced at Tate, as though Savannah should have seen what she considered an obvious connection.

Savannah just waited.

"I don't know what you're talking about."

Either Keira had a relationship that was completely surface level with her husband, or she was oblivious. Savannah said,

"The last time I saw him, the DA told myself and my colleagues that he was in fear for his life. Someone was threatening him."

"I have no idea who that could've been. But Nolan had a very important job, sending all kinds of unsavory bad guys to prison. It was probably one of them, trying to get revenge."

"How about his personal life? What can you tell me about your relationship?" She needed to gauge how much Ilkins confided in his wife, considering she seemed to have only a general understanding of his job.

"It was fine."

"Things were good?"

Keira shrugged, the tissue in her gloved hand all but forgotten.

"No one's marriage is perfect, but that's why I ask. Because every situation is so different."

"Nolan and I were married nearly fifteen years. That long, things get…old. You know?"

Savannah nodded, even though she didn't know.

"So we made an arrangement that was mutually beneficial."

Tate spoke from the corner of the room. "How long have you had this open relationship?"

Keira's eyes widened.

Savannah said, "Answer the question, please."

"A few months."

"Do you know who else he was involved with?"

"Of course not." Her eyes flashed.

Savannah didn't believe her. "We will find out. It's only a matter of time."

Keira's face washed with anger. Savannah said, "Anyone in particular who disliked your husband stand out to you? Maybe someone who'd threatened him. Or someone who had argued with him recently."

Keira started to shake her head. She was about to speak when the door flew open and Bernice Aggerton trotted in on 5-inch heels.

"Sweetie!" She flung herself at Keira, and the two collided in a tangle of pointy limbs.

Keira started to cry, delicate little hitches in her breath accompanied by dry eyes. Savannah waited a minute or two for them to have their conversation. They did share something, both being new widows.

Something told her they wouldn't be inviting Robert Gaynes—or Tate—into their group.

Savannah began, "Mrs. Ilkins—"

Bernice spun around. "How dare you! At a time like this?"

"Our conversation with Mrs. Ilkins is entirely necessary, Mrs. Aggerton. You know that." She kept her voice soft, even though she didn't want to. Besides, how did she know Savannah hadn't been about to say goodbye before she'd interrupted?

Mrs. Aggerton turned to her friend. "Don't let them strong arm you. You're the victim here." She squeezed Keira's shoulders. "We survivors have to stick together." Bernice tugged Keira around so they both faced off with Savannah.

She stood. "If I have any further questions, Mrs. Ilkins, I'll give you a call." She laid her card on the end table. "And if you think of anything I might need to know, would you do the same?"

She started to speak, but Bernice cut her off. "You won't be disturbing her anymore. Not at a time like this." Hot, angry tears rolled down Bernice's face.

If she didn't looked genuinely upset, Savannah might have considered that she was laying it on thick.

Savannah glanced at Tate, then said to Keira. "Thank you for your time."

She turned away.

Bernice said, "Thanks, but no thanks."

Savannah didn't look back. She wandered down the hall, past the study where an officer stood at the tape, cordoning off the area where Nolan Ilkins had died. The same way Aggerton had died. Now their wives were together, best friends supporting each other. She nodded, and the officer did the same.

Then he said, "Tate." The word itself like a verbal nod.

"Hey."

She heard a shuffle, and the clasp of hands. Savannah shoved the handle down and strode outside. Tate caught up to her at the car.

Her car.

She'd persuaded him to leave his car so they could take hers. Now she regretted pushing it. She didn't even like driving.

"You okay?"

Savannah turned and leaned against the car, folding her arms so the shoulders of her red coat were tight.

Tate stopped in front of her, waiting. Listening and attentive. When she didn't say anything, he gave up. "Have you ever done that?"

She frowned. "Killed my husband like it's the perfect crime?"

His head jerked. "Uh, no. I meant the relationship thing."

"Oh." Wow, she really read that wrong. "No, I don't cheat."

"Sounds like there's a story there."

"Not one I want to stand around out here talking about." She tossed him the keys. "Let's go."

He opened the driver's door and got in while she checked her new emails. He pulled out, headed for the center of town again.

"Are you going to tell me?"

She sent a quick reply to Conroy's question, then said, "There's no way I would ever have an open relationship. I was the 'other woman' at one point, and I didn't like feeling that way. I was just grateful he could be as cold and calculating at work as he was in his personal life, so he could still do his job after I broke it off."

She knew he'd ask, so she continued, "It was a case. He was a junior prosecutor back then. No one else would give me the time of day. I gave him everything he needed to prosecute a high-profile case and get him the promotion to district attorney, while he strung me along with empty promises of a relationship. Might as well have tied it up in a bow."

"What kind of high-profile case?"

"Corruption." She stared at her phone. "But don't think I don't know plenty about women conspiring to kill their husbands. Like that old movie. Two women meet and make a pact. They agree to off each other's husbands and provide the other with the perfect alibi."

"Wow, you're a suspicious person."

So he'd said it. She glanced at him. "Comes with the territory."

"How so?"

It was a weighty question. She could feel it hang in the air. Savannah had to admit—if only to herself—that she knew now how he'd felt last night. He'd kicked her out of the car not wanting to talk about his grief and his past. The Lord knew she felt the same now.

Savannah bit her lip, then said, "That corruption case?" She shifted to face him, wanting to see for herself just how much he could handle. "My father was the New Orleans Police Commissioner."

His eyebrows rose, and despite the fact he didn't need this to take up any brain real estate right now with everything else he had going on in his life, he still seemed content to learn more about her. She just didn't want to be a burden.

"It was two years ago. He'll be getting out of prison around my fiftieth birthday." Savannah shrugged. "If he lives that long." She winced.

"Savannah—"

"Don't." She shook her head. "Don't worry about it. I'm in Last Chance County now, and I just want to do my job."

This case wasn't about her. It was about Kenny Aggerton,

and Nolan Ilkins. It was about Rob Gaynes hurting his wife, and whether or not Claire had been murdered.

She wondered if either of the two women they'd just met with had been the one on the video going into Claire's room. There was no way she could get a warrant for their phone records, to see if the women were connected. Any of the three of them.

Had one of them paid that final visit to Claire's room? Only the doctor doing the autopsy could tell them if it was murder.

Tate said, "I appreciate you sticking up for me in there. Telling her I'm consulting."

"Come up with something good, and you're welcome." He smiled. She said, "I'll never turn down a pair of fresh eyes."

"I hope we get to the bottom of this."

"Me, too." And quick.

Most murders weren't solved all that fast, and she had other cases to work on as well. But bodies were piling up. The town would not be satisfied too much longer unless she came up with an answer. Why did it have to keep getting so much more complex?

This whole thing was bizarre. It was like staring at a plate of spaghetti, trying to figure out where the end of a strand was.

"Huh."

She shifted in her seat. "What?"

"Blue car. Behind us."

She twisted and saw the small SUV on their tail. The driver sped up, far enough and fast enough to nudge the back of Savannah's car.

Tate grasped the wheel with two hands.

She grabbed the door handle and held on tight, then twisted to look again.

"That's Bernice's car."

"Yeah, and this is highway fourteen."

"What does that mean?"

Tate said, "Half a mile up ahead? That's dead man's curve."

23

Savannah screamed. "Dead man's *what*?"

Tate kept his focus on the road, not able to let go of the wheel with one hand to give her a reassuring squeeze, even if he'd wanted to. Instead, he just said, "Everything is fine. We still have two miles before that stretch of the canyon."

She whimpered. "I'd rather not die here, if that's okay with you." Just when he was starting to think she was angry at him, she turned and looked out the back window. "I really hate you, Bernice!"

Tate had his foot almost to the floor as they careened down the highway, Bernice right on their tailgate. All the while, he had to bite back a smile. She was seriously cute when she was angry. This did not bode well if they were to have a future together, as it'd incline him to pick a fight with her just to see that fire spark and flame up.

"Why are you smiling?"

Tate wasn't going to touch that. "Call in. Get a black and white here. Yeah?"

She dug around in her backpack and pulled out a radio. "Forget cell phones. This is getting broadcasted. She twisted a dial at the top of the bulky handheld unit and lifted it to her mouth, "This is Detective Wilcox requesting backup from any available units in the vicinity of highway fourteen." She lowered it. "Where are we?"

"Mile marker seven."

She got back on the radio. "Mile marker—"

Bernice bumped them from behind again. Tate fought to keep them from spinning out.

"—seven," she finished. "In high-speed pursuit, chased by Bernice Aggerton." She gave a description of the car that included Bernice's license plate.

Bill, the police department dispatcher, replied, "Copy that. Unit responding."

Savannah sighed.

"It's not personal, you know."

She twisted to face him. Bernice hit them again, and Savannah said, "That feels pretty personal. Like it's going to feel personal when I slap Bernice across her face."

"Are you really going to do that?"

"No." She bit the word out.

"We'll be fine."

"If you tell me not to be mad because her husband just died, I'm going to…I don't know what. Because that's not an excuse for driving like this. She's reckless. All of our lives are in danger."

The highway bent, and Tate decided it was smarter to concentrate on the road in front of them instead of replying. She was just venting. He didn't blame her, to be honest. Tate was itching for a fight. This whole thing was hitting too close to home. And far too deadly.

"You aren't going to die here." He needed to say it, for her benefit as well as his own. "Neither of us are." He gritted his teeth, then heard sirens behind them.

"Who is it?" Savannah turned in her seat, peering out the

wing mirror on her side. "I think that's Frees. Good, we can use that to our advantage."

Savannah got on the radio and asked for Frees to switch to a different channel. When he came on, she said, "Good to see you."

His low voice came through the radio speaker. "Let's get this done, Detective."

"Fine by me."

"You driving?"

"No, Tate is," she told him. "What are you thinking?"

Before Frees could say anything, Bernice hit the brakes. Metal slammed metal with a bang and a screech as she slammed on her brakes—the police car's front bumper plowing into her back bumper.

Savannah spoke into the radio. "Frees?"

There was no reply. Tate glanced in the rearview. The cop car swerved to the side, out of control. Bernice veered the car off to the shoulder, taking a sharp turn that nearly flipped her car.

"Fire road." Tate tapped the brake, realizing too late what Bernice's plan was. He twisted the wheel hard to the left and pulled up on the emergency brake.

Savannah squealed and fell against the door as the car spun around to face the opposite direction. Tires squealed and they came nose to nose with Frees's black and white patrol car. He saw the guy's face, hard set and determined. Definitely a man to have your back in a serious situation.

Tate hit the gas and got Savannah's car turned around first. He bounced onto the fire road and tried to gauge how far ahead Bernice was already.

Basically just packed down dirt and some gravel, the whole thing was rutted by potholes filled with frozen rain water.

Tate tried to avoid one, hit another, and heard the ice crack. At least, he hoped it was ice and not the car's axel. He winced and followed the road around a bend where it inclined, up the hill.

"Up ahead."

He saw the car. At least the corner of it. "She pulled off."

"Probably making a run for it."

He pulled over behind her and Frees came around in his cop car, completely blocking Bernice's car from backing up at all.

They climbed out, drawing weapons as they moved toward the blue car. Tate glanced in the passenger window. "Clear." The front seat, at least.

Savannah opened the rear door. "Clear."

Frees popped the trunk. "Clear. She made a run for it, didn't she?"

Tate moved around the car, watching the ground as he went. From the driver's door, a set of footprints moved away from the vehicle. "She went this way."

He bent down to inspect the prints closer. They were bigger than he'd expect a woman's shoe size to be. These were at least a twelve. He didn't remember noticing her freakishly large feet while at Ilkins' house. The only conclusion he could make peace with was that they weren't chasing after Bernice—they were chasing after a man.

He set off, trotting alongside the footprints. They spaced out as though the person had started to run. Tate did the same, trying to catch up to whoever had climbed out of the car and raced off.

The person who had slammed into the back of their car and nearly killed them. He didn't mention to Savannah how close they'd come to spinning out. Or flipping over and crashing.

She probably knew, but he didn't want her to even get the possibility into her head. *I'd rather not die out here.* Because she wanted to live, or because she'd rather be somewhere else if she was going to breathe her last breath? It stung that she might prefer a place other than where he was.

Though, at the same time, Tate wanted to know where

"home" was to Savannah Wilcox. Then he planned to take her there so she could feel that sensation of returning to the place where her heart felt like it belonged.

"She just planned to disappear into the woods?" Frees asked.

Tate kept his gaze on the ground. "Or find a place to turn the tables. Get the drop on us."

Frees huffed. "Not likely."

"Also," Tate said, "we're not dealing with Bernice here, but someone larger with gigantic feet."

"Copy that."

Not that Tate didn't think Bernice completely capable of doing something like this. He figured at the drop of a hat she could turn into a shrieking tornado. Some people just buried their true potential well under a civilized surface.

The kind of people more inclined to snap and stab a person over and over in a rage.

Had Bernice killed her husband? She didn't seem to care that he was dead. Tate hadn't even been married to Claire, and he felt more over her death than Bernice seemed to about her own spouse. Although, it was possible she just held her emotions in check without letting anyone see the truth about her feelings.

It had been nice of her to show up at Ilkins' to support the DA's wife—also a new widow. Maybe too nice. There had to be some kind of ulterior motive there. Two rich women, trying to save face and keep their reputations and lifestyles intact, even after their husbands were murdered. Tate knew Aggerton at least had been cheating on his wife, and Keira herself said that she and Nolan had an "open" relationship. Could be that the wives had held grudges for the infidelity. Savannah herself referenced that old movie where two women made a pact to get rid of their husbands.

This was rapidly turning into more of a conspiracy than two straightforward murders. If the two women were behind it, and it was their idea to make it seem complicated, then they were doing a bang-up job. But they had to have had help to pull it off —who was the man driving Bernice's car?

There were so many suspects, he didn't know which had the most to gain by Aggerton and Ilkins being dead. But Tate couldn't get one man out of his mind throughout all of this.

Robert Gaynes.

Tate raced through the woods, following the tracks. They led him to the edge of a creek, splashed into the water…and didn't come back out.

Tate hopped to the far bank. "Huh."

He stared around.

"Lost them?"

Tate pressed his lips together. Frees didn't want to know what Tate thought of his tone. "Give me a second."

He studied the ground, thinking about who had been driving the car. A man. Someone who had stumbled into this creek and disembarked, using the water to disguise his new direction. Which meant he knew they were following him.

Tate bit back his frustration. "Savannah." He glanced around. "Where's Savannah?"

The words were only barely out of his mouth before a gunshot echoed through the woods. Tate set off running.

Frees raced behind him. "At the cars, calling in backup to search."

He pumped his arms and legs, all the way back, exactly where they'd come. Fear froze his insides, like being pummeled by wind coming down from the north. The kind of cold air that chilled to the bones. To the inside. *Savannah.*

He'd lost one woman he cared about this week. Tate wasn't about to lose another. Nor could the town afford to lose a police detective as good as she was. As dedicated.

Another gunshot rang out.

He could hear yelling, high in tone. Might've been her. He didn't have time to think on it and figure that out, though. He just needed to get there. She was already hurt. She didn't need this.

Frees huffed behind him. Tate saw the cars in the distance, heard an engine roar to life, and caught sight of Savannah's car pulling out. Where was she going?

"Savannah!" He broke through the trees, gun up.

He heard a groan and raced for it, around to the far side of Bernice's car.

Savannah rolled over and sat up. "Ouch."

He crouched. "What happened?"

"He shot at me. And stole my car." She stood and swayed, forcing him to stand as well.

He held his arms out to steady her and Savannah collapsed into them.

She stared up at him. Same as she had when she'd collided with him outside Hope Mansion. Blinking, trying to figure out what had happened. Not as cute as when she was angry, but it was pretty close.

"You okay?"

Frees cleared his throat. The two of them turned and the cop said, "I'll call in a BOLO on your vehicle, Detective. We'll find it."

He turned away, headed for his car, and got in.

"Right." Savannah cleared her throat and pushed away from Tate. "Bernice's car?"

He tried not to be disappointed. "You want to go after him?"

"It was a man, wasn't it?" She eyed him.

"You saw him?"

"Ski mask. Like the guy who cut you." She shrugged. "Maybe he left a print in the car."

Tate grinned. "Or he'll leave one in yours when he dumps it. On the run. In too much of a hurry to wipe up after himself. Fingerprints."

"DNA." She smiled. "Time to get down to business."

She grabbed a duffel from the back of Frees's cop vehicle and hauled it over to Bernice's car. "Ever dusted for prints before?"

"It's been a while." He rocked forward on the balls of his feet, then back to his heels. "But I'm sure it'll come back to me quick enough."

"Then let's get to work."

24

S avannah scanned the fingerprint she'd collected from Bernice's car into her computer so she could have the program compare it to the fingerprints they had on file locally.

Mia said, "Got it." And hung up her phone. "Frees said your car was found abandoned."

"He better not have taken my CDs."

"You still listen to CDs?"

Savannah narrowed her eyes.

Mia lifted both hands.

Savannah said, "So he's gone?"

"No sign of the driver. And the car was left on a residential street at the edge of town. No cameras, but everyone seems to have one of those Wi-Fi doorbells these days, so they're going to canvas the neighborhood."

Savannah nodded. Tate was out on the streets, looking for the car along with the rest of the cops. Doing the same secret, private investigator stuff that got him examined at the hospital the same night she'd been attacked.

She grabbed more coffee and came back to check the progress on the fingerprint scan.

5% complete.

She picked up her phone and dialed Ted's office.

He answered before the first ring finished. "You couldn't walk down the hall?"

She gritted her teeth at his question. No, as a matter of fact, she couldn't walk past the bathroom where she'd been shot. "Too much to do." True, but not the reason she hadn't visited him in his office to ask him. "Anything new for me?"

"You don't think I'd call or send you an email if I did have something?"

"Humor me."

Ted sighed. "Fine. I've got the DA's phone and computer files to go through. His whiskey was being poisoned as well, just like Aggerton's."

But that wasn't what had killed him. "The wives."

"You think?"

Savannah said, "Fingerprints on the decanter in each man's office would confirm their prospective wives touched it. That doesn't prove they put the poison in there, though."

She would have to first find proof they had purchased the poison—after the lab they contracted with at the State Police got back to her on what exactly it was. Financial records, maybe. Proof of purchase of a deadly substance? Assuming they hadn't covered their tracks.

"What else?"

Ted said, "I've got Claire's phone, which Tate passed over from her personal effects. Then there's everything the FBI sent me this morning, which is an entire zip folder of documents. Things they think pertain to the books for Ed Summers that the DA had information on. Which I also still have to go through."

She said, "Mia and I are helping. Sorry you're so swamped, but this thing is complicated. And getting more so every day it seems."

"I could do without hearing you were shot at today."

"I'm okay."

Ted was quiet for a second, then said, "Honest?"

"Sure." Her computer chimed.

40% complete.

He said, "Running a print?"

"Yes, and it's taking forever so send me something to work on. What's next on your list?"

"Comparing phone records we have to what the FBI sent me from the burner phone Tate found—the one they believe belongs to Aggerton."

"Right," she said. "Send it over."

She opened the attachment a minute later and exported the phone records into a program Ted had written that looked for matching numbers across all the files. That way, he could quickly tell who was associated with who. The second thing it did was assign names to numbers, and he also categorized conversations. Though if the phone's owners used a third-party messaging app instead of the default texting app, then they'd never get those conversations.

A second later the first match popped up. The text conversation between two phones was lengthy, with the calls and messages sorted into linear order by the program.

Starting six months ago, these two phones had been in contact daily. Brief texts. Long calls. Even periods where the two phones pinged the same cell tower and GPS indicated they were in close vicinity of each other. Usually in the evening, and usually only for a couple hours at a time.

She looked up the area on an online map.

Couple stores, a dry cleaner. A coffee shop maybe? Behind them was a hotel chain only out-of-towners used when they came into the area on business.

By all accounts, it appeared to be the exchange of two people embroiled in an affair. Savannah looked at who the two phones belonged to. The first was the burner Tate had given to the FBI. Was it really Aggerton's phone? She hadn't been able to ask him about that. She'd been too busy getting her face slammed against her car.

The second number belonged to…

Savannah sucked in a breath. The air got stuck, and she started coughing. Why had that number been included in this group? She wouldn't have added it to the program if she'd known whose it was. She had to cough, and took a sip of coffee to get her breathing under control.

Mia said, "You okay?"

"Is she okay?" That was Tate, standing across the counter, frowning. Kaylee wasn't there, as it was late, and she'd already gone home for the night.

Savannah nodded and finished coughing. Or tried to. Was she being poisoned as well? Maybe that was why she couldn't catch her breath.

Couldn't…

White spots blinked around the edges of her vision.

Sound rushed through her ears. She needed to get the search results off the screen. He couldn't see them… She needed to…

"Put your head between your legs." Tate's face swam in front of her.

She shook her head.

"Is she having a panic attack?"

He moved in front of her. Lifting her coffee cup, he sniffed the contents. "We should get this tested. She could've been poisoned."

"Like Aggerton and Ilkins." Mia leaned over her shoulder, one hand on the mouse as she scrolled down Savannah's copy of the email Ted had sent out right after their conversation. At least, she was assuming that's what it was.

Savannah couldn't even think straight.

"Both of whom had poisoned liquor in their offices." Mia sounded worried.

"There you go. Easy now." Tate smiled, his gaze on her face as he studied her. "I've always thought liquor was bad for you."

Savannah sucked in a long breath. It hitched a couple of times, and she had to clear her throat, but she didn't cough.

"There we go," Tate said. "Now another."

She inhaled, then blew it out.

"Easy peasy."

Savannah lifted one eyebrow.

"And you're back."

She shook her head. "It wasn't a panic attack. I was just… choking a little."

"Mmm."

Mia looked at Savannah's screen. "Because someone was having an affair with…oh." She stopped and backed up.

Savannah pressed her lips together.

Tate stood. She grabbed his hand, stood and tugged him away. "Don't." The last thing she wanted was for him to know Claire was having an affair with one of the victims.

He turned to her. "What are you hiding?"

"We don't know what it means yet. Why drudge up things that weren't intended to be made public?"

Spreading something wide for all to know—or telling someone who cared—was entirely different from uncovering information that would be included in a police report.

If Claire Gaynes's death had been murder instead of from natural causes.

"I'll get Conroy." Mia wandered off.

Savannah ground her molars.

"You'll regret the dental bill for that." Tate eyed her. "Sit down. Tell me what it is that got you into a panic."

Savannah wasn't even sure that was what it had been. How was she supposed to know? She'd choked a little, like she said, and things just escalated from there. She'd felt like she was drowning before and didn't like it then either.

"You've been working like crazy."

"I'm not burned out." Not yet, anyway. She was closing in

fast, but it wasn't like she could take time to slow down right now. Not when there were murders to solve.

She slumped down onto her chair.

"That's Claire's number." Tate's brows crept toward each other. "She was cheating on Rob?" His nose crinkled for a second. "Don't exactly blame her. Who was—"

"Kenny Aggerton." When Tate said nothing, she turned in her chair. "Maybe you should sit down."

"She didn't kill him. I'd put money on the wife."

He was right, as Claire had been busy getting beat to a pulp that night. As for the wife? "Bernice alibied out. It wasn't her."

"What about Ilkins's wife? Maybe it was Keira."

Savannah sighed. "You think a bitty little thing like her could've killed Aggerton? He was massive."

Tate looked a little sick. "I wonder if Gaynes knew. Maybe he retaliated over it."

"There's a theory." Savannah remembered the woman's health regimen. Maybe she was stronger than she looked. "We need proof if we're going to make charges stick. After all, that's the night Claire was attacked. We need his alibi, but it'll probably be that he was beating her at the time." She paused. "You don't need to be part of this investigation. The FBI can do their own liaising."

Conroy said, "Agreed."

She looked over, aware that Tate turned to him as well.

The police chief folded his arms across his chest. "Mia filled me in. Bernice was brought here to explain what happened with her car. I'm not satisfied with what she told the officer about the theft."

"There's a whole lot of entirely-too-coincidental stories flying around." She glanced up at Tate. "This could be the break in the case we were looking for all along. You brought us this phone, right?"

"Phil gave it to the FBI."

Conroy glanced between them. "Who is Phil?"

She said, "A friend of Tate's."

Before he could ask more, Tate said, "So long as it's helpful, can you look through this information for anything on someone called 'West'?"

Savannah did the search.

Conroy said, "I'll go talk to Bernice."

"I'll go with." Tate squeezed Savannah's shoulder and walked away with her boss.

She watched him leave. She wondered if Bernice would even tell them anything. Then she wondered which of the suspects killed Aggerton, and then Ilkins. Had it been over a relationship, or something far bigger?

The search yielded no results for West. She straightened as Mia walked back over. "I'm beginning to think this West person is just an effort at misdirection."

Mia sat. "Could be. Whoever killed Aggerton and Ilkins was angry."

"Maybe it was a professional hit, done to look like an angry, scorned person. Possibly a woman."

"You think so?"

Savannah shrugged. "Could be. I've had more bizarre outcomes than that. But I'd put money down on Bernice knowing who it was. In fact, since Claire was having an affair with Bernice's husband, I'd put money on her being the one who paid a visit to the hospital room. And sent her threatening texts."

Mia said, "I'll go tell Conroy to ask."

Savannah looked at the search results again. She tapped her foot on the side of her desk. A couple of seconds later, the fingerprint match was complete.

One result.

She clicked the name. A partial, so only a possible match but there was only one match in town: Patrick Dearnum, assistant to Robert Gaynes at City Hall.

She'd have to run it again through national databases they

could access. That would turn up more results, considering it was a partial. But this was enough she figured she could get a warrant to go through the man's personal and professional life. See if there was anything there.

Still, maybe she'd been right about it being a hired hit.

Or maybe he'd been coerced into murder.

Conspiracy.

Savannah's phone rang. A private number, not uncommon in her work. Some people wanted to remain anonymous. She swiped her thumb across the screen as she lifted it to her ear. "Wilcox."

"Back off this case." The voice was distorted, sounding electronic. Like something from a horror movie.

"Who is this?" She wanted to sound confident. Steady. But she didn't. She sounded like a scared little girl who'd just had a panic attack a few minutes ago.

The caller chuckled. "Back off this case. Or things will get a whole lot worse for you."

"What is—" Mia stopped. She whispered, "Savannah, why do you look so pale?"

Before Savannah could answer her partner, the caller hung up.

25

Conroy hadn't let him in the interview room, and Tate figured that had been a good choice. Given how belligerent Bernice was being, his presence would only have fanned the flames of that fire.

Tate didn't want to acknowledge that a whole town of people he'd worked for and lived with for years seemed to have suddenly turned on him. As though he was a waste of space, only good for pinning multiple crimes on. The perfect scapegoat.

Through the glass, Conroy said, "So you glanced out the window and noticed your car was missing."

Bernice lifted her chin. "That's right."

"Did you see anyone outside earlier?"

"No. I was there to be with Kiera. Consoling her." Bernice sniffed. "I know a little something about losing a husband, you know."

Conroy nodded. "Of course."

On the other side of the glass, Tate smirked. He didn't believe his friend's sincerity one bit. Or maybe it was that Conroy was perfectly capable of being a professional with empathy, and it was Tate who was unable to show sympathy to someone so hateful. He preferred to save his sympathetic energies for people who deserved it. Like Elexa. And Savannah.

Savannah had been having a panic attack. Tate knew what they looked like. He had friends who were in the military or retired from, and one struggled pretty badly with panic attacks. No way would he let her brush that off as nothing when he knew very well that it was something.

But he'd blown any chance of getting her to open up about anything more than just surface stuff when he'd refused to open up to her about his parent's deaths. She'd wrapped up the case involving her father and a conversation about her last relationship in one neat little conversation, devoid of all emotion he knew must still be active.

Tate blew out a breath. How did he get her to expand a little bit? Clearly there was more to these situations than her CliffsNotes account of what had happened.

Conroy said, "When did you first learn your husband was having an affair?"

Bernice's lips puffed out. "Do I care?"

Conroy turned his phone so Bernice could see the screen, and all Tate could see was the back of his hand. "Seems to me like you cared enough to send threatening text messages to Claire Gaynes, warning her to break it off with your husband. *Or else.* What does 'or else' mean, Bernice?"

Bernice said, "She should know better than to touch my husband. Everyone should."

"So you take it as a personal affront that she was sleeping with Kenny?"

She shrugged one shoulder. "Don't expect me to sit back and do nothing."

"Like sneak into her hospital room and finish the job Robert Gaynes started? Get rid of the problem once and for all."

"Not like anyone would miss her."

Tate's hands curled into fists.

Conroy said, "She has a daughter."

Bernice's lips puffed out again. "Am I supposed to care?"

The police chief said nothing.

"Anyway, what does this have to do with my car being stolen?" Bernice shifted in her seat.

Conroy said, "Evidence suggests all of this is linked. Including Claire Gaynes's death."

Tate knew for a fact the autopsy had not been completed on Claire. Her death hadn't been ruled a homicide. Yet.

Bernice said, "None of it had to do with me. I'm the victim here."

"Yeah." Tate realized he'd spoken aloud to the room, which was currently empty—well, except for him. "Keep spinning that line. See where it gets you." He heard a woman chuckle and spun around. "Savannah."

"The one and only." She shut the door behind her, looking much better than she had before. Color had come back to her cheeks. She glanced at the window and listened for a minute, then winced. "So I guess you know."

Tate said, "That Claire was having an affair?"

She nodded.

"We hadn't been married for a long time. It doesn't bother me like you'd think. And as far as I know, I didn't give her a reason to step out on me when we were together."

"So it was Gaynes' doing?"

He shrugged. "I'm not saying it was justified, because I don't believe in that. But she was looking for something, and she obviously wasn't getting it from her husband."

Savannah studied her boss and the woman through the glass. "It's so sad." She sighed. "I'm not supposed to feel it. I try not to. But sometimes it just…gets to me. You know?"

He squeezed her shoulder.

"I'm sorry. You lost Claire." She turned. "This shouldn't be about me."

"You're allowed to have your own feelings at the same time I'm having mine." He wanted to pull her to him, give her a hug.

But after he'd shut her down in the car, he wasn't sure he had a right to do that.

Instead, Savannah stepped toward him. She wrapped her arms around his waist. He hugged her back, leaning his cheek against her blonde hair.

"I'm sorry you lost her."

"Thank you." Tate laid a kiss on her hair. "It's Elexa I feel sorry for, though. Her future is uncertain. She's lost the only decent parent she ever had."

She leaned back. "So what are you going to do about it?"

Tate shrugged. "Make sure she's all right at the mansion with Maggie."

"Teenage girls need more than that. They need a father figure. A solid, good, role model."

He grinned. "You think I'm a good guy?"

"Don't change the subject. I was a teenage girl, you know?" She gave him a pointed look. "Trust me, she needs someone like… No, not just someone. She needs you, Tate."

He'd never considered himself that guy, or worthy of being that guy before. "I don't even know where to start."

"Good. Because teenagers can spot a fake. She knows she can trust you and that you give a hoot about what happens to her. That's how you start." She tugged her arms loose from his.

Tate followed, not willing to let her go just yet. Her eyes widened a second before he lowered his face close to hers. And kissed her.

Short. To the point. Careful to not tweak her broken nose. He'd almost forgotten about it.

He pulled back an inch. "Thank you for being someone I can trust, someone who gives a hoot about what happens to me."

Humor lit her eyes, and he felt her breath on his lips as she exhaled.

"My parents were killed in a car accident. They were hit by a drunk driver."

She pressed those lips together now. He knew she'd known, but had wanted to say it out loud to her anyway.

She grabbed his hand and squeezed, then turned aside, watching the conversation through the glass as Conroy asked Bernice about a person who might want to steal her car. "He doesn't know about the partial print found on her steering wheel." She glanced at him. "Local result gave me one match. Robert Gaynes's assistant."

He hadn't thought she would tack on that last word. "The skinny guy?"

"His name is Patrick Dearnum."

"Right." Tate nodded. "You think he's in on this?"

"At least that he ties the murders to Gaynes."

Tate blew out a breath.

"This type of corruption makes my skin crawl. People who think they can do whatever they want—hurt whoever they want—just to further their own ends."

"Isn't that everyone?"

"Not like this." She shook her head, but there was no humor in her gaze. "Not like my father."

Tate stood silent, giving her time. The way she'd done, even after he'd shut down. If he boxed her in and tried to force her into talking to him, he figured she'd also shut down.

She stared, unseeing, at the scene through the glass. "When I figured out what my father had done—*what was he even thinking?*—I was glad my mom was dead. Living to see that would have destroyed her. But then I had to wonder if the corruption didn't start because she was gone."

Tate wanted to hold her hand, or hug her again. But that would jolt her out of whatever zone she was in now. Deep in her memories.

She shrugged. "By the time I realized what was happening, he'd built an empire. It started out as payoffs, but he got in deep with some people. Hits were ordered, and he squashed cases. Hired muscle. Coercion. Corruption."

"A RICO case?"

"He wouldn't tell them who he was working with. Took the fall for the whole thing, him alone except for a couple of stragglers. The DA tried to persuade him to name names, get a witness protection deal." Shook her head. "Even brought me in to try and get him to talk. Didn't work. All it did was put me on their radar so the death threats and attempts on my life got worse. I gave the DA everything I had, took my mother's maiden name on a new ID, and walked away."

Tate kept himself still. "Why would they kill the DA in New Orleans now?"

She shrugged one shoulder. "Maybe it's unrelated."

He slid an arm around her shoulders so he could give her a quick squeeze. Solidarity. Comfort. "Eric can find out."

She nodded. Through the glass, the conversation Conroy had been having with Bernice erupted into a fit of screaming.

Bernice was on her feet. "If course I threatened her! What do you think I'd do with that tramp?"

"I really could slap her." Savannah sighed.

Tate suppressed a laugh. Slapping a citizen wouldn't be a good idea. He said, "Feel like taking a field trip?"

Savannah moved from the glass to the door. "Sure. Fresh air would be good." She looked at the clock on the wall. "I'm waiting for the warrant to come through so we can go pick up Patrick."

"I'm not sure the air will be fresh where we're going."

Half an hour later, he pulled the car into the parking lot of the county jail.

Savannah's eyebrows rose. "You really think Summers will talk to you? I thought Phil was contacting him."

"He didn't get anywhere yet. But it's worth a try isn't it?" He didn't get out. Instead, he shifted in his seat and covered her hand with his. "You okay?"

She shrugged.

"Don't brush it off."

"We have multiple cases to solve." She reached for the door handle. "That moment in the viewing room was a nice interlude." She steadied her gaze on him. "Very nice. But it's time to get back to work."

She got out.

At least she had called it "very nice." But was that "very" nice, or did she mean *very nice.* Then he realized she was waiting for him, so he got out of the car.

He'd always said before that he didn't mind complicated women. But that was when life was simple. Right now things were erupting all around him, and he hardly knew where to step first for fear of getting burned.

In the middle of it all, there was Savannah.

When had she become such a central part of his life? They'd been at odds, pretty much since the day they met. They didn't work the same way. Their lives hardly meshed. But they'd both lived through pain as a result of someone else's poor decisions. They'd both tried to do the right thing. To live with integrity and honor. Sure, on the surface they had wildly different methods. But deep down, they were the same.

He grabbed the door handle and pulled, holding it open for her. "Kindred spirits."

"Uh…what?"

Someone inside yelled, "Tate!"

He greeted the prison guard, a friend of his from high school. Small talk got them on the log, and the guard radioed for Ed Summers to be brought to an interview room.

"You really think he's going to tell us anything?"

Tate stated it as plainly as he could. "Lost causes is what I do."

Savannah blinked, but he was pretty sure he saw the sheen of tears before she turned away to face the approaching guard.

"Follow me." He showed them to a small room where Summers already sat. He didn't look well.

Savannah glanced back. "How long has he been like this?"

The guard shrugged. "Flu is going around."

Tate walked to the table where Summers was sweating. Coughing. "You okay?"

He tried to speak but could only cough some more. His already skinny body was practically emaciated.

"Or it's withdrawals." The guard shut the door, leaving them in there with Summers.

"We can do this quickly," Savannah said. "If you're up for it."

He looked at her, face flushed and eyes glazed, then glanced at Tate. Summers seemed to recognize him. He opened his mouth to speak.

Right then, his whole body keeled over and hit the floor.

Tate held Savannah back. He knelt and pressed two fingers to Ed's neck, then looked at her. "He's dead."

26

———

Savannah paced the hall outside the room where the prison doctor was bent over Ed Summers performing his own examination. "This whole thing is a mess." She took two steps and said, "Chief? You still there."

"Yeah." Conroy was quiet a couple of seconds. "He's really dead?"

"Ed Summers won't be going to trial."

"I guess that's why the prison warden is on my other line. Probably calling to commiserate."

She muttered, "Or something."

"What's that?"

"He died here. I better be satisfied with the investigation, or there are going to be problems."

"Because you don't have enough cases right now?"

She turned back at the end of the hall. Tate glanced over at her, breaking off his conversation with his prison guard friend. She wanted to take that second he seemed willing to offer her. Have a moment with him, since those had gone pretty well so far. They'd been getting considerably closer lately. He'd even kissed her earlier.

If she was a sentimental person, she might consider him some kind of safe haven. A harbor in a storm.

If.

He frowned. She shook her head, feeling the slight curl of her lips.

"Wilcox."

"What?" She spun away from Tate and said, "Yep. Chief?" Heat flooded her face. A man was dead, and she was mooning over a guy she liked. Savannah touched the bridge of her nose, wishing she could squeeze it. Even a light press made her face throb. A good reminder of the stakes.

At any moment something else could happen. "This is a nightmare."

"You're telling me," Conroy said. "I wanted to watch Summers go down. Now I'll never get that chance because he managed to get out from under this as well."

"By dying. Not exactly a way to skate justice."

"Hmm. True."

Savannah said, "Sorry."

"Why are you sorry? You didn't kill him."

"So I can't have sympathy, because it wasn't my fault? I know how hard you worked to get him in prison." She'd helped him do that, happy to get Summers off the street at last.

Mostly that had been because, at one point, it had looked like Tate was working with him. Or for him. She wasn't clear on that. However, now that she'd met both Phil and Elexa, she knew there was a whole lot to Tate that she'd never understood. If he'd been there, inside Ed Summers's house, there was a really good reason. And he wasn't obligated to tell her what that reason was. Though, she figured Phil might actually be the reason.

"Fair enough."

"The doctor is done."

Conroy said, "Find out what happened."

Savannah hung up. The doctor peeled off his gloves. An

older man, the shirt buttons over his belly gaped to expose the white undershirt beneath. His tie didn't hang to his belt and his hair seemed to have given up right in the middle of a half-hearted attempt to grow.

"Verdict?"

The doctor sighed. "I'll have to make my formal assessment, but I'm thinking it wasn't the flu."

"Like maybe poison?" She didn't want to plant an idea in his head, but that had been a reoccurring theme so far. "Because I've got two dead from vicious stabbings, only there was evidence that they were also both poisoned."

He frowned. "Why stab someone if you're already poisoning them?"

"Probably you wouldn't do that…but if you didn't know they were already being poisoned…" She didn't need to discuss the details of her case, so she pulled a business card from her back pocket. "Please include me in your final report. I'd like the details."

"Thank you, uh…" He looked at the card. "Detective Wilcox."

She walked away, Tate shook the guard's hand, and they met halfway down the hall.

He said, "My guy says he has no idea who could've slipped Ed Summers something, but it's not like that would be hard. They serve each other meals."

Savannah said, "What's the likelihood we'd hit the right guy even after interviewing every single prisoner in this place?"

Tate scratched at his jaw. "Exactly." He rubbed a hand back over his hair. "So we look at surveillance?"

Hours and hours of whatever prisoners did when they knew full well they were being watched. Not exactly her idea of a fun night. Plus, knowing her luck, it would be another shot of some guy wearing the sweater Phil had stolen from Tate—the one Phil said someone had then stolen from him.

"We need to go talk to Gaynes's assistant. Find out what he

can tell us about Bernice's car, and who might want people silenced."

Tate nodded. "We have three dead guys, all lower level. All with secrets that someone—possibly this 'West' person—didn't want getting out."

She said, "So they're desperate. Enough to know we shouldn't talk to Summers, but that only confirms something we didn't know. Namely, the fact this wasn't Summers hiding his own business from fully getting out."

Tate nodded. "This is bigger."

"I have a special dislike for people who abuse their own power by lording it over other people's *lives*."

He knew now. She'd told him exactly who her father was and what he'd done. The secret was out. Savannah didn't have to hide the truth anymore. Her dad had taken an oath to be honorable. Upright. A police commissioner who was supposed to stand for everything a cop should be.

Instead, she'd been tarred with his brush. And those who didn't believe she'd been a party to it the whole time had considered her a snitch. Someone not worth their time, let alone their respect. As though exposing corruption was akin to being responsible for it, rather than simply doing the right thing.

In the end, she'd come here to a middle-of-nowhere town called Last Chance, of all things, to realize there were good cops still after all.

And she was one of them.

Conroy. Mia. Frees. Donaldson. Basuto. All of them, even Kaylee, though she wasn't a cop. They were good people, even if they didn't always make perfect choices. They knew what honor was. They knew what was true—what was right and good for them to do, rather than making choices based on their own selfish motives.

The warden stopped them. "I've got a guy." He tossed his head, in the direction of his office. "He wants to talk to you."

Savannah turned to him. "Yeah?"

He nodded. "Says make it fast, before he changes his mind."

She glanced at Tate, who shrugged, then told the warden, "Lead the way."

He took them to his office where a prisoner stood by the wall. A guard held post at the open door, watching.

"Thank you." The warden passed him and stepped inside.

The guard shot Savannah a look, like he didn't think much of the warden's choice to have him leave. She returned with a commiserating expression even though she had no intention of building a rapport with the guy.

Tate shut the door.

"In a second, I'll step out," the warden said. "Give you some time to talk."

Savannah eyed the prisoner. Greasy hair, tattoos. She knew his face. One of Ed Summers's guys. "Thanks. That'd be good."

The warden shut the door behind him.

She said, "Brian Matthews, right?" When he nodded she said, "Any relation to Anderson Matthews?" She was curious to know if he was family to the church elder with the gambling problem.

"My dad."

She said, "Why talk to us now? Surely someone will hear you snitched. Won't go so well for you."

He took in Tate, who hung back at the wall. Content to let her take the lead. Matthews said, "Not like I'll do something for nothin.' So put in a good word for me with whoever takes over for Ilkins. I figure they'll be all fired up to take care of business now that people are dropping like flies."

She wouldn't have put it like that, but he wasn't wrong.

"Besides, you got a deal for Hammer right? That's why I ain't seen him in here. He talked. Got sprung."

"I have no idea who that is. But there are some guys who worked for Ed that we didn't find." She and Conroy had surmised they heard about the raid beforehand somehow and skipped out. Stayed under the radar.

"Don't matter." Matthews shrugged one shoulder. "I still want a deal."

"Deals are contingent on an exchange. That means, in order for me to offer you something of value, you first have to do the same for me."

"Tit for tat?" The whole question had a *tone*. Suggestive, and aggressive.

Tate said, "Easy." A low, harsh word he bit out.

Savannah was used to guys looking at her, or talking to her, a certain way. She was small and blonde. Not like she could make herself taller without wearing higher-heeled boots. And she wasn't going to dye her hair. That would look ridiculous.

"So tell me," she said, drawing on the weight of authority her badge gave her. "What've you got?"

He said, "Summers worked for Aggerton. Kind of. Maybe it was more like they were different parts of the organization, you know?"

She didn't know, but nodded anyway. "They work for Gaynes?"

"Robbie?" He laughed. "No way. That guy's a joke." He glanced at Tate. "No offense."

Tate said, "Why would that offend me?" But he didn't need Matthews to answer, he just asked a question of his own. "Who did they work for?"

"Whoever killed them."

"And the DA?" Savannah asked.

"Can't let him dig. It'll all get out." He shrugged again. "Why not get rid of him?"

"And steal the books."

He nodded. "Right. Those books Aggerton kept."

"Tell me something I don't know." She was waiting for him to mention "West" since that name had cropped up so many times already. "Otherwise I can't do anything for you, and every one of your friends will know you talked to me. You'll hang out to dry."

"Fine." He shifted, the cuffs on his hands clinking together. "Everyone hates Gaynes, but he's been trying to get on the inside for years. Probably thought he could work his way up or something, but the guy's a joke. He's got no restraint, and he doesn't care who knows it. The boss doesn't want him in. He's a liability."

"Better. Now give me something good."

He flashed gritted teeth.

"I'll give you a clue," Savannah said. "How about you tell me who the boss is?"

His eyes widened. "He'll kill me."

She nodded. "Especially if I have nothing to get you a deal, no protection. He'll not only know you talked, but he'll be able to get to you."

Tate said, "Who is West?"

"A ghost. The guy's nothin' but mist—you'll never get to him, and you can't protect me from him."

"If you think he's so scary," Savannah said, "why come to us? You know it won't end well."

"You got Hammer out! He's safe, right?"

She glanced at Tate. He mouthed *Phil.* She pressed her lips together. "Tell me *now* who West is, and you'll be in protective custody immediately. He'll never get to you."

Matthews shook his head and began mumbling to himself. "No. I thought I could do this." He trained his wild eyes on Savannah's. "You're closer than they even know, and he'll kill me. He'll kill my *dad.* Guard!" He moved to the door, yelling, "Guard!"

The door flung open and two uniformed guards pulled him out while Matthews yelled about them hauling him out for no reason and "putting the screws to him as if he would roll over."

His voice rang down the hall, "As if I would talk!"

She sank into a chair.

"Does it feel like every time we turn around someone else drops dead?"

She lifted her gaze. "I shudder to think what's going to happen next."

27

Tate pulled up to a stoplight. He rolled his shoulders while the light was red, trying to ease the tension in his muscles. "Feel like this has been the longest day ever?"

She nodded. "Yes."

They probably both needed a nap, but tell that to Savannah. The woman was happy to admit she was fatigued, that she was struggling with the enormity of this case—and he was too. But at the same time, she had no intention of allowing it to stop her or even slow her down. Just a chance to acknowledge how she felt, and then back to work.

They were on the way to interview Robert Gaynes's assistant, hoping he was either at work or at home. No point calling ahead for an appointment only to spook the guy.

"All your cases like this?"

"No." She shook her head. "No way. Not in this town, at least."

"And back in New Orleans?"

She let out a huff that sounded like sardonic laughter under her breath. "Never anything as messy as this, but close. I was about to hit ten years as a detective."

He figured there was a story there. She didn't go on, though. And Tate didn't push it. She could tell him in her own time, and he figured they had enough of that in their future. Maybe a lifetime of it. He'd discovered something here with Savannah Wilcox.

Life wasn't perfect, but you made perfect moments in the middle of the chaos. You stood together to weather what came—something he'd never done with any other woman. He'd always been the one who stood in front, taking it full force. Just like Millie had done for him. She'd taken him on when she was still a kid herself, but she'd protected him.

With Savannah, Tate didn't need to do that. He could, and he wanted to. If she needed it, he would absolutely protect her so she didn't have to feel the threat.

But they stood together.

They faced things together.

Tate's phone buzzed. He handed it to her, pressing his thumb on the screen as he passed it over. "Can you see who that is?"

She held the phone. "You're letting me look at your phone."

"I'm driving. And what do I have to hide?"

"Uh, plenty. I'm guessing."

Tate shrugged and took the next corner. "The text?"

"It's from Maggie. She says Elexa wasn't getting her paper done, so now they're taking a break and making cupcakes."

"Good."

"Do you want to go over there?"

"Later is good. I'm not sure what more I could do that Maggie isn't already doing."

Savannah said, "My guess? You could do plenty." She locked his phone and set it in the cup holder only to pull hers out so she could answer it. She swiped the screen after the third vibration. "Wilcox." Then said to him, "It's the chief."

A second later, she hung up. "We have to go to the office."

"Did he say why?"

"No, but he didn't sound happy. I think something happened."

Tate sighed and changed directions to head to the police station instead. "Patrick Dearnum better not leave town before we get to talk to him."

She said, "I can get a uniform to sit on his house while we wait to hear back from the judge. But he'll know we're looking at him if we do that."

"Probably better to let him believe he's not a person of interest, unless you can get a plain clothes."

She typed on her phone. "I'll put in the request."

Tate pulled into the parking lot, and they hustled inside. Kaylee let them into the bull pen and they moved through to Conroy's office. She tapped on the door, opening it with her other hand.

"What's up, Chief?"

"Shut the door, Wilcox."

"What about me?" Tate wasn't a cop. Did this involve him?

"Get in here."

Tate shut the door. Savannah sat, but he leaned against the door.

Conroy looked up, his expression blank. "Care to explain why I recently received copies of a series of emails that go back and forth between your two accounts?"

Savannah relaxed against the back of the chair. "That's it? We've been emailing each other." She started to stand. "We need to—"

"Sit down, Detective." Conroy shook his head. "You really think I'd call you in here for regular emails?"

She glanced back at Tate, then said, "No...what are they?" Her words were cautious.

Tate didn't like this at all. It couldn't be good if Conroy had called them in, right to his office. He moved to the desk as Conroy opened a file. Savannah stood.

They read the printed pages together. Multiple short emails

exchanged back and forth between them. He said, "When did they start?"

"The night you were attacked at your office. Last one was sent early this morning."

Savannah slid her finger down the top paper. "*We have to do this. Man up and get it done.* What on earth? *Make sure you leave the knife exactly where I told you to.* Wow, I sound like I'm really cracking the whip."

She backed up. "You know this isn't us, right?"

Tate kept reading. "Makes it look like you and I are in cahoots, evidently trying to cover up the fact I murdered Aggerton *and* the DA. Huh." He tapped his chin. "Where have I heard that one before?"

Conroy shot him a look. "They're good whoever they are. Ted said they look legit and until he does some more digging, he won't know who sent them."

"Uh…the killer?"

Tate glanced at her.

She planted a hand on her hip. "Did you read this? I sound like a shrew." She sucked in a deep breath and used a high-pitched voice. "*Don't screw this up, Tate, or we'll both be in trouble. I won't let you leave me hanging. If I go down, so do you.* Wow, I sound like a piece of work."

He almost smiled but caught her gaze.

"This isn't funny. I'm not like that."

"It's not personal, Savannah. Unless you consider that they're trying to frame us for murder."

She made a pfft sound. "I didn't kill anyone. You?"

Tate shrugged.

"I don't like people talking about me."

He started moving toward her, but she held up her hand. Palm facing him. Tate stopped.

"Which is why I don't care what they're trying to do." Savannah folded her arms. "Frame a police detective? Please. That's never going to work."

"Yes, it is." Conroy intertwined his fingers on the desk.

Savannah and Tate both swung around to him. She said, "What?"

"Yeah," Tate said. "What?"

"They think this is going to work. And it will." Conroy said, "So give me your badge, and your gun, because you're off the case. Officially, at least."

"*What?!*"

"Savannah." Tate took that step toward her.

Conroy said, "To whoever did this, it needs to look like it worked."

"No way." She waved a hand at her boss. "You seriously think these might be real?"

"Of course not. Though, officially I can't take your side until an investigation has been completed."

"And in the meantime?"

Tate said, "We figure out who killed Aggerton and Ilkins."

"That's what I was *trying* to do when I was pulled in here!"

Tate pressed his lips together. Conroy said, "Badge and gun, Detective Wilcox. Mia will continue to investigate this case. But because of this accusation, you're *officially* off the case."

Tate picked up on what the police chief was saying. "Copy that."

Savannah whirled to him. "You're not the one who has to give up your badge and gun."

"He could get the state to revoke my private investigator license. I may not get out from under this completely unscathed."

"Like you're not going to carry on as though nothing happened, Mr. Cool and Collected?"

She'd fired that at him like an accusation. "Would it be a bad thing? The killer thinks he took out the police department's best shot at finding him. So he's cocky now, which means he'll get confident and wind up making a mistake and exposing himself. Do you plan to be on vacation when that happens, or just laying low?”

Savannah pressed her lips together. She glanced at Conroy, who nodded, then back at Tate.

“What’ll it be?”

She shook her head. “I’m not turning in my badge.”

Conroy said, “I figured the gun would be the harder sell.”

“You think I don’t have another gun?”

“Only one is your duty weapon. Hand it over, along with your badge.” Conroy said, “Also, yell a lot. Like you think you’re being fired.”

She didn’t move.

Tate got the feeling she could muster up the emotion to start screaming and crying right now—without pretending. But handing over the badge and gun? He wasn’t sure she could do it. Being a cop was everything to her. Honor and integrity—all that her father was not—were who she was.

“Savannah.” He moved closer but didn’t touch her. “This won’t work if it doesn’t look good. They need to think they won.”

She lifted her gaze to his, fire and tears there. “And when do I get to punch someone in the face for thinking they can do that to me?”

“I’ll see what I can do about that.”

“I’m sick of this.”

“I know.” He turned to Conroy. “What if I get publicly fired? Or maybe you could arrest me, release a statement that you guys figured out I really did do it. There are other ways to get this done.”

Savannah shook her head. “They need to think it worked. That I’m out of commission. Not a cop anymore—” Her voice broke on the last word.

Conroy’s voice was low. “I didn’t know it would be *this* hard.” He sounded sorry, even if he didn’t apologize.

Tate had known. But there was no time to absorb the fact he apparently knew Savannah better than her own boss, a man she'd befriended and worked with ever since she first arrived in town.

Savannah looked like she wanted to say something, but didn't. The bruises on her face were angry. She'd gone up against these people already, as had he. Both of those fights had been vicious—and unfair. Like this, she'd been caught unawares. The bad guy had delivered his hit and disappeared into the dark.

Conroy said, "Mia will talk to Gaynes's assistant." When Savannah swung around he added, "I'll go with her."

"Good." Tate had to break the silence from their side of the table somehow.

"Take the van. We'll get you a feed."

"You could plant a bug while you're in there," Tate suggested.

Finally Savannah spoke. "Not unless we have a warrant."

"Darn."

He saw the edge of a smile on her face, and he said, "Do it fast. Like ripping off a bandage. Then we can get back to work."

She pulled both her gun and her badge in one stealth move and planted them on Conroy's desk in front of him. He let her stride out by herself, thinking it would look better that she was disgruntled and alone. They could meet back up outside.

Savannah shoved Conroy's door open so hard it hit the wall. The eruption of glass breaking was so loud Tate flinched. Conroy, too. Savannah grabbed her backpack and coat and walked to the back hall toward the EXIT door down past Ted's office.

"This isn't good."

Tate turned to him. "Just text me where to be for the interview of Patrick Dearnum. Yeah?"

Conroy eyed the shattered door. "You'll make sure she's okay?"

Tate didn't bother answering such a dumb question.

28

———

The van door opened, and Tate climbed in carrying two paper cups of coffee. Savannah accepted one so he had a free hand to close the door. "Thanks." Then she said, "I figured you'd be Ted."

"I don't think he's coming." Tate sat in the second chair, which was basically a stool.

The van was a regular, windowless cargo van, decked out with computer tech Ted had put together. And he wasn't here to run it?

"Weird." She'd called him, but Ted hadn't called back yet. Or returned her follow up text.

"You doin' okay?"

Savannah scrunched up her nose. "I'm kind of trying not to think about it, mostly."

"I read all the emails."

"Yeah?" She sipped her coffee, stared at the computer monitor and tried to pretend she didn't care what they said.

"Mostly I figure they were thrown together, but there had to have been a plan to get them into our email inboxes already in the works. That part, at least, was well crafted. Someone who knows their way around planting evidence and leaving no trace—"

"Ted hasn't looked at everything yet."

He said, "You think he'll come up with a suspect?"

"He usually does." She shrugged.

The whole thing was beyond irritating. She kept shifting, expecting to feel her badge or gun on her belt. But they were gone. She wasn't a cop right now. Except that her boss had told her to sit in the van and listen in on the whole conversation he and Mia were going to have with Gaynes's assistant.

She knew they were placating her. No, it wasn't that bad since she figured they actually valued her help. But exactly what could she do for this case when she had no official authority?

Tate said, "Do you have the footage from Aggerton's office, of that guy in my sweater?"

"Wasn't that your buddy Phil?"

"Yeah, but I wanted to see if the SUV is in there," Tate said. "Since Robert's guy drives one."

She got on the computer and copied the file to a flash drive, which she handed him so he could plug it into his computer.

"Thanks." He didn't let go of her fingers.

Savannah looked at him. "What?"

"I know maybe it doesn't feel like it, but this will work out. It'll be okay."

She shook her head. "No guarantee." She quoted, "In this world, you *will* have trouble." The words of Jesus had been spinning in her head since Mia texted the verse to her a couple of hours ago.

Savannah wanted to find it funny, since trouble was exactly what was happening. But it wasn't funny at all when she was losing everything right now.

There was one thing she couldn't get past.

"Conroy sold out to the pressure."

"Sav—"

She held up her hand. "He did. Even if it only looks like

that's what he did, and I'm fine with everything until I can officially come back. Doesn't matter. Everyone thinks I got suspended. Whoever did this, they know they won."

"Because what people believe is true?"

"No. They'll believe whatever they want, for whatever reason they have, and it's all based on preconceived notions and experience. The truth? That hardly matters."

Tate said nothing.

"Same thing happened when my father started his smear campaign. Didn't matter that he was just lashing out because he knew I was right, and so did everyone else. They all went along with it anyway. Not one person cared about the truth. Only what they thought was true."

"Honey."

She shut her eyes. No way did she want that soft tone, the first time he'd called her an endearment other than the shortened version of her name. Which she hated. Her father had called her "Van." Like it was cute.

Right now, she couldn't take sympathy. Even if what she wanted was another hug, this wasn't the time. And she would hate it if this was the reason.

"Just let me feel sorry for myself." She shrugged. "So I can't handle not being a cop. I probably need therapy."

"Who doesn't?" He chuckled.

"I don't think I've met with my shrink in…months. Maybe a year?" She shook her head. "Guess I'm overdue."

Tate shifted in his chair. Out the corner of her eye she saw him turn toward her. "What happened? With your father, I mean."

"The DA—the one who was gunned down? He's the only one who believed me. But that was only because I threatened to tell his wife he tried to start a relationship with me." And wasn't that a whole other conversation? "I told him to look into my father, or I'd tell her what he'd done. He did and when it became clear I was onto something, he ran with it. All the way to a promotion."

He said nothing, so she continued. Not to fill the silence, but because she wanted him to know. "I wasn't in a good place. The culture, it wasn't like it is here. Going to church wasn't encouraged like it often is in small towns. Or you just go and who cares? It's none of their business. I got sucked into Sunday sports when I wasn't on shift. Just never worked out for me to go to church.

"It was like a slow creep. When I realized what the DA had done, that he'd tried to have a hook up with me and wanted to use the case to further his own career, I sat down and finally admitted to myself how he had treated me, even though he was married…" She hated to think of who that Savannah had been. "I looked in the mirror, and I didn't like the woman I saw. So I did the right thing. I made sure my father paid for what he'd been doing under the table for years. I decided for once I was going to be the person I wanted to be."

"And you've been her ever since."

She turned to him then. "Sounds like you might know something about that."

He shot her a sardonic smile. "The FBI establishment accepted me, but I never toed the line. I guess they figured I'd have unique ideas and a different perspective until I figured out how to walk the walk." He shrugged. "Eric was a good buffer, but I saw the hits he took. So I went for more and more undercover jobs. I burned out. Quit. Came home. Got married, that didn't work. Tried to find it in a career. That also didn't work."

"Have you found out what it is you need, yet?" She had, but now all that was in jeopardy. Now she was questioning her decision to throw herself into the life of a detective. She'd defined herself by that alone since she got here. Maybe she should've added more to it.

"I think I have, actually. But I'm still working out the details."

"Oh." Maybe it had to do with Phil, or whatever Tate had been doing liaising with Ed Summers. She wanted to believe the details had to do with her. But she also didn't want the responsibility of being everything to anyone.

No one needed that much pressure.

But now that she'd learned again how to put God first, it was time for the other parts of her life to shift into correct perspective. At least, she figured she was ready for that to happen.

Conroy's voice cut across the comm channel. "This conversation is riveting, but Dearnum just pulled in. And you were right, Tate. The SUV could very well be the same one your guy reported seeing outside Aggerton's office. Dark color, right?"

"Yep." Tate glanced at her. "You think Gaynes's assistant killed Aggerton and the DA?"

Savannah shrugged.

Conroy said, "I guess we'll find out."

Mia's voice came through as well. "Let's go to work."

"Give me a camera check, Detective."

Savannah confirmed her screen was operational. "You're coming through, clean and clear. We are recording."

Conroy said, "Let's roll."

Savannah heard doors shut. Boots on the pavement, Mia's low-heeled shoes. She muted their end of the communications so Conroy and Mia could focus and asked Tate, "Think they'll get a confession out of him?"

"The guy is pretty squirrelly. I guess we'll see." Tate said, "What's your theory on who killed Aggerton and Ilkins?"

"I figure it could've been Gaynes's assistant, if he has that in him. I can't reconcile it being Gaynes when it was the same night Claire got hurt."

"Unless someone else hurt her, and Lex just assumed it was Robert."

Conroy called out, "Mr. Dearnum. I'm Chief Barnes. This is Lieutenant Tathers."

"Uh, yes. Of course." The man's voice was higher pitched than most guys. He could probably hit those high notes like some male singers on the radio did. "I know who you are."

The picture on screen quit tiling and Savannah caught his face from the body cam Conroy wore. "Someone slapped him." Sympathy pangs twinged in her nose. She wanted to rub the bridge, but she thought better of it, remembering the pain it would cause.

"How can I help the police today?"

"In your work for Councilman Gaynes, did you ever work with Kenny Aggerton?"

Dearnum said, "Or DA Ilkins? I'm guessing the fact they're both dead is why you're here." He laughed, but sounded nervous.

Tate said, "I'm going to pull his picture and compare it to the surveillance from my office."

Savannah took the flash drive from him and saved a screen clipping to it before passing the drive back to him.

"Thanks."

Mia asked, "Anything about their deaths you think we should know?"

"Dunno what that might be." He chuckled again. "I thought your guys' job was to catch the killer. Mine is to pick up Robert Gaynes's dry cleaning and fetch his coffee."

"That makes you a pretty big part of his life, right? You know all about what he's up to."

On screen, Dearnum shrugged his slender shoulders. What was it with all the skinny, tall assistants with slim cut suits? Savannah figured there was either something in the water, or they all shared diet tips with one another.

"He probably gives you all kinds of errands to run."

"Sure, all the time."

Mia said, "Cleaning up his messes afterwards. Making calls for him."

"I've sent a few break-up gifts in my time." He lifted his chin. "He's no different than anyone else I've worked for."

Conroy said, "Is that really true?"

Mia asked him, "You probably get to know all the dirty secrets of whoever you work for, right?" Her tone was light, as though they were just having a gossipy conversation and this wasn't a police questioning. "And not just what they got on their collar." She added a giggle Savannah thought might be overkill.

Dearnum laughed. It sounded forced. "You have no idea."

"And you get paid to make it disappear."

"If I want to keep my job. And I happen to be very good at it."

"What about Fenris? He worked for the DA," Conroy said.

Dearnum glanced to the side. "I don't know him that well."

Savannah didn't think that jibed with his body language. "That was a lie."

"Yeah," Tate said, "no kidding."

Conroy said, "But you do know him. What's your take on him?"

Dearnum shrugged. "Not a bad assistant. Spends more time at Ilkins's house than the office. Making sure he keeps a lid on the wife, you know? I'm in the office most days working on city council business."

Conroy said, "Collecting dry cleaning and sending breakup gifts."

"I signed a nondisclosure agreement on anything of a business nature."

Mia said, "Like hiding a knife at a crime scene because your boss is a murderer?"

Dearnum gaped. "What?"

"Which is how it came to have your print on it, right?" Conroy said, "Because you touched the knife that killed Aggerton and Ilkins, and you hid it in Ilkins's study after you or Gaynes *killed* him."

"I… He…" Dearnum couldn't speak past stammering. "I want my lawyer!"

Conroy said, "Let him know you're going to have to come up with a good explanation as to how your print got on the murder weapon."

29

———

Tate needed to get face to face with this guy to know for sure, but he figured he'd obtained enough footage. He'd seen this man in his own hall with his own eyes. Dressed in a ski mask, wearing a coat as he swung that knife and sliced it through Tate's forearm.

He looked at the guy now, on the screen. The two images were side by side. He'd pulled the surveillance picture from his cloud storage to compare.

"I think it's him." He turned to Savannah. "The guy from my office, who took a swipe at me."

His arm still hurt, along with his head and everything else. What was new? The last few weeks had been insane, but he wouldn't trade even the destruction of his reputation for the time he'd spent with Savannah. Regardless of how it all turned out.

He cared about her.

Maybe even had begun to fall in love with her.

Did she feel the same?

She stared at the image. "Agreed, but how will we confirm it when he was wearing a mask? It's not conclusive."

Tate tried to figure out an answer.

"That could be when his print got on the knife. Maybe showing up at your apartment and killing you was part of cleaning up Gaynes's mess."

"So the boss gives him the knife and he comes by my office." Tate thought about it. "He takes a swipe at me, poorly I might add. And when you show up, he runs off. Trying to kill me? Or maybe his plan was to leave the knife there and frame me for Aggerton's death?"

"But it didn't work."

"And now there are two deaths. So—what?—they decide to do Ilkins after I was cut? An add-on, I guess?"

Savannah said, "For whatever reason."

"Question is, how far would he go for Gaynes?"

They drove back to the police station, where Conroy and Mia already had Dearnum and his lawyer in interrogation.

Conroy said, "Tell me why you broke into Tate Hudson's office. To kill him, or to keep up this charade of framing him every time your boss decides it's time to murder someone again?"

As much as Tate would have liked to see Gaynes go down as a murderer, it didn't fit that he'd killed Aggerton. Not given it was the same night Claire had been attacked. She'd been having an affair with the DA, sure, but that gave Gaynes all the more reason to take out his anger on her.

Dearnum stammered.

"We have a witness who can put you at the scene. Which makes that a poor choice." Conroy said, "Now, you can go down for just what we can prove, or we can make sure to tack on another murder charge, as well. How does that sound?"

Dearnum's lawyer leaned over and spoke low in his ear.

"You know who did it." Mia's words were clipped. "And you're willing to help cover it up. Frame an innocent man. Which means you'll be in jail alongside the murderer. I'm sure it'll be fun times reliving the good old days of when you tried to pin it all on Tate Hudson."

"He wasn't supposed to be there! I was just going to leave the knife in his drawer or something."

"Your boss jumped the gun after that, didn't he?" Conroy asked. "Since he still wanted to kill Ilkins."

"It was just supposed to be one." Dearnum pressed his fist to his mouth.

The lawyer shifted in his seat. "My client has been more than forth—"

"Aggerton should have been the only one," Dearnum cut across him. "He promised."

"Patrick," Mia said, softly. More softly than Tate would have deemed appropriate. "Who killed Kenny Aggerton?"

"He said it would be fine. Tate would go down for it, and we'd be in the clear."

In his pants pocket, Tate's phone started to ring.

Conroy asked this time. "Who killed Aggerton, Patrick?"

"My client needs assurances."

Dearnum didn't wait. "We had to do it, or he'd have ruined everything." He cried out then, as he realized the secret was finally out. They knew what he had done. "He'd have ruined everything. I had to do it."

Savannah gasped. "He did it. He killed Aggerton."

Tate pulled the ringing phone out of his pocket. It vibrated in his hand, the screen illuminating. "It's Lex."

"Go," Savannah said. "I'll clean up here."

Tate moved to her, touched her cheek and pressed his lips to hers. "Be back."

She nodded, a smile curling her lips, then shoved him gently toward the door. "I got this. We're on the road to the end now."

"I know." He let himself out, swiping the screen of his phone and bringing it up to his face as he moved. "Hey, you okay?"

Tate smiled as he headed outside. Things were finally looking up. Police work had broken the case. Together, as a team, they'd found Dearnum and gotten a confession.

"He's here." Elexa's voice trembled. "Robert is at the front door, pounding on it and yelling."

Ice rolled through his body, and all the celebration evaporated like someone had just thrown a grenade on the moment. "Lex—"

"He told Maggie I have to come out. Said I have to go home with him."

He'd never heard so much fear from her, even the night her mom had been beaten unconscious. What could Gaynes possibly want with her?

Whatever the answer, Tate was going to find out.

"Dial 9-1-1. Don't let him in."

"Maggie already did."

Tate raced for his car. "I'm on my way, and I'm close."

Ten minutes later he pulled up outside Hope Mansion, which was lit up from inside. He saw someone standing and watching at almost every ground floor window.

Maggie was on the front lawn, talking with Basuto and his partner. Tate sprinted over. "Where is he?"

"Ran off." The older woman's hair was in curlers, and she wore a robe over pajamas, her feet in rubber boots. "That way." She waved toward the wooded area that surrounded the house. The woods the residents loved to walk in.

And Gaynes wanted to take away the safety they felt, living here? Some of them had serious trauma in their backstories. Now he wanted to rid them of whatever peace they'd managed to find? Anger burned hot in Tate's stomach. He wasn't going to let Claire's husband do this. Not when she had been lowered into the ground because of his actions.

Not only that, but Gaynes wanted to hurt others now. The man had forced his assistant to kill Kenny Aggerton, as if there was no other choice. Then they'd planned to frame Tate for it. Ilkins was dead as well, and they were still trying to bring down Tate, Savannah, and the police investigation. Pinning crimes on Tate. Destroying both of their reputations.

He agreed with her—people who thought their power was justification to hurt others were the worst kind of people.

He wanted to call her father's prison and demand a word with the man. To stand up for the woman he wanted a future with. But first, he had to find Gaynes.

"Tate!"

Lex stood at the door. He detoured and went to her, touching her elbows. "You okay?"

She nodded, then launched herself at his chest, hugging his waist. Tate gave her a squeeze. "I need to find him."

"I won't go with him. I can't." Her eyes filled with tears that reflected the street lights. "Please don't let him take me."

Behind her he heard a small child start to cry.

"You're not going with him." Her stepdad was responsible for murder, but Tate didn't need to get into his theory right now. "I promise." He touched her cheeks. "I'm not going to let him take you."

"He scared the kids." She sniffed. "He was screaming. Mom always—" Her voice broke and she planted her face against his jacket.

"I know, baby." He held her for a second, then said, "I have to go look for him."

She shuddered.

Tate had to admit he felt the same, but he wasn't going up against the man unarmed. He had his gun. "I want him in jail."

She nodded.

"Go inside now. Be safe."

He gave her one final squeeze and waited until she shut the door. Then he called Savannah.

She answered after the first ring. "Wilcox."

"Gaynes is at the Mansion. I'm looking for him now."

"You need backup."

"I have Basuto and his partner."

The sergeant heard his name called and looked over. Tate motioned with his hand that he was going to search the area.

Maggie went back inside as Basuto nodded, then said something to his partner that involved more motioning towards the woods.

"He's coming with me. We'll find Gaynes."

"Good," Savannah said. "You need help?"

Honestly, he didn't. Tate planned on having Gaynes in custody before she got there. Plus, it couldn't be discounted that having two cops help him apprehend Gaynes held more weight than a detective on suspension.

"Never mind." She sighed. "It's fine. Just keep me posted." She hung up before he could say anything else.

Tate was just glad he'd kissed her before he left. Might be the last one he ever got from her at this rate.

He drew his gun then. Heard the door close behind him. And went hunting.

Usually he searched for an entirely different kind of prey.

Basuto stepped up beside him. "Maggie says he ran off that way. The road to the north runs close to the woods up ahead. Lot of people she takes in come from that direction, as it's unmarked."

"There's a road?"

He shook his head. "Just a path. Leads all the way to the road, about two miles."

"You guys spread out, make sure he's not hiding so he can double back when we clear out. I'll jog up, see if he parked at the road and ran to escape."

"Copy that." Basuto turned and instructed his partner.

Tate didn't wait around to hear their plan. He raced to the path, and headed along it using his phone's flashlight to make sure he didn't trip on any tree roots or downed branches. The last thing he needed to add to his injuries was a sprained ankle. Those took forever to heal, and hurt like nobody's business.

He had enough trouble just trying to breathe with these bruised ribs.

The end of the path came soon enough. A car was parked

in the dark. Tate saw no one around it. He shut off the light and let his eyes adjust, slowing his pace so he could hear. He scanned the area and made his way to the vehicle.

The hood was warm to the touch. Recently driven.

A twig cracked behind him. Tate spun to it and saw a deer emerge between two trees, visible in the moonlight.

Heavy weight slammed into his back.

Tate hit the ground and immediately rolled to his back, gun up. A heavy boot kicked the weapon from his hands. He cried out at the pain from the impact, then swung again. Tried for purchase.

A crack sounded half a second before he saw sparks.

Electricity coursed through his body and everything went black.

30

Savannah tugged her red coat on. "I'm going to head home. See how the search is going for Gaynes."

"Want my help?"

Considering Mia was her lieutenant, it wasn't like she needed Savannah's permission for a manhunt. Everyone available was now at the mansion looking. She was only going there because it was her home, and there were residents in danger.

It was only a little because she wanted to backup Tate, in case something happened between him and his ex-wife's husband.

"It's not because you can't help me, or because I'm trying to protect you from a potential situation where gunfire could be exchanged. It's because I don't trust myself to sit there and listen while Dearnum explains in detail how they decided to destroy me and Tate, our lives and our reputations."

She reached for a gun she no longer had. Of course they noticed. Savannah gritted her teeth, walking out the back hall again.

Same as when he'd put her on suspension. She pushed through the door to the back hall where Ted's office was—and the bathroom where she'd been shot.

Memories flashed in her mind as she raced down the hall to the EXIT door, and out to where her car was parked. She had to get out of there. Leave the memories behind. Cold night air hit her, and the heavy door slammed shut.

Savannah felt something. An instinct. She glanced around. Slowed.

Still heading for her car, she palmed her phone. Even if she couldn't get a call out, she could use it as a weapon if needed.

No one was there.

What had sparked the flash of instinct?

Savannah checked her backseat, because everyone knew that was where attackers hid. Empty. She drove home with her lights and sirens flashing.

The parking lot was full of police cars, a sight that would calm her probably for the rest of her life. She'd grown up a cop's daughter. Regardless of the fact she'd had to put her father in prison, she still believed in the job and always would.

Too many times she'd wondered if she counted the job more important than family. It was more that she understood people were human. All actions had consequences, some were bad. Some involved her pulling out every stop to make sure the people she lived with were safe.

Protected.

She raced over to where Basuto stood, giving orders.

"Got it?"

Everyone around him nodded, six uniformed cops and a K9 from state police trained to find people that were hiding. Not a scent dog that tracked only one specific person. This dog flushed out any number of people who were hidden.

Tate was missing?

The K9 officer said, "Yes, Sergeant." Then started up at a jog, giving the command for the dog to come with him.

"What's going—"

Basuto lifted a hand. "Tate is missing. We've regrouped, now we're going out organized. Not as the hodge podge we were."

"Any sign of Gaynes?"

He shook his head, then glanced aside as his attention was drawn away. "Go talk to Maggie. I'll keep you posted."

"Yes, Sergeant." Savannah pressed her lips together.

She would much rather be out there, looking for Tate. But there was a full contingent of cops—and even a dog—looking. No one cared about the Mansion or the people who lived there more than her. Still, it was hard to trudge to the front door. Savannah prayed as she went that God would give the cops wisdom. That they'd figure out where Tate was, and what had happened to him.

Maggie stood in the doorway, dressed in her robe. Her hair was in curlers, and she hugged a shotgun to her chest.

"Any sign of him?"

Savannah wanted to ask for Maggie's weapon but figured that wouldn't go down well. Maggie Filks had been protecting this home and the women and children who lived here long before Savannah showed up in town.

She said, "They just headed back out to look."

"Always was a wild boy." Maggie shifted so Savannah could step inside. Then she shut the door. "At least, that's what everyone always said. I didn't believe it."

"No?" The hall and front parlor were empty. Everyone in their rooms, probably. Some residents trying to sleep, others avoiding being spotted by a male—or a cop. Or both.

Maggie shook her head. "He was a good boy. Just got tarred with a certain brush because his sister took him on. Everyone expected him to go off the rails, so any indication he was about to, he was immediately tarred with that brush."

"Self-fulfilling prophecy?"

She shrugged, turning away to shuffle into the kitchen. It was industrial-sized, bigger than a normal house kitchen. Maggie could cook for thirty but usually only did so for the thirteen who lived here. Fourteen now that Elexa had moved in.

The teen sat up on the counter, holding a mug.

"Girl, what did I tell you about sitting up there?"

She slid off. "Sorry, Maggie." When she saw Savannah, she said, "Where's Tate?"

"I don't know." Savannah felt as powerless as she figured the girl did. She gathered the teen into her arms and gave her a quick hug like she figured Tate would've done if he was here. "But they'll find him."

She prayed they would, anyway. What else could she do? When Savannah had finally figured out who was behind the corruption in NOPD, and that her father had not only condoned it but actually authorized a whole lot of it, she'd prayed. It had been the first time in a long time that she'd needed help above what she could do herself.

Right now felt a lot like that.

Tate could be injured. Gaynes could have gotten to him. Savannah tried to get her stomach to quit roiling.

"You sure look like you believe that."

She glanced up at Elexa. "I'm sorry you lost your mom."

"I'm not going to lose Tate, too. God wouldn't do that to me."

Life didn't work like that. There were no guarantees. God's favor, or His love, didn't have squat to do with a person's goodness or their performance. She of all people knew that. Trying to do the right thing, or be the right way, didn't mean life would go right.

"You don't believe me."

Savannah said, "That's not it. The cops will find him if he's out there to find."

"Just so long as Robert didn't hurt him." She flashed gritted teeth.

"If he did, you let me deal with it. This isn't for you to wade into just because Gaynes is a bad guy." Savannah didn't need to go into detail on what they'd only just learned. Before Elexa could ask what that was about, Savannah said, "All you need to do is make sure you're safe. Let the cops do what they're trained to do."

She didn't seem super impressed with that, but didn't argue either.

Maggie said, "You done with that mug, hon?"

Elexa handed it to her. "Yeah."

"You should try to get some rest."

She shook her head. "I won't sleep until I know he's okay."

Savannah said, "I'll text you as soon as I know. Okay?"

Elexa nodded. "I'm going to wait in the parlor."

They both watched her leave. Maggie had put the shotgun on top of the refrigerator. Now she was wiping down the stove top, which seemed to be clean enough already.

"You doing okay?"

Maggie didn't turn, she just kept wiping. "Two murders. Claire Gaynes is dead." She shook her head. "It's like bad mojo. If I even believed in that."

Maggie was "saved" as most people would define it. She also went to church every Sunday and led a Bible study for residents out of the parlor on Wednesday nights. However, she was also very spiritual. The kind of person who seemed to be sensitive to those deeper things. She would often get a sense she needed to pray for someone—at the exact time they were in danger. She'd told Savannah that she'd been on her knees for half an hour after Savannah had been shot in the bathroom and knocked out. Maggie'd had no idea what was going on at the police station, yet she'd been compelled to pray.

Savannah was never going to turn down that intercession. "You think Tate is okay?"

"Because I'm a fortune teller?" She glanced over. "Girl, faith don't work like that."

Savannah shrugged. "Fine. Just pray, yeah?"

"Haven't stopped."

Savannah padded over, kissed Maggie on the cheek, and walked out of the kitchen. She noticed Maggie's eyes widen as she pulled away from her, but there was no time to wonder why. Was she having one of her hunches?

She checked on Elexa, who was in the parlor on the couch looking at her phone screen. "I'll be back."

The girl nodded but didn't look up from her phone.

Savannah hit the front step, locking the door as she went out. *Where are you, Tate?* He needed to be here for Elexa. For her, too. She wanted him here, and the fact he wasn't here, wasn't a comfortable feeling at all.

She sent Basuto a text to see if they'd found Tate yet, then walked around the outside of the huge house. Just in case someone was there. Or hiding. She didn't even know where Tate had gone when he'd gotten here. Just that he'd shown up and then went to find Gaynes.

Savannah sighed. Her boots crunched grass. Twigs. Gravel, a path in the backyard area. She circled the rose bushes and ducked under tree branches, going around to the other side of the house.

When she got back to the front, she saw movement over by her car.

Gaynes?

Savannah picked up her pace, reaching for her weapon. Which she didn't have. Not a cop right now. On suspension. She hissed out a breath. "Who's there?"

No one answered.

Savannah started to dial her phone but hadn't yet hit the "call" button when a boot slammed into the back of her knee.

She cried out and went down. Pain shot up her leg, and she braced the ground with her hands. Her phone fell, skittering away from her. She scrambled for it and made it two feet before being kicked again, this time in the stomach. She rolled and came to her back.

Savannah looked up. A woman stood over her. Savannah realized right away who it was as a whole host of pieces to the puzzle dropped into place with two words: *Krav Maga.*

Keira Ilkins lifted her fists and shifted her weight.

Savannah saw it coming and rolled to the side. But there was no room, and she came up against a hub cap.

Before Keira could kick her, Savannah got up. Pain sliced into her knee. She cried out and turned to meet her attacker.

Keira was already swinging at her. Savannah tried to grab her forearm. The slam of bone to bone sparked pain and her hand immediately numbed.

She hissed out a breath. "What are you doing?"

"He said I'd need a stun gun." Keira huffed. "Didn't need one with Claire—don't need one with you." She backed up and came at Savannah again.

Savannah kicked her in the stomach.

Breath whooshed from Keira's mouth, and she stumbled back two steps.

"You beat Claire Gaynes?"

Keira huffed, muttering choice words. Savannah couldn't decide whether they were about her or Claire.

"You're under arrest."

The DA's wife laughed. "Not likely. No one will ever believe you."

"They don't need to." Savannah grabbed for Keira's arm so she could get cuffs on. But she miscalculated.

Keira took the cheap shot. She stiff armed Savannah in the face, hitting her right on the shattered bridge of her nose.

Savannah dropped, head low and about to be sick. The world swam around her.

Keira grabbed her hair and cracked Savannah's head on the closest car door.

31

Tate heard a low moan. It took a second before he realized he was making that noise. He blinked. All around him was dark, except for some light in a high window. Looked like a basement. Exposed pipes. The air was chilled and smelled like mold. Like his grandma's house, before she moved into a retirement home and the new owner tore the house down to rebuild.

He tried to move, and it all came rushing back.

"Gaynes!" He yelled the man's name, pouring all his confusion and frustration into the word. Only a squeak came out of his mouth, though. Tate coughed. Pain tore through his abdomen. His hip hurt, his knee. His shoulder and head.

Like he'd been shoved off a cliff. Or dropped. He looked around and saw wooden steps leading up to a door.

Thrown down stairs.

He winced. Even that hurt. Tate let out a breath that sounded too loud in his ears. Above him, a single chain hung from a bare bulb.

Someone's basement.

Gaynes. He'd gone after Elexa, drawing Tate out. So he could take him like this? Tate didn't want to think what that meant. Too bad his brain continued to spin as he lay there. Tate wasn't entirely sure he could get up. If he even wanted to.

Tate gritted his teeth and pushed up to sitting. His entire body felt like he'd been hit by a truck. It hurt so bad his stomach roiled. If there'd been anything left in there, he probably would have tossed it up on the floor. Maybe that would be better. Get the sick feeling out, so he didn't have to suffer with the added pleasure of stomach acid swirling around.

Upright now, the room spun. He waited it out, taking long breaths. Trying to ignore the pain in his stomach. *Don't think about it.* Except he couldn't ignore it. Tate had watched enough medical TV shows—which he would never admit to watching— to know that internal bleeding was a bad thing.

He sucked in a series of choppy breaths. Each inhale felt like someone stabbed him in his bruised ribs. They were probably cracked now.

He flipped so he was on hands and knees and pushed up. The quicker he got straight again, the better. It made the room spin, but his stomach did not need to be bent in half.

Tate blew out a long breath and reached for the cord.

Pulled it.

The room was suddenly washed with harsh, yellow light. He turned and surveyed the small basement. Cardboard boxes, old and rotting. Corners chewed by rats now had material spilling out. Storage containers labeled *Christmas* and *Mementos.* Someone had moved on, and this stuff had been forgotten. Whoever moved in next would clear this place out, thinking they might luck out on something valuable.

Unlikely.

Tate eased over to the window. It was dark outside. With the light on in here, he couldn't see anything through the cloudy glass of the window. Packed against it in one corner was a mound of what looked like leaves.

He lifted his arms to the latch.

Pain tore through his middle. Tate groaned and nearly bent

double. He wrapped one arm around his stomach and used the other hand to grasp at the latch.

The light from the bulb flickered and popped. Darkness.

His hand twisted the latch. It didn't budge.

Tate slammed at the frame with the flat of his hand, not sure why he was even bothering. No way could he fit through there. The wiggling alone would make him pass out from the pain.

He moved to the stairs, grasped the rail, and just breathed. Then he started up the steps. Probably futile, considering the door was likely locked.

He should have been tied up, right? Maybe they decided it wasn't necessary because he'd been unconscious. Who knew? Maybe they just didn't want the ligature marks that would come post mortem from him being tied up prior to his death. Too much evidence.

Plenty of reasons or explanations. Enough to occupy his brain so he didn't dwell too much on how much it hurt climbing these stairs. Or how slow going it was.

He had to do that old man shuffle his grandpa used to do. One foot up a step. Pause. Bring the other foot up. Pause. Fine, if he had earned this shuffle the way his grandpa did. By the normal wear and tear of the body. Tate wasn't used to pain. He didn't like it. Which probably made him a selfish, self-absorbed jerk, but that was how he felt.

He'd been kidnapped. He could feel about it how he wanted to feel.

Great. Now you're whining. Get your act together, Tate.

Tate pushed out another breath, gripped the rail, and ascended the next step while the world spun around him. Again. Concussion. Internal bleeding. What else was wrong with him? Maybe he was out of it, confused, and not thinking straight. What if he put himself in more danger because he didn't know what he was doing?

Halfway up the stairs, the door handle twisted. Tate had a

split second to make a choice before whoever was on the other side of the door stepped through the threshold to discover he was awake. Should he go back down the stairs and hide, or remain where he was. A split second. Not nearly long enough.

A dark figure loomed at the top, backed by more of that harsh, yellow light. A man? But the shape was all wrong.

The figure shifted. Tate realized too late what was happening as a heavy weight slammed into him. Strength and softness.

He lost balance and fell back, clutching the weight to him.

Tate's back hit the floor, and the world blinked into darkness to the sound of maniacal, low laughter and the door slamming.

He planted one foot and pushed off the floor, rolling his hips, depositing the weight to the side. Her head hit the floor beside him and she moaned.

"Savannah." He patted her cheek.

The hiss of breath that puffed out her cheeks was the best sound he'd ever heard in his entire life. Tate braced his weight on his forearm and said, "Hey."

"Ouch."

"Yeah. I'm guessing your nose doesn't feel too good." Probably felt about as good as his stomach did right now. "But I need to see your eyes."

She blinked. Her face was swollen, and she probably couldn't see too well. Already bruised, she would probably be even more black and blue tomorrow. Or blue and purple. "Hi."

"Hey." He touched her cheek, back in front of her ear. "Today isn't going very well."

She tried to talk and wound up wincing, then said simply, "Sit rep?"

He told her about getting jumped, and that they appeared to be in the basement of a house. "Gaynes got to you?"

"No." She faintly shook her head. "Keira Ilkins."

"Wha—"

Before he could finish she said, "Krav Maga." Her brows

gathered together. "She beat Claire, and maybe she's even the one who killed her."

"Gaynes is the only one I've seen here."

"I think they were working together this whole time."

Tate shut his eyes for a second. They were down, but not out. Still, it wasn't looking good. Gaynes and Keira Ilkins probably thought they had the upper hand. That they were the ones wielding the power.

Making it look like Tate and Savannah were in league, trying to cover up the fact Gaynes and Ilkins had murdered two men and a woman by framing them. Was that what had happened?

He could hardly believe it. Dearnum had killed Aggerton. Which of the three of them had killed Ilkins?

"I'm sorry. I know you cared about Claire."

He opened his eyes. Hers were focused over his shoulder. "I'm just figuring this all out, yeah?"

"I'm still sorry."

"I loved her a long time ago, Savannah. The man that fell for her isn't the man you know now. I'd like the time to convince you of that, but we'll have to get out of here first."

"You don't need to. I know who you are now, and there's no one I'd rather be stuck in a basement with. Only…"

He frowned. "What?"

"Can you get off me? I have to pee and you're making it worse."

Tate backed up. He hadn't realized he was leaning on her. "What did she do to you?"

"Aside from smack my face?" Savannah let out a frustrated sound. "I'm going to arrest her. And it's going to feel really good."

He liked her spunk. Down but not out. He helped her sit up. Tate winced, feeling the discomfort in his stomach. He didn't even know how to describe it. Except to relate it to having eaten something with a serious temper that was just now making its presence known. This couldn't be internal bleeding, could it? He'd be passed out. Needing surgery. In serious danger of losing his life imminently. He knew he needed to get out of here and get to a doctor, but beyond that, all he knew was that Dean likely couldn't fix this.

"Can you get up?"

"I did. I mean, I was up, before Gaynes threw you on me."

She glanced at him. "Tate, that doesn't sound good."

He figured he didn't look so good either. He repeated the move he'd done before. Hands and knees, then push up. Pain rippled through his body, and he collapsed back down, breathing hard. Sweat dripped down his forehead and onto the floor.

"Hey." She touched the back of his shoulder. "What did Gaynes do to you?"

"He fought dirty with no honor, like the bad guy that he is."

"Oh, baby."

He liked the sound of that, even if he didn't like the reason. "We need to get out of here. Or, at least find a way to call for help."

"An ice pack would be fantastic. Along with my gun, my badge, and a cell phone."

He bit out, "In that order, or are you not picky?"

"Thank you for staying with me. I wouldn't want to have to face this basement on my own."

He rolled to his side and reached for her. She stretched out her hand and they clasped fingers with a whole lot more strength than he had alone right now.

"I've lived through more than my fair share of crazy. God has always been there, but it's been the best with you here too."

Tate said, "That might be the nicest thing anyone's ever said to me." But the last couple of words got stuck and he had to cough. The spasm shot knives of fire through his chest. He rolled and coughed onto the floor.

Blood spotted the concrete.

"That's not good." She scooted closer, squeezing his fingers. "I'm thinking that's *really* not good." She kissed his cheek and let go of his hand. "Please don't die before I get us out of here. The paperwork will suck."

Tate's chest shook, and he wheezed out a couple more coughs. "My rib punctured my lung." It was a guess, but it was a good one. He didn't want to think about those medical shows, where they plunged a needle into someone's chest to drain the blood build up and reinflate the lung. "Does feel like slowly drowning."

"No." Her face was suddenly right by his. "You're not going anywhere before I put on a dress, and you take me somewhere nice."

Tate would've laughed. He wanted to but doing so would hurt. "Steak."

"And a loaded baked potato." She leaned down and kissed his cheek. "Hang in there. I'll figure this out."

So, basically…she was his dream woman.

Love you.

"I'm gonna hold you to that steak, though it's the potato I'm really after."

Tate felt her squeeze his shoulder, and then her shoes tapped the concrete away from him. *God, help us. We need saving.*

He'd never needed saving before. But Tate had to admit this was bad. He was completely incapacitated. *Help her get us out of here.*

Tate heard the door at the top of the stairs bang open.

She clambered up the stairs. "It's over, Gaynes."

A gunshot blasted through the room.

Savannah screamed, and he heard her tumble down.

32

Savannah gasped. "You almost shot me!"

Keira laughed, trotting down the stairs. "Just getting a feel for it."

Gaynes came down after her, moving to the middle of the room. Savannah backed up on the floor until she was up against Tate's prone body. Her heart squeezed in her chest until she thought it would stop altogether. If it did, she'd never be able to get him help. She worked to slow it by taking deep, gulping breaths.

He yanked on a cord. Nothing happened. He swore. The word sounded harsher in the dark of the basement, even though she'd heard that word so many times before. Didn't mean she appreciated hearing it.

"People will be looking for us. They were already looking for Tate."

She tried to make out their faces from the upstairs light that spilled down from the open door. Shadows abounded. She wanted to banish them.

Gaynes huffed, but it was Keira who said, "No one was out in that parking lot when I threw you in the car. And no one followed me here, either."

"Where is here?"

She felt Tate's fingers curl into her hip and she put her hand over his. He intertwined their fingers. Companionship. Solidarity. They were going to face this together. Like true partners.

It just irritated her that she had to feel that now, in this situation. Why couldn't she have something good like this when things were normal?

"Shut up, Keira." Gaynes said, "We need to do this quickly. Like she said, people will be looking for them. And I didn't set all this up so you could screw with it. Just because you've decided you need to 'get a feel' for murder."

"Are we still going to Hawaii?"

Savannah turned to her. "You guys." She shook her head. *Should've realized it.* "Claire was having an affair with Aggerton. I get why Bernice wanted her dead." Tate's fingers flexed in hers. She wanted to apologize for not picking up on the obvious answers embedded in this case sooner and hoped she'd get the chance to later. "But why kill him?"

If she could get them talking, they would hopefully say more than they meant to. Plus it might give Basuto and Conroy more time to realize they'd both been taken and be able to find them.

In the meantime, she had to seriously stall.

"And the DA?" Savannah blew out a breath. "Why did Nolan need to die? Because as it is, you're just piling charges on charges. You'll never get out of prison." She glanced at Keira. "You'll die there."

"No, we won't." Gaynes said, "Because the two of you are taking the fall. For *all of it.*"

If he thought Conroy would believe that, he was crazy. And there was no way Elexa would believe it, either. She'd scream to the rooftops of his innocence. *Elexa.* Savannah's heart squeezed again. An ache in her chest.

The girl would have no one if Tate was put away.

She'd have Maggie, and all the residents at Hope Mansion.

But she wouldn't have her mother or Tate. Family. "You'll never get away with it."

Gaynes laughed. Keira did as well, the sound harsh against Savannah's ears. "We already did," Keira screeched. "We kill you, and we're free."

"Two more bodies? That'll never fly."

Keira said, "Murder/suicide. It's the perfect crime."

Savannah didn't even know what to say. A murder, followed by a suicide. Conroy would fight to prove what had really happened, but if Gaynes and Keira did it right, it could be difficult. Not impossible. Added to the emails and everything else swirling around her and Tate, it certainly painted a bad picture. Collusion. Crime.

Her breath hitched and Tate's hand shifted. She realized she was squeezing his fingers, too hard, and she loosened her grip.

Keira and Gaynes both had guns. She and Tate were both unarmed and seriously injured. *God, help*. Tate had been so sweet. He'd touched her face and spoken gentle words to her. Probably the best moment of her life. She didn't even know being close to someone could be like this—and she could predict the danger their relationship would present to the both of them.

Their physical attraction to each other could not be denied any longer, and the trauma of enduring this crazy situation together was already forging a bond between them. She had always tried to live what she believed, and here she was, in this basement, finally being honest about her attraction to Tate. They would need to be careful they didn't go too far before rings were exchanged.

And why was she even thinking about that stuff right now? It wasn't like they'd made a commitment to each other. She and Tate had to actually get out of this situation alive first.

Which meant it was up to her to make that happen.

Savannah shifted her fingers away from his, feeling his reluctance for her to let go. She gritted her teeth and stood. Keira shifted, gearing up for another attack. No way would she get the drop on her now. Savannah sidestepped and grabbed her wrist, eyeing the weapon in Keira's other hand.

Keira screamed in frustration and the gun went off.

Savannah twisted Keira's wrist up behind her back. Gaynes lifted his gun. The DA's wife cried out.

"Drop the gun!"

Keira dropped it from her other hand and it clattered to the floor. Savannah didn't let go of her arm. The woman cried out again. "Ow!"

"Krav Maga didn't teach you how to take the punishment, just dish it out?" Savannah gritted her teeth together.

"Shoot her!"

Gaynes shook his head, but he held the gun pointed at the two of them. She wanted to pray that Tate was taking advantage of this moment. Sliding across the floor, going for Keira's gun so he could shoot Gaynes and they could escape.

Keira lifted her foot. She brought one shoe down, trying to stomp Savannah's toes. Savannah just kept moving. Kept Keira in front of her.

If Gaynes was going to shoot her, he'd have to shoot his girlfriend first.

"This won't work," she told him. "You have to know Conroy will never fall for it. He'll never stop asking questions about what happened. Not until he unravels the whole thing."

"Doesn't matter. I'll be where I want to be."

His tone… she didn't like it. Not one bit. It sounded like he wanted to get ahead. Ambition alone didn't get you to Hawaii with your girlfriend, a pile of bodies left in your wake. This didn't make sense.

Unless there was more. A "more" that had led to Aggerton and Ilkins dying and Summers being poisoned.

That Matthews kid in prison had called Gaynes a "joke." Was he still trying to get in on the operation with West?

"You're saving your own butt. Conroy will figure that out." She shifted again to avoid Keira's boot heel. She'd lose her grip on the squirmy woman soon enough, but not yet. "You'll never be out from under suspicion."

She saw a flash of his teeth in the dark. The gun exploded, a combustion of light and sound in the enclosed space.

The force of the blast hit Keira who slammed into Savannah. They both went down. A tangle of limbs, landing partially on Tate.

He shifted. Savannah's ears rang, and she thanked God that Mia wasn't here to permanently lose her hearing. No way would she have knowingly brought her partner and lieutenant into a situation like this. And she had no intention of ever doing so. Not if she could help it.

No matter what Conroy or Mia wanted.

Did I really just figure out right now that I'm not prepared to risk her?

She struggled to get up. Keira's weight lifted off her, and she realized Gaynes was hauling her up, ready to toss her to the side. Like she was nothing.

Savannah scrambled in the direction Keira had dropped the weapon. Hands and knees. She skittered across the floor. Her palm landed on something sharp, and she gasped.

A boot slammed into her back and she went down, crying out as her chin hit the floor. Black descended. She fought it off, blinking. Trying to hold onto her thoughts.

Trying to move.

He couldn't shoot her in the back. That was the only thing she could hold onto. A murder/suicide plan—if that was even still his plan—wouldn't work like that.

Savannah reached. Crawled. Her palm was slick with blood. Her face felt like it was about to explode. Her eyes were nearly swollen shut.

A whimper escaped her throat.

She reached for the gun.

Gaynes stood on her hand.

Savannah cried out. He stomped her fingers, and she pulled

her hand back to cradle it against her chest. A reflex. Huddle. Hide.

Keira shrieked. In the dim light, Savannah saw her launch up from the floor. She saw the flash of a muzzle. She had the gun? Keira screamed. She fired at Gaynes, but missed.

He fired at her.

And didn't miss.

Keira slumped to the floor, blood pooling around her body from a second gunshot wound. She lay with unseeing eyes, staring. Close enough to touch.

Savannah scrambled back. She bumped something and boxes tumbled over. She sat up, recoiling from the critters that came scurrying in her direction. The last thing she needed was a tangle of displaced rodents crawling over her and in her hair.

Sweat rolled down her temples, even though the air was chilled. "How are you going to explain that?" She motioned with a chin lift. "You killed her." She was talking nonsense, stating facts that were plainly obvious to all of them. And doing it in a whimpering voice that made her sound like she was fifteen.

Gaynes shifted. She flinched. But he didn't shoot her, he got out his phone and made a call. Savannah looked for Tate. He was unconscious. Was he dead?

Another whimpering breath escaped her lips. She needed Keira's gun. It hadn't done the woman any good.

Keira's strengths lay elsewhere. She might punch like a heavyweight, but she wasn't a trained police officer. Just because Savannah didn't have a badge, or her duty weapon, didn't mean that every inch of her was not still a cop.

"It's Gaynes."

While he was occupied with his call, Savannah inched across the floor. The only hope she had was to get to that gun. *God, help.* She needed Him now more than ever. There was no fear in trusting God when she had nothing left. No way out. He had rescued her every other time she had called on Him, for anything, and she needed that surety now. He was the strong foundation she had based her new life on. He would come through like He always did.

"I've got Hudson and the cop. What do you want me to do with them?"

She slid another inch, wincing. Though, even that was difficult. She could barely see. Hardly breathe. Things were not good. And it occurred to her that Tate was in a worse situation. That his injuries were possibly not survivable.

He might die down here in this basement.

She would be alone.

Savannah bit back the whimper. Gaynes would hear. He would know she was moving. Going for the gun.

"Because I'm letting him decide!" Gaynes's voice boomed.

Savannah froze.

"That's the whole point here. What does he want me to do with the cop?" He listened. She could hear the murmured voice of whoever was on the other side. "Of course we're going to get rid of them! They know too much. That's what I've been setting up this whole time!"

Savannah's fingers touched the gun, still warm from being fired by Keira.

She flexed her fingers, grasping for it with the tips. It slid toward her.

"Fine!" Gaynes let out a cry of frustration and jabbed at his phone. "Idiots."

Savannah's fingers curled around the grip of the gun. She swung it around, rolling to her back as she moved.

She squeezed the trigger. The weapon discharged.

Gaynes cried out. He stumbled back, pain and surprise washing over his face. "You shot—"

She fired again. The gun clicked.

Empty.

He lifted his gun, pointed square at her chest. "Nice try."

Tate's leg swung out. From the floor, he kicked Gaynes in the back of the knee. The councilman cried out and half collapsed. He caught himself. Tate kicked out again.

He landed on one knee, crying out some more.

In a last ditch effort, Tate launched at him.

They fell back, scrambling. Rolling. Both going for the gun. Savannah scrambled up, slipping on the blood that puddled on the floor. The last beats of Keira Ilkins's heart.

She reached for Gaynes.

The gun went off. The sound was muffled between them, and she didn't know who had been shot.

"Tate!"

Gaynes shoved him away. He got up, ramming her as he went, and raced up the stairs.

33

***

Tate gasped. His body bucked and pain tore through him. More pain. Like he wasn't already in bad enough shape. Now he had a whole host of other problems.

"He shot you!" She scrambled to him, breathing hard. She didn't look in tip-top shape herself.

Tate gritted his teeth, both hands planted above his hip, the warm blood now seeping from his side. He winced. Even though it was from close up, he was pretty sure he'd just been grazed. "It's just a flesh wound." He used his best high-pitched voice and everything.

"This isn't the time for jokes!"

She was wrong. The fact she caught his attempt at lightening the mood with his favorite movie line meant it was most certainly the time for jokes. "I think you might be the perfect woman."

"If I was, I'd have shot him dead!" Her eyes flashed. "Instead, he just ran out!"

"Honey." She was scared. Tate saw it. He just wasn't in a position to be able to do anything about it. "Check Keira for a phone." When she didn't move, he said, "Savannah. We need help."

"Right." She nodded, clutching one hand to her. "Okay."

When she turned away, he allowed his raw emotions to surface. No point hiding it when she couldn't see his face. Savannah didn't look good. Her face was seriously swollen. Whatever complications she might have to endure from rebreaking her nose, he wasn't sure, but it couldn't be good.

What happened to her hand?

"I found one!" She scrambled back over. "I'll call Bill, and—hello?" She paused. "And Tate." She glanced at him, holding the phone with her good hand. "We need serious help. Tate's been shot." Her voice sounded nasally, like she had the world's worst sinus infection. "Okay. Okay, yes, I'll hang on the line." She lowered the phone and tapped the screen with her thumb. "It's on." Pause. "Okay, just hurry." She said to Tate, "Ted isn't there, but Bill is tracing the phone's GPS."

"Good."

Her gaze got distant and she said, "Copy that." She lowered the phone.

Bill's voice came through the speaker, sounding tinny. She'd put it on speaker. "Dean is on his way."

"Good," Tate said again. She still looked scared, even knowing now that help was on the way. He needed to comfort her. But it wasn't like he could hug her. He'd probably pass out from the pain of it.

Savannah lifted his hands away from the wound. She grabbed ahold of the tear in his T-shirt and ripped it all the way open.

"Savannah's taking my clothes off!"

Bill chuckled. "Good thing you're not dying. Things might get interesting, and you wouldn't want to miss it."

Tate felt the corners of his lips curl up.

"This isn't funny!" Savannah looked like she was about to cry. "Keira Ilkins is dead in here. Gaynes ran off, but he could be upstairs doing who knows what."

"Dean is two minutes out, Detective."

Tate was going to go for a different tactic. He kept his voice soft and said, "Honey."

She balled up his shirt and pressed it against the wound.

"Honey, look at me." He moved his hand to touch her but realized it was covered in blood. She didn't need more of that on her.

She lifted her gaze to his. "It doesn't look bad but that doesn't mean there aren't a whole load of other problems you've got going on." She winced. "My hand really hurts, and you've been shot."

"Tell Dean I've probably got internal bleeding." He said, "You know, in case I pass out."

Her eyes flared.

Bill said, "Copy that."

"Savannah, we survived this. You prayed, didn't you? Well, so did I. And we're going to be okay."

"Gaynes is still out there." A tear rolled down her face.

"So we regroup, and then we'll get him. With backup. And you can get your badge and your gun back. After you get your hand and your face looked at. Though, it seems to me like you've proved you're still good without the badge and gun." He grinned. "Nothing's gonna stop you from bringing in Gaynes. Right?"

She sniffed and nodded. Then she moaned. "My face really hurts." Another tear rolled down her cheek. She shifted her hand and winced.

Through the phone, Bill said, "I'm sure Dean has an ice pack, Sweetness. Listen to Tate. You'll be all right. Yeah?"

She nodded, then said, "Yeah. I will. If you don't call me 'sweetness' again. Ever."

Tate had never been more proud of anyone in his life. If he could've sat up, he'd have hugged her. Probably picked her up and carried her out of here like some hero. Saved the day. Brought Gaynes in, guns blazing. Of course, she'd have swooned.

"You're drifting." She whimpered. "Please don't pass out. I know Bill is on the phone, but I really don't want to be alone with a dead woman."

Bill's voice came through, buzzing against the speaker as he yelled, "Tate, wake up!"

Tate blinked. "Hey. What?" He shifted his legs and pain rolled through his abdomen. "I'm here."

"Wilcox!" The call out came from high above. In the house.

Savannah lifted her chin and called back, "The scene is *not* secure."

Tate sucked in a breath. All he could do now was moan. Who was here? Dean? It sounded like an army as multiple booted feet hit the floorboards above. It sounded like the house was going to fall down around them. Seconds passed and he heard, "Clear!"

"Clear!"

"Clear!"

"I've found them." That was Dean. Who the others were, Tate didn't know and he didn't have the brain power to guess. "Back up the truck. And find me something to carry him on." Dean landed on his knees beside Tate. "Time to go, brah."

"Yep." Tate didn't want to know how badly this was going to hurt. "Good plan."

He felt shifting around the wound, and the press of fingers through rubber gloves. Dean winced. "I don't like the look of your belly."

Tate shifted, planting a hand on his sternum. "Chest."

Dean felt around, then hissed out a breath. He pulled a stethoscope from his bag and listened. Two seconds later, he pulled the thing from his ears. "Get me that stretcher. *Now!*"

"What is it?" Savannah said, "What's happening?"

"He needs to be in a hospital." Dean said, "His ribs are broken. If one shifts and punctures his lung, we're going to have more problems than we already do."

"Tension pneumothorax."

Dean's head whipped around to pin Tate with a stare. "How do you know what that is?"

Tate named the show he liked to watch.

"Finding out all your dirty secrets." Dean patted his shoulder with a grin. "Don't go dying on me when I think we just might be friends."

Tate liked the idea of that. Dean was a good guy. He was also someone who knew how to keep his mouth shut. The two of them understood each other. They got the value of need-to-know and how far trust went. Like Savannah. With her, trust went all the way. No secrets.

She said, "I have to secure this scene and wait for Conroy."

Dean shook his head as footsteps thundered down the stairs. "Not with your face like that, or your hand." He gave her a gel pack. "Put this on your nose. Or your hand. Or better yet—" He placed the pack on her nose and gently put her hand on top —"like this. Put it on both. One of the boys will stay here and wait for the chief."

"Okay." Her voice was small, drowned out by the shuffle and press of people.

Tate got a glimpse of a beanie. Then a black, thermal shirt. Someone's forearm, with a tattoo he'd never seen before.

They rolled Tate, hip and shoulder, onto his side before he could ask these guys who they were. He felt the press as they shoved something under him. Then he was up, and multiple pairs of hands held him steady as he was hauled up the stairs. He blinked and saw the ceiling inside the house, then felt a rush of cold air. These guys were fast.

"Who…"

"Tate?" Savannah's face came into view. "Don't worry. Everything will be fine."

He wasn't sure he believed her but now wasn't the time to argue. He needed her to believe it. Probably as much as she needed him to. Fact was, they were alive. They'd survived being kidnapped—nearly killed, actually—in an elaborate murder/suicide plan.

Thank You, God.

There was so much more to pray for, but his brain just sort of sputtered out. He saw stars. He felt better when he realized he was staring up at the night sky. It wasn't just his head spinning. The stars were real.

They slid him into the back of the truck, and he felt cold metal beneath his elbows. An engine turned over. She clutched his hand and the truck started moving. Someone threw a blanket over him. Savannah tucked it around his body.

"Are you with me?"

He blinked. "Sorry."

"Goodness, why?" Savannah shook her head. "You've saved my life so many times I've lost count. You helped me keep the faith tonight, when I would've lost it any other time. I'd have been alone. We wouldn't be alive. I would be dead."

She called Conroy and explained everything in a couple of terse sentences. After she hung up, he said, "Can I have the phone?"

"What's wrong?"

"I just need it." He could barely hold his hand up. How was he going to hold the phone? But he knew he had to make this call.

"Give me the number. I'll dial for you."

He told her. She put the phone on speaker and set it on his chest, holding it steady as she scanned the streets around them. Watching for Gaynes? Tate wished he'd have caught the guy, but that would have to come next. Gaynes wasn't going to get far. Not once Conroy and Eric learned what had happened.

"Hello?"

There was the sound of a hand covering the mouthpiece and a muffled voice. "No, baby. Mama's on the phone."

Tate's breath caught. "Sis?"

A tear rolled from the corner of his eye.

He heard some static, and his sister was back on the phone, "Tate? You okay? You sound weird."

"Got shot." He sucked in the biggest breath of cold air he could. Enough to say, "How are the kids?"

His sister chuckled. "Ornery as usual. But that's not what we're talking about. Are you okay?"

"Love you." He stared at Savannah as he said it, hoping she understood the full extent of what he meant.

Maybe it hadn't been long enough, but he truly did love her. As much as he cared about his family. And then more. He wanted Savannah here with him every day of his life, for the rest of his life. Regardless of anything else he wanted that.

"I love you too, kiddo."

Tate squeezed his eyes shut.

"You still there?"

Savannah said, "He's here. Um, so am I."

"Are you Savannah?"

"Yes." Her words were tentative. "You know who I am?"

"Eric told me."

"Oh."

"And he's walking out the door now. I'm sure you'll see him soon." Tate heard her kiss her husband, and answer, "Yes" to whatever he said. "He's on his way."

Tate managed to choke out, "Thanks."

"I'll pack up the kids. They love road trips."

He wanted to laugh, but that would not be good. "Love you."

"So you said. And yet you continue getting injured. Though, I don't mind Eric's overtime check, all those hours he puts in pulling your butt out of the fire."

"We're at the hospital now." Savannah shifted. "They're coming out with a bed for Tate."

"See you soon."

Tate got out a, "'K." and then his sister was gone. He closed his eyes. When he opened them again, Savannah was still there.

But he was inside the hospital now. The dull, yellow lights made him wince, but also filled him with relief.

"I have to go now."

He tried to speak.

Savannah leaned down and kissed his forehead. "I'll see you soon."

Tate's eyes drifted shut.

34

Three days later

"**A**ny word?"

Savannah dumped her backpack, still fighting off the after effects of the sleeping pill, taken the night before so she could rest despite all the aches and pains. "Tate?" When Mia nodded, she said, "He's awake and moving around a little. His brother-in-law is there, at the hospital. His sister is at his apartment with her kids and Elexa."

"Oh. Good."

Savannah didn't even touch that.

"How does he seem to you?"

She shrugged. Savannah hadn't actually seen Tate since he'd been taken back to surgery to repair all the damage done to his internal organs. He'd been bleeding into his abdomen, and he'd had to have his gallbladder taken out.

His sister was the one who'd told her that. When she'd called to ream Savannah because she hadn't been to visit him yet.

"Savannah, why are you here?" Mia's question yanked her from her thoughts.

She hit the button and fired up her computer, which of

course took way too long to load. "There's work to do. Did anyone get word on Gaynes overnight?"

Out of the corner of her eye, she saw Mia shake her head.

"Then we'd better have another crack at Patrick Dearnum. Make him tell us where Robert might've gone to hide."

"He's probably in Mexico by now."

Savannah said, "Canada is closer."

"How are you?"

She glanced at her partner. Mia knew something about suffering major injury. She also knew a whole lot about trauma, specifically kidnapping. She should talk to her. Work through it. Instead, Savannah said, "Let's get Patrick up here. Have a conversation."

Mia sighed. "Your call, Detective."

"Yes, it is. *Lieutenant.*" She shot her partner a look.

Mia actually smiled a little.

Savannah didn't want to unload on her. Not just because her superior would realize just how rough things were right now. What she really wanted was to talk to Tate. But how could she face him? Her actions had drawn him into this.

Sure, Gaynes had a personal vendetta against him. But if she'd solved this case faster, if she hadn't been so distracted by her attraction to him, then she would have been able to prevent the two of them from being taken in the first place. She'd have realized the answer was right in front of her the whole time.

As soon as she'd confirmed with the officer to bring Dearnum into interrogation, Savannah hung up. She could only maintain the façade for so long before reality crashed back in.

She'd failed.

Tate had nearly died.

"How do you wanna play this?"

Savannah said, "You're the lieutenant, remember?"

Mia leaned back in her chair. "Humor me."

Savannah shoved her chair back. "I'm going to ask him where Gaynes would go to hide."

"In return for…what?"

"Me not shooting him?" She shrugged. "At least for starters."

"Don't make me have to tell Conroy you threatened a prisoner. You'll get suspended again."

Savannah couldn't stop the shudder that moved through her. She'd woken up in the hospital from a nap—a nap made possible by the lovely meds they'd given her that made her feel all warm and fuzzy—to find Conroy by her bed. The first thing he'd done was give back her gun and badge. Not that she'd needed her gun in the hospital, but to a cop that was trust. It was respect, and a nod to the responsibility she had earned to get where she was.

It was a symbol of who she was.

The kind of woman who bravely walked this road. Who wouldn't rest until Gaynes was brought in.

Yesterday, after Eric had told the nurse he needed to see her about the case, she'd checked herself out of the hospital before he could have that chat with her—against medical advice. No reason to stay there and do nothing when there was so much work to do. She'd been beat up and uncomfortable, but the doctor had given her a handful of prescriptions. He'd wrapped her hand, and checked her nose.

Not like Tate, going into surgery. His family rushing to his bedside.

Savannah had Maggie pick her up and take her back to the mansion. She'd slept for sixteen hours straight, eaten, and then slept again. Now it was time to find Gaynes.

She walked into the interview room with Mia, pulled out a chair and sat down. "You don't want your lawyer?"

Dearnum lifted his gaze. He looked about as rested and peaceful as she felt. "He told me not to talk to you."

"So why'd you come up?" He had the right to refuse the conversation.

He shrugged. "I'm bored of staring at the wall. Felt like seeing what you wanted."

"We haven't found Gaynes, yet." She had to wonder what kind of relationship they had, the councilman and his assistant. Seemed kind of like hero worship by the look that passed across Patrick's face at the news his boss still hadn't been located. "Any idea where he might be? Places he liked to go, somewhere he'd lay low."

Dearnum said nothing.

"Is he really worth protecting? It's only a matter of time before physical evidence places you at the scene, corroborating what you've said about Aggerton's death. You think we won't pin Ilkins's murder on you, too?"

The knife had come back clean of prints. No prints at all. It had been wiped before being hidden behind books on a shelf in the DA's study, where Tate had found it at the scene of the murder.

Dearnum's cheek muscle flexed. "Keira Ilkins killed her husband."

"So you say. She's dead, so it's not like she can defend herself. I figure since he was killed the exact way you killed Aggerton, it was probably you."

She was having the doctor compare both victim's stab wounds to be sure. An attacker's height and weight played into the angle of the cuts, making it possible for them to surmise— under oath—whether it had been the same killer or a different person altogether.

"Either way," Mia said, "Gaynes was behind all of it. Pulling the strings. Only it wasn't because he had business dealings with Aggerton. This was about circumventing him. Gaynes wanted him out of the way for another reason. Not just revenge. Right?"

Dearnum shrugged.

Savannah decided then to try a new tactic. She'd remembered a few things last night in the middle of a particularly vicious part of her nightmare. Something she'd forgotten until then.

Gaynes, asking someone on the other end of the line what he should do with Tate and Savannah. Like they were a gift to the person—their deaths, at least. "Was he looking to get on board with West's operation? Is that it?"

Dearnum's eyebrows widened.

"I figure that's why he wanted Aggerton out of the way."

"Gaynes deserved to be a part of West's operation. Not Kenny, sleeping with Claire and getting in the way when Gaynes already hated him." Dearnum shifted in the chair. "Claire didn't know what she had, and she threw it away." He practically spit out the words.

"So Keira killed her."

Dearnum shrugged one shoulder.

"And she also killed her husband. For Gaynes. Just like she killed Claire."

He huffed.

"Gaynes was moving on, from Claire to Keira." Except Keira was dead now. Savannah continued, "Leaving you behind."

Savannah figured Dearnum had already been left behind before Gaynes fled the abandoned house where she and Tate had been held. He'd had Keira to do his dirty work, probably since things were getting too hot with Aggerton's murder and the police investigation. Keira had thrown the case off course, making it harder to solve.

It was a good tactic, even if Kiera had planned to punish them all. Probably until the day she died. After all, Savannah had been running in circles trying to figure out what happened.

Claire seemed like she'd been collateral damage. Keira had killed her, presumably as punishment for betraying Gaynes. But also so Keira could be free to move on with Gaynes since her husband was now dead. The autopsy report had come back. Bruising on the neck indicated a nerve and artery in Claire's neck had been pinched, cutting off blood from her brain and causing her death. The video had shown Keira entering her hospital room to finish the job. Seconds later Claire had coded.

But what good did that information provide? Certainly no closure, not even for Elexa. Justice would never be served.

The killer was as dead as the victim.

Dearnum said, "Robert Gaynes will be in the governor's mansion one day. And I was gonna be right there by his side."

"Maybe that's what he told you. Seems like everyone else involved with this has been strung along and then dropped like a hot potato."

She didn't even want to think about Gaynes getting a foot in the governor's mansion. That was a horrifying thought, giving a man like that so much power. She shuddered. "Like you. I mean, you murdered Aggerton but you did it for Gaynes. So it was basically coercion."

"I knew what I was doing." Dearnum spat, "It's not like he hypnotized me. I can think for myself."

She spread her fingers and kept them pointed out on the table. "My bad." She shifted in her chair like this was just a casual chat. "So why'd Kenny have to die?"

He pressed his lips together, as though conceding some point. "Since you know about him, it doesn't matter—Aggerton was about to make a deal with West. But Gaynes couldn't let that happen. Summers and Gaynes had to freeze out Aggerton, but he wouldn't go down without a fight."

"Which you brought to him."

He shifted, almost preening. "That's why Aggerton let the cops find out about Summers's books. Retaliation. Summers goes to prison, and Aggerton goes forward with West. Free of any entanglements that would get in the way."

Mia said, "Aggerton didn't tell the police about those books. That information was given by an informant."

She was right, as that informant had been her sister, Meena.

Dearnum said, "How do you think she found out?"

Mia closed her mouth and sat back.

Savannah said, "So this whole thing was about Aggerton wanting to bring down Ed."

"And Gaynes."

"So Gaynes fights back, has Aggerton killed." Savannah paused. "Who poisoned Ed in prison?"

"Maybe Aggerton set it up before he died?" Dearnum shrugged. "Maybe it was West. All I know is, it wasn't Gaynes."

"Where is he?"

Five minutes later, she stepped out into the hall. Conroy stood out there. "Well?"

Savannah folded her arms. "His dad had a cabin. It's up in the mountains, and he lets West use it to stash shipments of drugs when he needs a place to stockpile while heat dies down."

She moved to walk past him, but he snagged the sleeve of her sweater.

"Not so fast."

Mia came out of the interview room and raised her eyebrows. "Whatever you guys are doing, I'm guessing you won't let me tag along."

"We need…" Savannah tried to figure out how to word it. "Someone to man the phones here. Run the command center."

Conroy said, "Yes, perfect job for our best lieutenant."

Mia sighed.

Savannah said, "My ears rang for hours after that basement fiasco." Among other lingering problems like the headache to beat all headaches. "You think we're going to risk you having permanent hearing loss?"

"Plenty of people live without hearing."

Conroy's gaze softened in a way that made Savannah wonder if she shouldn't give them a minute. She started to inch away while he spoke softly to his fiancé.

"Savannah."

She ignored his call for her. There was an operation to set

up. She had to bring down Gaynes. For Tate, because she loved him and needed to fix this colossal screw up.

"Detective Wilcox!"

She flinched and turned around. At the end of the hall, past Conroy and Mia, Special Agent Eric Cullings stood with a thunderous look on his face.

This was bad.

She couldn't talk to Tate's brother-in-law when Tate nearly died because she hadn't done her job well enough. She might have brought down corruption in New Orleans, but all she'd done here was get Tate hurt.

Conroy said, "She's got a lead on Gaynes."

Savannah shot him a look. Such a traitor.

"Great." Eric waved to the bull pen. "Let's get the team together and plan this operation."

35

The door to his hospital room opened. Tate braced. It hurt, but his entire body tensed with anticipation over who it was. Wishing it was a certain person. Figuring it would probably be the doctor, or his sister again.

Instead, Eric stuck his head in. "You decent?"

Tate had a hospital gown on. But he said, "No."

Eric grinned. It was short lived.

"What happened?"

"I filled in the police chief." Eric stood at the end of his bed. "We've got Detective Wilcox locked down at the police station formulating an operation to get Gaynes."

"Maybe you should fill me in."

"Sure you want to know?" Eric cocked his head to the side.

"Why don't you let me decide what the answer to that is?"

"She hasn't been here, right?"

Tate wanted to shrug, but his whole torso hurt. Even lifting his arms was problematic right now, though he could make it to the bathroom and back by himself. He was just starting to get antsy about being here. They were waiting for…whatever the doctor was waiting for. Then they would release him.

Tate said, "Just tell me what happened."

"The DA in New Orleans, the one who was gunned down?" When Tate nodded, he said, "Investigation led to discrepancies in a few of his cases. Turns out he's been in the pocket of a cartel for years now. Every case he ever prosecuted is now in question, convictions are getting overturned, and defendants are getting released left and right." He paused. "Including Savannah's father."

"Where is he?"

"Local PD have no idea. He's in the wind because someone screwed up and dropped the ball." Eric said, "I passed the case up through federal channels and just got word. He was sighted outside Denver by a Colorado state trooper."

"He's headed here."

Eric nodded. "That's what we think."

"To get revenge on Savannah?"

"You don't know that. Maybe he misses her and wants to apologize for what he did, betraying his oath and hiring contract killers to try and take her out."

Tate felt his eyes bug out.

"I'm guessing she didn't fully brief you on that part."

He didn't waste time, "We need to mobilize. She should be under protection, not guarded and kept in the dark."

"Conroy and I talked about that, too." Eric scratched at his jaw.

"Don't agree with his assessment?"

Eric said, "Not for me to agree or disagree. You guys know her better than me. This isn't my case. I just happen to be in town and available. Though, not in an official capacity."

"Did you report her whereabouts back to the FBI?"

"Of course not. But I asked specifically about her father. Anyone with enough brain cells to rub together will figure out there's a reason why I asked only about him."

Savannah.

Tate didn't want to have hurt feelings over the fact Savannah hadn't been here when he woke up from surgery. He was confined to this bed, in this room, and she'd been released. Which meant she was perfectly free to come here to pay him a visit.

So why hadn't she?

Last he'd seen her she'd had stark fear on her face. Tate squeezed his eyes shut. "She…"

He was quiet long enough Eric said, "She what?"

"She was so scared." And yet, so brave. She'd gone toe-to-toe with Gaynes while Tate had been injured and unable to fight alongside her. One kick didn't count.

Gaynes needed to be brought in. Now. So this nightmare could be over.

But it wouldn't be, would it? Her father was on his way here, and Tate didn't think it was for the purpose of a happy family reunion. A corrupt police commissioner, exposed by his own daughter. A police detective. One of his own cops.

Talk about a hit to the pride. An entire police department, and the one cop he hadn't been able to control was his own daughter.

Eric settled on the side of the bed. "None of that has gone anywhere."

"What do you mean?"

"She might not be in that basement anymore, but the fear is still there. I figure that's why she doesn't want to come here, if doing that means you'll get worse. She's trying to protect you, Tate. Or maybe she just doesn't want you to see the fear. Knows you have enough to worry about."

Eric stared at the wall for a second. "She's doing her job, but that's all she's doing. Conroy should have sent her home as soon as she showed up. Why he's letting her work right now, when she should be dealing with what happened, I have no idea."

"So he can keep an eye on her. Make sure she's all right." He figured it was not so much that Conroy wouldn't be able to manage whatever fallout there was for Savannah when she finally fell apart. More like Mia and Conroy wanted to keep their friend close. Be there when it all caught up with her. In the meantime, they knew she did good work. Tate knew it was probably helpful to have her mind occupied with what she thought she needed to be doing.

Gaynes, still out there.

Now her father was coming.

"We need to tell her." Tate said, "Maybe she'll see reason, and we can persuade her to go into protective custody with the FBI until her father is found. We can dissuade him from approaching her."

"You think that will work? She's bent on getting Gaynes right now."

"I need to talk to her, so I can at least try to convince her." Tate said, "How did you get her to not move right away on Gaynes?"

"Conroy had uniforms go sit on the house where they think he is. Do some recon, so they can gear up and go out in full SWAT."

"Sounds like fun."

Savannah was busy. She was working, throwing herself back into things she was secure in. Being a cop was what she knew. It was who she knew she was.

Tate had to admit it made sense to him that she'd fallen back on what was familiar, and the unfinished business of arresting Robert Gaynes.

That didn't mean he had to like it, though.

She hadn't come to see him. Tate was going to have to go to her, do this in person. Find out why the woman he'd woken up knowing he was in love with insisted on ignoring him, throwing herself too quickly back into work.

They'd been through too much to not have the conversation she had to know was coming. Why was she refusing to face him? Tate didn't want to be needy, but she had to feel something for him. Right?

"Did getting hurt jog your feelings loose?"

"Shut up." If he'd had something to throw at his brother-in-law, he'd have done it.

"You tell dogs to shut up, dude. Not people."

"Don't call me dude."

"Don't tell me to shut up." Eric said, "And don't teach my kids to do it, either. You're a bad influence as an uncle."

"Too bad I'm the only one they've got."

"You better convince her to marry you." Eric looked like he'd just been delivered bad news. "Otherwise you'll only get worse."

Tate wasn't sure what to do with that. He liked the idea that Eric thought Savannah would make him better. He already knew that was true, but it was nice to hear. Though, not the part about getting worse if he couldn't convince her.

And he wasn't going to let Eric get away with saying it.

"I just had surgery. Maybe you should have a little more sympathy and get me my shoes." They'd patched him back up. Taken out what he didn't need and repaired the damage. He wasn't going to be working out anytime soon, but he could be useful.

"Didn't Millie bring you the get well pictures the kids drew?"

"Sure. They're cute." Tate motioned to the drawer beside the bed. "Shoes."

"Why do you need your shoes?"

"So we can go keep Savannah safe. Obviously." He wasn't about to sit here doing nothing.

"You're trying to misdirect me." Eric frowned. "So I don't realize what you're actually doing."

"Uh, duh." Tate sat up. "Is it working?"

"Where do you think you're going?"

"Considering you think I'm such a bad influence—" Tate shoved back the covers and shifted so his legs hung off the side of the bed. "—I figured I'd get out of your hair. Go where I'm wanted. Which is home, so West and his goons can show up and finish what we started."

Eric waved a hand. "Phil and I have that under control. At least for right now."

A pang of fear registered in him, bringing with it the idea that maybe Savannah didn't want him. That could be why she hadn't shown up here. Instead of her just being scared and not wanting to see him hurt, maybe she'd changed her mind. They'd gotten too close. He'd come on too strong. Things had been too intense. She didn't feel about him the way he felt about her.

"I'll coordinate with my team. Set up a trap for her father. Just in case he shows up." Eric didn't even comment on Tate's complaint. He just handed Tate his shoes like nothing was wrong between them.

Tate hadn't ever had a brother, until Eric. He figured this was pretty much how it went. Support each other. Ignore the fact that one of you was being an idiot. "I'm not being an idiot."

"We're just not going to talk about how you are in no way well enough to be getting dressed right now." He handed Tate a pair of sweatpants Millie had brought when she'd come by the hospital with the kids and those get-well cards.

Tate pulled his pants on, ignoring his entire abdomen. When he'd gotten the waistband over his underwear, he pulled off the hospital gown. His torso was wrapped in bandages. A good thing, considering he didn't want to know what he looked like. Probably some kind of mangled freak show, scars and stitches everywhere.

"Easy." Eric steadied him with a hand on his shoulder, the other hand clutching Tate's T-shirt.

"Make yourself useful, and go tell them I'm leaving." Tate didn't need an audience to watch him as he struggled to get his shirt over his head.

Eric sighed. He tugged the tee over Tate's head and helped him get his arms through. "This isn't a good idea. You shouldn't leave the hospital until you're well enough to hold a gun."

"Give me one."

"You might be able to fire it, but what use is it if you can't even lift your arm to aim?"

"I'll figure it out."

Eric kicked Tate's shoes across the floor until they were in front of his feet. All he had to do was stand up and slide his feet in.

"Get me a wheelchair."

"Not if you're going to try and get up while I'm gone. You'll keel over, and I'll have to lift you back into bed."

Tate toed his shoes closer and slid his feet in. "There. Now get me out of here."

Eric didn't move. "She loves you."

"I don't need you to make stuff up to try and make me feel better." Eric knew that was basically lying, right? Tate didn't need to be placated. "I need to talk to her. And I need to know she's safe. That doesn't include sitting here, doing nothing when her dad could show up at any moment."

Eric squeezed Tate's shoulder at the base of his neck. Hard enough it made Tate wince, though he didn't let that show. Eric strode out, leaving the door open.

Tate sighed, knowing Eric was right. He probably would keel over if he tried to walk. Who knew what would happen to his balance when he tried to stand? But he couldn't let that stop him. He knew she would be on that operation to get Gaynes, regardless of how she felt.

And she had to be feeling her injuries, even if they hadn't warranted surgery or a longer stay in hospital.

She loves you.

He didn't know if that was true, or if it really was just Eric placating him.

But he wanted to find out.

Eric walked back in, pushing a wheelchair. "Let's roll."

36

"You're not coming."

Savannah just stared at her boss.

Conroy said, "There's been a development in another case."

She waited for him to explain, but he didn't. So she rounded him and headed for the door. This was her operation, and they'd just spent two hours going back and forth planning it. She wasn't going to get left out now.

Not when staying here meant being out of the loop. Not busy working on the problem in front of her to keep from realizing she had a handful of other problems looming right behind it. And she definitely didn't need to have down time. She'd just end up thinking about Tate.

"Detective Wilcox!" Mia's voice rang out across the bull pen.

Savannah froze, knowing what was coming. Her lieutenant was going to pull rank on her.

"Unless you'd like to find yourself on suspension again, you'll do as ordered and stay here. With me, your BFF who's asked you to be a bridesmaid, unless you've forgotten that."

She turned around. "Low blow. Making it personal."

"I need company. So you should stay."

Savannah pressed her lips together. Conroy glanced between them. "I'm gonna go run this operation."

Savannah bit back the sarcastic comment she wanted to say. They were benching her. After all the work she'd put in? Gaynes was going to be cuffed, and she wouldn't even be there to see it.

As soon as the door shut behind Conroy, Mia turned to her. "Get your keys."

She blinked. "Uh, what?"

"Your car keys." Mia took two steps forward, her gaze on the front window where multiple department vehicles were pulling out of the parking lot. "Get them."

Savannah just stood there. "I'm not following." Maybe they were going for pie, or something. It was what they did occasionally. When one of them needed a sugar high or the other one wanted to offload about something.

She didn't want to talk, least of all about Tate. But doing anything would be better than sitting here doing nothing.

"Fine." Savannah grabbed her backpack. "What's the flavor of the week?"

"You don't know?" Mia gaped. "Wow, you don't feel good. Do you?"

Savannah shrugged. "I've been too busy to check my browser."

Mia said, "I'll drive. If we hurry, we should be able to watch." When Savannah just blinked at her, she added, "The takedown."

That was what she— "Go. Go. Go."

Mia chuckled. "Don't tell Conroy."

They loaded into the car, and Mia drove. She hit the highway and wound north. The cabin was out of town a bit and would take at least thirty minutes to get there. Thankfully Mia didn't seem to feel the need to talk to Savannah. Try and get her to open up. About her *feelings*.

She'd rather pretend everything was fine.

Until it wasn't.

Then, she planned to take a day off. To deal. She shouldn't need more than one day. *You wish.*

"So…" Mia dragged out the word, then said, "How are you doing?"

"I'm hungry. I thought we were getting pie."

"You'd rather do that than watch Gaynes be brought in?"

"No."

"Then why are you complaining?"

"I'm not." Savannah said, "I'm simply stating facts."

"Why don't you tell me about Tate first? Have you, uh… talked to him?"

"You know I haven't."

Mia sighed. "You know I'm not good at this friendship thing."

"Really? I hadn't noticed."

Her lieutenant and partner smiled. "Thank you."

"Just stop asking me about Tate."

"Why on earth would that be a sore subject? He didn't hurt you, right? And he's been in surgery, so you haven't said anything that would hurt him. So what happened in that basement? Did you leave something out of the report?"

Savannah stared out the window. "No." Yes. "Finding Gaynes is the priority. Then this can be over."

She would find a way to avoid Tate, and if she couldn't, well, then she'd find a way to avoid that awkward conversation they were bound to have. She wanted anything other than to have that chat—the one where he'd tell her he'd been thinking about things. He'd try to break it to her gently.

She'd have to pretend her heart wasn't breaking all over again. The way it had when he got hurt. When she'd realized how badly she'd let him down, allowing Gaynes to get away.

"How's your face?"

"I can't sniff because it hurts. I'm hoping I don't catch a cold until my nose is back to normal size and the cartilage is actually healed, otherwise blowing my nose is going to be excruciating."

"Yeah." Mia shot her a commiserating smile.

Savannah saw a sea of cop cars ahead. "This is it?"

Mia drove closer. The cabin was beyond the cars, their people all over the yard. "Looks like it might be done already."

Savannah stared. Long enough her eyes burned. Finally she saw Conroy walk Robert Gaynes out of the house, handcuffed. He loaded the man into a police cruiser and shut the door, then his gaze snagged.

On them.

"Uh-oh."

Savannah patted her friend's arm. "Go. Go. Go."

Mia said, "No. We face the music. I'm not running because we did nothing wrong. He said to stay safe, and we are. Did we get out of the car? No, we did not."

Conroy kept his attention on them, pulled out his phone, and made a call.

Savannah said, "That doesn't look good."

Who was he calling? There was a thunderous expression on his face, but neither of their phones rang.

He hung up.

"Should we go?"

Savannah turned to look out the back window, to see if it was clear for Mia to turn around. Maybe they should just go get pie right now. That would be better than going back to the office to wait for Conroy—and the lecture that was to come.

A big SUV barreled up the street behind them. Lights came on, then a siren. "Whoa."

The vehicle stopped, almost touching the back bumper, and the driver swung out leaving the door open. He rounded the hood and came to her door.

Special Agent Eric Cullings opened her door, reached in, and hit the button on her seatbelt. "Get out. On the double."

"Excuse me?"

"You're coming with me. No arguing." He tugged on her arm. Not hard, but she also recognized that she wasn't being give a choice but to do as he said.

Mia yelled from the driver's seat. "What do you think—"

"Stay where you are, Lieutenant." He held up a hand to her, bent to look in the car and said, "This is a federal matter now."

Savannah sputtered. "A federal…"

He walked her to the SUV and pulled open the back door. "Climb up."

She looked inside. Tate sat in the backseat, other side. He just stared at her. She turned to Eric. "I don't think—"

"We're exposed right now. Get in."

She climbed into the seat. Eric shut the door and trotted around the car. He lifted two fingers to Conroy, who was currently facing off with his irate girlfriend. Fiancé.

The chief returned the gesture.

"Savannah."

She ignored Tate, waiting until Eric got back in the car before she said, "What's going on?"

Eric backed up the car. "Tell her, Tate."

"You're now under federal protection. Until we believe you are no longer in danger." His voice was soft. "As soon as your father either presents no threat to you, or that threat has been extinguished."

"My father?" She spun around. "I thought you just wanted to *talk to me.*"

The skin around his eyes flexed.

"You look awful. Shouldn't you be in the hospital?"

Eric barked a laugh. "You're sure this is the woman you want, bro?"

Tate's lips pressed into a thin line.

Savannah wanted to curl up and be absorbed by the seat. Just disappear. Maybe suffocate. Quickly. She squeezed her eyes shut and leaned her head back. *My father.* They thought she needed protection.

Tate's fingers touched hers. She started and opened her eyes.

He pulled back.

Savannah said, "Are you okay?"

She was messing this up. Making everything worse, and it was already pretty bad.

"No, I'm not okay."

What was she supposed to say to that?

"Are you okay?"

Savannah shrugged. "I'll be fine." She said, "We got Gaynes."

"I saw that."

"It's good, right?" She figured she had redeemed herself with that, even just a little. Even though it had been Conroy who'd cuffed him and brought him in. Sidelining her and Mia in the process.

She wanted things to go back to normal. With a desperation that probably wasn't cute.

He nodded. That was all.

"Should you really be out of the hospital?"

"No."

Savannah went to say something else but couldn't think of anything. This was too weird. Too awkward. He'd been so gentle. Then she'd ruined it by being herself. Now it was worse, because he was protecting her from her father.

Eric pulled up behind Tate's office. "Don't get out. Give me a minute."

Two agents stepped out, badges on their belts and bullet proof jackets over their shirts.

One had a shotgun.

Eric opened Tate's door. "Ready?"

He nodded, scooting around to face his brother-in-law. "On three?"

"Sure."

Tate counted, then Eric helped him stand. Savannah's

stomach flipped over. She scooted to his back and touched his elbow, wanting to help.

He leaned on his brother. Eric called over one of the other agents. He stuck to her back as she walked inside with them.

Eric had Tate lay down on the couch in his office and handed him a Sig Sauer. "It's loaded."

Tate nodded.

Then he turned to her. "You don't leave, not for anything. The two of you stay here until I say it's safe."

At least she had her gun, too. She said, "Where is my father?"

"You let me worry about him." Eric shut the door.

Savannah stared at it.

"Sit down. You're making me nervous."

She pretty much stomped to the desk and slumped into his chair. With enough attitude the wheels rolled back a foot.

"There are cops other than you who are capable."

"It's *my* father. And Gaynes was *my* collar."

"So that basement didn't teach you that leaning on other people is okay?"

She stared at him.

He lifted one brow.

Savannah huffed out a breath and folded her arms.

"I'd have told you that. If you'd have come by to see me at the hospital."

"You didn't want me there." She said, "And I didn't want to hear you say it."

"Where did you get a silly idea like that? What if that's not how I feel?"

"How else would you feel? I didn't get Gaynes. Now I can't even protect myself from my father. And my nose got obliterated. I look like a freak."

She'd seen her reflection. Turning around in the bathroom this morning she'd accidentally caught sight of it. Then she'd cried awful, painful tears that made her nose feel worse. It had taken an hour for the puffiness to go down so she could go to work this morning.

"Savannah, can you come here?"

Hot tears burned her eyes. He sounded like he had in the basement, gentle and sweet. The Tate he didn't show many people.

"Please."

That got to her. She padded over, leaving her shoes under the desk. Her backpack on the floor by the chair.

He took up the whole couch, so she sat on the floor beside him, leaning her shoulder against the couch cushion. His eyes flared.

"I know. I look hideous."

He touched her chin, and she lifted her gaze. "You look strong."

She didn't believe that for one bit.

"You look like you survived."

"Because you were there."

"Isn't that how it's supposed to be?" He stared at her. "It was my pleasure. As is this, making sure you're safe. With Eric's help."

She took his hand, tears spilling down her face. "I don't want to see him. I can't."

"Your father isn't going to get anywhere near you." He squeezed her hand. "I promise."

She opened her mouth to respond but didn't get to say anything.

Beyond the closed door, a gunshot rang out.

37

Her whole body flinched in a way that looked painful. Tate slid his hand to her neck, the pad of his thumb on her cheek. "Stay with me."

Whatever was happening outside that door, they couldn't help with it. And the last thing he wanted was for her to leave now when he hadn't had a chance to say what was in his heart.

Her face paled, that fear sparking again in her eyes. "What if Eric is hurt?"

Tate was scared for that, too. Mostly for his sister and her kids, but also because there had been far too much loss the past few weeks. "He knows what he's doing. They all do."

She nodded, her eyes closing for a second.

"Your father isn't going to get in here. There's no chance of that happening."

She still seemed scared. So scared. Why couldn't he help her? She either trusted him, or she didn't. Those old fears reared their heads. Insidious voices, telling him he wasn't enough for her. The insecurity he thought he'd put away, now trying to convince him that the woman he'd fallen for didn't actually care about him. That he'd made it all up.

Another shot rang out, then several more. Tate knew what that sound meant. "It's over."

Her father had come to harm her. The FBI agents she had watching her back hadn't let him get through the door before they were forced to put him down.

Okay, so he didn't know about her location. But the principal was the same.

Her father had shown his intention. And if the FBI didn't take him out, he'd have put one of their lives in jeopardy. Before he tried to get to her.

"Savannah."

She didn't look at him. What she did do was lean forward and touch her forehead to his hip, her cheek on the seat of the couch. Eyes closed.

She almost looked asleep. Except for the angry purple bruises across her face and the white bandage covering her nose.

She looked like she'd been in a war. Which, in a way, he figured was true. A fight for her life, for the truth. For the future they might be able to have together.

"Everything is going to be okay."

A muscle flexed in her forehead. That small amount of defiance. It wasn't distrust, it was fear.

"I'm not going to let anything happen to you." He decided to just lay it out. "Because I would never let the woman I love go into an unknown situation without backup. Regardless of whether you are fully capable of taking care of yourself, or the fact you might be scared out of your mind, I'll still be there."

Right now he was a little more than completely useless, but he'd still be there.

She lifted her gaze to him, fear being replaced now by something else. Something he liked the look of a whole lot.

"I needed you." Tate figured it was out now. This might hurt, but he needed to tell her the truth. She should know. "I woke up. There was so much pain, you wouldn't believe.

Figured you'd be there. Then I thought something happened to you. Millie told me you were already home, so I called. You didn't call me back."

"I didn't know what to say." She swallowed, lip quivering. "How to face you."

"What are you talking about?"

"I didn't do anything right. I never do anything right." Her breath hitched. "I always try to do the right thing, but it doesn't work."

"Putting your dad away? Bringing down Gaynes, and Ilkins's wife. Summers. You think you're not gonna find something on Bernice Aggerton? Get her smug face in jail for whatever it is?" He had to be getting through to her. "Honey, you can't clean up the whole world. You just have to do the best you can."

"Even if it's never good enough?"

"Talked to Elexa."

She frowned.

Tate said, "She said you stayed up with her, almost all night. Sat with her. Talked about losing your mom, so she knew you'd been through something like what she went through. You're telling me that's not good enough?" He lifted up off the couch, far enough his head and shoulders were up. It hurt like crazy, but he didn't care. "That's everything."

"But—"

"Did you ever give up even once this whole investigation, even for one second?"

She closed her mouth.

"I didn't think so." He said, "Do you *ever* give up?"

She said, "No." Very quietly.

"Then don't start with me."

Fresh tears spilled onto her cheeks. "You needed me?"

"I needed you. And I don't want to lose what we've got now. Because I've fallen in love with you, Savannah."

The door opened.

Eric stuck his head in. "All good."

"Good. Now get out."

Eric shut the door, laughing.

"That was rude."

"Don't care. But honestly, that's another reason I need you, to tell me when I'm like that. Remind me how to be a nice guy."

She narrowed her eyes. He figured she'd say something. He was just about to interject his own comment, when she finally spoke. "I needed you, too. I just didn't want to admit it."

He studied her face. Taking it in, the fact she was here with him.

She said, "I'm sorry I didn't come to the hospital. I should have. I don't know what I was doing. I was just…lost. More lost than I had been after my dad went to prison, and I'd realized I'd given up everything. I had no family, no career, and no home. Then I came here. I found you, and even though I didn't want to need you…I do."

"It's not weakness. We make each other better. That's what relationships do, when you're in it together." He just hadn't known exactly how that worked, until Savannah.

"I've never had that with anyone."

"Me either." He said, "Think we can figure it out?"

Humor lit her eyes. "I think we'll have fun and misfortune figuring it out."

He figured she was right. This would be rocky, but that was life. And he was in it for the long haul if she was, too.

He said, "So long as we add making out to that list, I'm in."

Her lips curled, and he saw the start of an adorable blush on her cheeks. "You're hardly in any shape to do that right now."

"Yeah, well, I'd be scared of hurting your nose, anyway. So I guess we're even." He quieted, his thumb moving across her cheek. "I'm sorry it hurts. But you're still you, beautiful and strong."

"And damaged."

"We all are. Don't you think? You don't have to be whole before you're good enough. You just have to be honest."

Savannah said, "Honestly, I think I love you."

Tate felt the words move through him. It was like pieces of him finally fell into place. "Can you please come here and kiss me? I don't think I can sit up."

She didn't think that was funny, and it probably wasn't meant to be, but a giggle escaped as she lifted herself up and brought her face over to his. She leaned down and gently laid her cheek against his.

Tate wrapped his arms around her, not caring how it made his chest feel. She kept her weight off him but slid her cheek along his until their lips touched. He let her control it all, figuring she knew which way to move to keep her nose from nudging his. He wanted to kiss her, but he didn't want to hurt her.

Savannah leaned back barely an inch and whispered, "Love you."

The door flung open, hitting the wall.

Savannah leaned back as Conroy and Mia raced into the room, guns drawn. "Really you guys?"

Conroy glanced between them. "Eric said your dad was here. We just booked Gaynes in and came right over. Where is everyone?"

"We thought you were in trouble." Mia frowned. "Have you been crying?" She shot a glare in Tate's direction. "Did you make her cry?"

Before he could speak, Savannah said, "Everything's fine."

More than fine, as far as he was concerned.

Conroy shifted, glanced down the hall and then said to Tate, "Elexa, your sister, and the kids wanna come down. I think they want to know if you're all right."

Tate sucked in a breath and called out, "I'm all right!"

He heard a teenage voice call back, "Well, excuse me for being worried about Savannah!"

Beside him, she chuckled. Then Savannah yelled, "Thank you!" to the hallway.

"You're welcome," drifted back to them.

Mia evidently found the whole exchange hilarious. Conroy, it seemed, not that much.

Savannah's smile dropped. "Is my father really…" She knew he was gone. This wasn't a question she was asking.

Still, Mia gave her a short nod. "Do you want to see him?"

"No." Savannah settled onto the floor beside him. "No, I do not."

He still had her hand in his. Tate gave it a squeeze. "If the coast is clear, the kids can come down."

A second later, they were bombarded by his nephews. Tate introduced them to Auntie Savannah, which made Millie sigh with a smile. She had a quiet conversation with Savannah in the corner, while he listened to a story about some game the boys had played and how they were going to beat him at it when he came over.

"We'll see about that."

Elexa perched on the far end of the couch, on the arm.

He said, "You okay?"

She looked at Savannah, then him. "She's good for you."

"That's the idea."

Elexa shook her head, a smile on her face.

"What?"

"What?" She shrugged in that teenage way.

"Spill it."

She rolled her eyes. "I need a job. I missed too many shifts, and they fired me from the ice cream shop. I heard you're hiring."

"Are you kidding—" He started to sit up.

"Whoa."

Everyone rushed at him.

"Stop!" Tate slumped back down. "I'm fine, okay? Everyone chill." He frowned at her. "What do you mean, they fired you?"

Elexa shrugged. "Some other teen showed up, and they put her to work instead. Whatever."

He didn't believe she didn't care. He knew her better than that. Tate glanced at Savannah, looking for help, but decided Millie might be a better bet. Maybe his sister had an idea how to help out a teenage girl. Savannah just looked like she wanted to…fluff his pillows, or something.

He got a little distracted by it and said, "Hey nurse! I might need mouth-to-mouth later. If you're available."

His sister made a gagging face. Elexa laughed, the first he'd seen from her since her mom died. A beautiful sound he hadn't heard in a long time. His nephews rolled on the floor making puke noises.

Savannah blushed. Full out.

Tate looked back at Elexa, "I'm not hiring."

Elexa almost looked disappointed for a second, then he said, "But you can have the job anyway. If you keep your grades up and stay at Maggie's with no problems."

The teen nodded. "Done."

"It won't be easy. There's a lot of—"

"Whatever, Dad." She rolled her eyes. "I said I'd do it. You don't have to beg."

She waltzed to the desk and sat, inviting his nephews to watch a movie on *his* computer. Savannah had her hand over her mouth, but he was pretty sure she was laughing behind it.

Millie apparently also thought the situation was hilarious.

Savannah wandered to him. She set her hands on the couch on either side of his shoulders and lowered herself like she was doing a push-up. "I love you."

"So you said."

"But I still want that steak dinner. When you're fighting fit again, and I don't look like a mutant."

He started to object so Savannah laid her lips over his.

And that was that.

I hope you enjoyed *Expired Secrets*, please consider leaving a review, it really helps others find their next read!

Turn the page for the first 2 chapters of the 3rd story in the Last Chance County series: *Expired Cache*

EXPIRED CACHE

LAST CHANCE COUNTY BOOK THREE

Trade Paperback ISBN: 979-8-88552-036-2

Publisher: Two Dogs Publishing, LLC. Idaho, USA

Cover design: Ryan Schwarz

Edited by: Jen Weiber

1

———

"**E**leanor!"

Everything in her screamed, *ambush*, a half second before she was engulfed in French perfume and cashmere.

Ellie gave the woman a squeeze. "Ruby."

"It's so good to see you again, hon." The older woman's skin shimmered like glitter. She did her makeup like a pro, and her white hair had been trimmed to a pixie cut. Ruby had been working the same style since she'd taught Ellie's fourth grade Sunday school class. Ellie had to admit, it really did work.

"You, too."

"Smile a bit," Ruby said, "and I might actually believe it."

"I never could pull one over on you."

"Can't kid a kidder."

Someone at the far end of the coffee shop called out, "Sugar free vanilla soy latte with whip."

"Ooh, that's me!" Ruby retrieved her paper cup from the end of the counter.

Ellie glanced from the elderly woman's red skinny jeans and white sweater, to her own flats and skirt with her most comfortable jacket. When Ruby came back over, Ellie pushed her glasses up her nose.

"What brought you back to town this time?"

Ellie said, "Meeting with the lawyer. We're going over grandad's will."

Her last trip to Last Chance had been for the funeral. She hadn't even stayed overnight. This time she'd be here for a long weekend, enough to help her younger sister go through their grandfather's things.

"And your mama? Is she still…"

Ellie didn't want to get into that. "She wasn't able to get the time off work."

"I see."

Yes, Ruby probably did. Ellie tried to smile. She moved back to the map on the wall she'd been looking at before the ambush hug.

"The Founders' Map."

Ellie glanced over, her frown enough of a question.

"That's the first map of Last Chance. From the year the town started." Ruby pointed to the copyright in the corner. July 4th, 1975.

"It's fascinating."

Ruby nodded. "Long before I came to town, but I read all about it in a series the newspaper put out a few years ago." She pointed to the foothills. "This whole section of the mountains was deemed safe, and that's where all the hiking paths are now. The area above that is out of bounds. According to the signage posted."

Ellie frowned at her.

"A couple of friends and I hiked up there." She leaned close like she was telling a secret. "We didn't see anything dangerous. It was fine."

"Oh." She wasn't sure what to say.

Ellie's gaze strayed to the bookshelf below the framed picture. A dozen or so books, all used, by the look of them, had slid sideways. In the middle was a thick tome about the Civil War. *When Freemen Shall Stand* had been a runaway bestseller, written by Professor Eleanor Ridgeman. Unless, of course, the reader was one of the hordes of people who'd hated it. Despite sales, people seemed to be pretty much in two camps—they'd either loved it or decried it as an emotionless regurgitation of facts.

Ellie winced at the sight of it. She hadn't written a single thing since.

The same barista called out, "Extra shot, extra-dry, dairy-free cappuccino."

"That's me." Ellie stepped away from her old Sunday school teacher. "It was nice to see you again, Ruby."

By the time Ellie approached the door with her paper cup, the older woman had joined a friend at a table off to the side. She lifted her cup with a parting smile and stepped outside onto busy Main Street. *Everything's fine. Deep breaths.*

She took a sip of coffee. *Ouch.* Too hot.

"Your hot tea is gonna be hot, smarty pants." Her sister strode onto the sidewalk, a thermos she'd brought from home in one hand. Jess, four years younger than Ellie, was dressed in what she referred to as her "church clothes" whatever that meant. She also had her hair in a ponytail.

Ellie shot her a smile like everything was fine and side-stepped a young woman with a stroller. She glanced over her shoulder at the cars and people passing on the opposite sidewalk.

Going into the coffee shop for a drink was supposed to have settled her.

Why did she still feel like she was being watched?

"You okay, El?"

"Sure." She smiled at her sister. "Let's get to our appointment."

They headed down the sidewalk to the office of Holmford and Watts, her grandfather's lawyer. Where the will would be read. Once she got through the rest of this legal stuff, she wouldn't have to come to Last Chance again.

Her sister was Officer Jessica Ridgeman, formerly with the NYPD. Currently an officer with the Last Chance police department. As though moving to a small town and taking a job with a tiny department eight months ago could ever compare to the career of a cop in New York. But their grandfather, the previous police chief, had been terminal.

Jess was the one who had sat beside his bed those last few months to ensure he had family around him. It had just made the most sense, considering Jess lived here. Ellie lived on the East Coast.

Now their Grandfather was gone and buried. Ellie was back here long enough to get the paperwork done, help her sister pack the house and deal with the old man's things, and then she'd be off on sabbatical.

Write another book, Eleanor. She winced, picturing her boss's face right in hers. Close enough she could feel his breath. *You need to pull your weight, and we need a bestseller for this department.*

Jess glanced at the screen of her phone, then slid it into her back pocket. "As soon as we're done with Mr. Holmford, I have to get to work. We have a new case and things are starting to get interesting."

Even having grown up with a police chief for a grandfather, Ellie still didn't know what that meant.

Jess spoke again. "How are things going at the university?"

"Things are fine," Ellie said. "Why wouldn't they be?"

"If you'd actually breathe, I might believe you mean that." Jess glanced over again, assessing her.

Ellie hadn't liked that "cop" stare when their grandfather did it. She didn't like it now from her little sister.

"You get that I'm trained to interrogate people, right?"

"Criminals. Not your own sister. And we all have the right to remain silent." Ellie sighed. "Let's just get to the lawyer's office and get this done."

There had been zero choice in coming back this time, just like there hadn't been for the funeral. She couldn't have left her sister to do all this alone. Being back in the old house with her sister felt good, but the memories in and through the rest of town put her on edge. That was the only reason she felt under a microscope.

Ellie was a history professor. She didn't know how that science stuff worked, but probably whatever scientists watched that closely—that *intimately*—knew they were being studied.

"You think there's anything in the will? Besides the house, at least."

"What about his cabin, or the car?" Ellie took another sip. Hot liquid encountered the burned taste buds on her tongue and she winced.

Across the street, a man parked in his car watched them pass. *It's nothing, just ignore it.* Would she always be suspicious of every man who glanced her way? No. That was no way to live her life. She might have avoided Last Chance for years, but innocent people should never be a source of fear for her. That wouldn't be fair to someone just trying to live their life.

Ellie had been targeted specifically by one person—and his friends. But that had been years ago. And it was done now.

If she was inclined to thank God for anything, she would start with the news report she'd read a few weeks ago. The one that gave her peace. Some, at least. There was no reason for her fear now.

"Who knows what all there is?" Jess shrugged one shoulder. "But the chief wasn't exactly hiding anything. You know he never could keep a surprise."

Ellie chuckled. "That is true." The old man had ruined more than one surprise party.

Their grandfather.

The police chief.

Jess had connected with him as a cop and had called him "chief" even in middle school. Ellie had existed at odds with the old man. Her grandfather hadn't understood her.

He'd tried to help her when she needed it. But at the time,

Ellie couldn't accept it. Not from him or anyone. She knew he'd felt rejected by that. Life had never given them the opportunity to fix that. They'd exchanged emails for years. Catching up on each other's news. But they'd never really made amends or worked to deepen their relationship. With Ellie's book becoming so successful, and then her busy teaching schedule, there just hadn't been time.

Ellie felt the burn in her eyes and glanced up at the sky so her lenses would transition to sunglasses and her sister wouldn't see the sheen of tears. Not that Ellie would cry. She never did. Crying didn't fix anything, and she wasn't one to wallow.

"Thanks for coming."

"I know." Ellie smiled at her sister. "You said that already."

Jess shook her head. "What with you being busy and all, I was kind of surprised you came at all, to be honest."

Ellie didn't take offense. She and her sister told the truth to each other, even when it might hurt. It was called honesty and it was key in healthy relationships.

She said, "I'm glad I came, too." Not exactly what her sister had said, but she understood the sentiment. "The will is supposed to be read to both of us."

Soon as it was done, she would get back to the East Coast and begin figuring out which New Hampshire rental house she was going to live in while she was on sabbatical. Ellie only had six months to research and then write a book about the Vietnam war.

It had better be juicy, Ridgeman.

Her department chair wasn't going to let her ride much longer, writing papers while refusing to "come into the new millennium" as though there was a void in social media that should be filled by academia. As if they should stoop that low. It was tantamount to selling themselves in the name of entertainment.

Still, Ellie had to give him what he wanted or she had to get out. And there was no way she'd let him push her aside. She'd worked hard. For years. Now she was going to make him see how much of a mistake it would be to force her out.

Ellie pushed all that aside for later and took a closer study of her sister's face. She seemed over tired. Because of the big new case or their grandfather's death, or both? Jess had adored their grandfather, which was probably why she'd become a cop. Of course she would deeply grieve the loss of her mentor and the only stable male figure in her life.

Ellie hadn't needed him in the same way, but she was still grieving.

Ellie said, "I'm sorry you lost him."

"You lost him too."

"You know what I mean."

Jess shook her head again. She seemed to do that a lot.

"It's hard to suddenly have your mentor gone, a man you looked up to personally and professionally."

"It wasn't sudden, El. He fought a long battle. No one thought he'd last that long. The kind of cancer he had is supposed to take a person quickly. Viciously." Jess paused. "I actually thought he was waiting for you to come and say goodbye."

"You know that was impossible for me, in the middle of the semester." She touched her sister's shoulder. "He had you. But that also means you feel the loss more. It's okay to be upset."

Jess said, "I might be comforted, if I thought this conversation was more than an intellectual thought exercise, professor."

"I'm not a psychologist."

"No, you're not. Just smarter than everyone in the room at any given moment."

"We're outside." They were walking along the street in the center of town in broad daylight. Why was Jess comparing the two of them right now? Was Jess more distraught over their grandfather's death than she'd thought, and trying to deflect?

Her sister shook her head. "Never mind." Her attention snagged on something across the street, and Ellie saw Jess's head turn sharply. Did she see it too? Did Jess feel what she did, that there were eyes on them?

Ellie spun to see what her sister was looking at. She heard Jess mutter, "Dean" as though the name was a curse word.

"Who is that?"

Ellie didn't recognize a guy with that name from high school. He was about their age, and he was huge. His face… she'd have remembered someone with those features. Dark hair. A strong jaw. The kind of guy who knew exactly the effect he had on women.

She saw men like him on campus every day, striding past huddles of tittering college girls like they thought they were walking through busy city streets. Heroes off to war.

"Dean Cartwright."

"As in…"

Jess nodded. "He's Ted's disapproving older brother."

Ellie glanced over.

"Yes, we figured out we have that in common." Jess grinned and nudged Ellie's shoulder away. "But trust me, he's way worse. Dean was a Navy SEAL, so of course he has that hero complex all guys like that have. The 'hop to it' and 'yes sir' stuff, with the hospital corners when you make your bed. Every day. Without fail. Ted's a computer genius."

Ellie nodded as though that topic jump made any sense whatsoever. Her sister's last email had been all about the police department's super cute—apparently—tech specialist. Given the handsome level of his brother, she didn't doubt he was good looking.

"Dean just can't stand to see Ted doing anything he doesn't approve of."

"Sounds like grandpa." Ellie grinned, trying to lighten the mood.

Jess laughed. "Back in your 'wild' days, getting picked up at the golf course at two in the morning, drunk as a skunk, in junior year."

Ellie groaned. "Oh, I remember that. Officer Frampton didn't let me live that down. He made me do the perp walk and everything."

Jess was still laughing. "Classic…until you got all weird senior year. Then you never did anything."

All the humor she felt dissipated in one fell swoop.

"Shoot. Sorry, I shouldn't have mentioned it." Jess sighed. "I know something happened. Grandpa never told me what, but you changed. That was obvious."

Ellie figured that, given her sister's experience as a police officer, she might've worked out what occurred that Friday night at the home game victory party. She might have been younger, but Jess had never been dumb.

Ellie stepped off the curb onto the crosswalk.

"El, watch —"

Car tires screeched. Ellie gasped, then turned to see a champagne-colored car barreling toward her. She jumped back. Landed on her behind on the street. Her hip glanced off the curb, and her palms slid across the asphalt.

She cried out.

Her purse dropped, and the contents dumped everywhere. The car's engine revved, and they sped off down the street while Ellie fought to catch her breath and figure out what had just happened.

"This is Officer Ridgeman. There's been a hit and run."

She twisted to her sister, blinking. Pain rippled through her side, and she cried out. When she touched her hip, it was with bloody hands. She winced, a breath escaping between her pursed lips.

"Careful." A figure entered her peripheral.

Ellie sucked in a breath and twisted, instinct causing her to jerk back from the dark figure.

"Easy." Dean Cartwright reached for her. "Let's take a look at your hands. I'm sure it's not too bad."

Beyond him, Jess frowned down at the former Navy SEAL.

Ellie felt his warm hands under hers, cradling them. She yanked her hands from his and shifted back. "I'm fine."

"Ma'am—"

"I don't need any help."

He towered over her. Big shoulders. A disapproving stare, as though she needed more of that in her life.

Ellie looked at her sister, who took three steps to her and held out a hand. This was going to hurt. She grabbed Jess's wrist anyway and let her sibling pull her to her feet while Dean Cartwright straightened to his full height. Good grief, he really was huge.

And still frowning.

Ellie lifted her chin. *Ouch.* "We're good. But thanks anyway."

2
—————

Dean looked down into her brown eyes and everything just...stopped. Then he remembered the roar of the car engine. Jessica's cry. The car hadn't even attempted to slow down.

The injured woman was scared. Probably woozy as well, from the shock of almost being flattened in a hit and run. He glanced at Jessica and saw the resemblance in their features.

His brother Ted, who worked with Officer Ridgeman at the police department, had told him that Jessica's older sister was coming into town again, this time to hear the reading of the will. She'd flown in one day for the funeral and not even stayed overnight.

He'd seen her from across the field during the service but hadn't stayed long enough to pay his respects. Now he kind of wished he had.

"Eleanor, right?"

"Ellie." She held a hand out to shake. It was tentative. Then she realized why he wasn't going to shake her hand.

"Dean Cartwright." He swung his backpack off his shoulder and slid a water bottle from the side pocket. He twisted off the cap. "Hold out both hands."

She held them to the side, and he emptied the water onto her palms.

"Rub a little, if you can. Get the dirt off." While she did that, he pulled out two gauze pads and ripped open the packets—she could use them to dry her hands off—and then grabbed a tiny packet of Neosporin.

Officer Jessica Ridgeman, the younger sister, stuck her hand on her hip. Dean was almost positive his brother was in love with her, given how he talked about her. Truth was, they knew practically nothing about her. Or the sister. Dean had wanted to run background checks, but his brother's reaction meant he'd tabled that discussion.

For now.

Dean caught her gaze. "Hand?" He tore open the cream packet and held out his hand so she could place hers in it.

She just frowned.

"I'm certified as an EMT if that's what you're worried about."

"I'm not." She took half a step back. "I'm fine, though. I don't need help."

Yeah, she'd said that. Dean wasn't used to treating patients who couldn't admit when something hurt. Though he dealt with his fair share of alpha personalities, so it really shouldn't surprise him to come across someone inflated with sheer stubbornness. Normally he didn't find it quite so attractive.

Usually those he treated knew they needed help. In their own ways, they'd allow him to do what he could to help them.

Her dark hair had been pulled back into a bun with a silver pen stuck in it. Now loose strands floated around her face. Her glasses were askew, in a way that made him want to reach over and right them for her. Attraction stirred. The librarian thing. He blew out a breath. It had always been a weakness for him, but that didn't mean he had to listen to it.

He wasn't in the place in his life where he was ready to look for a relationship.

At least, not yet.

Dean tossed the Neosporin packet to Jessica. "Make sure she puts this on her cuts."

"Aye aye, captain."

"I might've been Navy, but I was never an officer. Thanks for the vote of confidence, though."

Jessica's eyes flashed. "It was unintended."

Ellie glanced between them. She could see he wasn't going to pretend there was any love lost between Officer Ridgeman and himself. Truth was, no one would be good enough for his brother.

Dean's watch alarm beeped. He canceled the tone and pulled his backpack on. "I have an appointment." He glanced between them but asked Ellie, "If you're good?"

He almost wanted to tack on the question of whether he could call her later and make sure. Ellie nodded, the hint of a smile on her face. "I'm good. Thanks." Like she knew exactly how she'd affected him.

Great.

"Dean!"

He twisted around. The door to the coffee shop was open, and Doctor Gilane waved a hand. Dean's appointment.

He held up one finger, and the doctor nodded.

A police car pulled over at the curb and the uniformed officer climbed out. Sergeant Basuto. He waited for the guy to make it all the way over and they shook, then Dean left them to it. As a rule, he didn't get involved in police matters. Jessica had this covered. He didn't need to get in the middle of this when he had a meeting with the doctor to get to.

One last glance back let him know Ellie had forgotten all about him. She was smiling at the sergeant in a way she hadn't looked at him.

Dean tried not to let that sting. Especially considering the fact he'd never been needy before. Why start now, with a dark haired, tiny nosed intellectual who checked every box he had?

No way was it a thing when no other relationship he'd had in his life turned out the way it had promised to be in the beginning. He was done being ditched, broken up with, tossed aside and otherwise moved on from. Dean was making his life what he wanted it to be.

He was about to start a new venture, one that would begin with securing backing from the doctor on his new project. He had plenty to do. And that didn't include wondering why a driver had tried to run Ellie down.

It wasn't an accident. It had been a deliberate attempt to hurt her.

But he wasn't a cop and Ellie Ridgeman didn't have any connection to him.

"Latte?"

Dean said, "Cappuccino."

A few minutes later, they sat at a small round table and Doctor Martin Gilane pulled Dean's portfolio from his briefcase. He set it on the table between them but didn't open it. The doctor's white hair was perfectly styled. His face was tanned like his arms and hands. A man who did good work but also regularly treated himself to exotic vacations with this wife, who was twenty years younger and closer to Dean's age than his own.

Dean had lived in this town long enough to know that Doctor Gilane knew his father. Knew some of his history.

The doctor tapped a manicured nail on the portfolio. "This is good stuff."

Dean hadn't been expecting that. He also wasn't sure what it meant. He lowered his paper cup, waiting for the inevitable "but."

"A treatment center for those suffering PTSD." Gilane tipped his head to the side. "When you came to me to sign off on your therapy hours, I can't say I thought this was where it was going. You've more than exceeded my expectations with everything you've done. You're an asset to the medical community in Last Chance, Dean."

He'd been hearing that from the doctor for a while now. The same as with all those other times, he just couldn't let the words settle in. Not in a way that it satisfied what was inside him. Dean only used the words to fuel him on.

He'd survived his childhood with his sanity intact. That had been a feat in itself. Then, Dean had gone into the Navy. He'd done one of the toughest jobs in the world.

Had he come out of that with a sense of satisfaction? Not the way most would think.

Will satisfaction come with this new venture?

God hadn't answered his question yet.

"This isn't going to be a medical facility. It'll be a voluntary residency, and a place people can attend group meetings or get one-on-one treatment that's highly specialized. I want to take on a certain client group."

People who had been where he'd been, and needed help the way he had. Dean was determined to give back. To be the man he knew he could be. Someone people wanted in their lives. Sure, he had friends. But there was so much he was missing.

Love. A family.

"The case studies are fascinating. I had no idea you've been doing all this since I helped you get licensed."

His stomach clenched. He felt like he was trying to pass an interview for the career he'd always dreamed of. "Having your support will go a long way to legitimizing a treatment center."

"You know, I'd love to put in some hours alongside you."

"You would?" The doctor had helped Dean get all his licenses and certifications, he'd been invaluable signing off on Dean's work so far.

"The chance to be on the cutting edge of PTSD therapy? Fascinating." The doctor took a sip of his coffee. "You know, I have a friend at the Pentagon. I'm going to make a call. He might be interested in taking a look, maybe secure some backing to get you referrals. Cases they'd like you to take on."

"You think so?" When the doctor nodded, Dean continued,

"It's been nearly four years since I left the Navy. A lot of my contacts there have dried up." So far, he'd treated a few friends and a couple of locals who'd sought him out.

"Even with those roommates of yours, word hasn't gotten out?"

Dean said, "They all work private security now. There are occasional government contracts, but those aren't the norm."

His roommates were currently halfway across the world, working a job. Only one was home with Dean and Ted. Dividing the chores between the three of them until the rest of the boys got back was going to earn them at least a month of freedom. The house was fifteen thousand square feet. It took forever to clean all that, even with Ted's squadron of seriously modified robot vacuums.

"I'll bend some ears. See what I can come up with."

"But you think it'll work."

The doctor nodded. "More than think. This is a great idea, Dean. Something noble the town should be able to get behind."

"Thank you." That was high praise. The kind that made him want to sit taller in a way that usually didn't happen outside the military.

"You really think you can take it on, on top of your…work?"

Dean said, "Being the town's informal EMT is something I don't think I'll ever stop doing." Even if the constant phone calls sometimes drove him crazy. "Though, I've thought about shifting it to more of a concierge thing."

"You'll charge people?"

"Of course not." He shook his head. "I prefer the muffin baskets anyway."

Gilane looked at him like he'd grown another head beside the one he already had.

Dean said, "I'll figure it out. If folks know I'm working on something that can help those who need it, they might chip in and take some of the strain. Or, they'll have a mind to what I'm doing and call less for incidental injuries."

"Or you could take on a partner. Get help with the EMT duties."

"I always figured that would come from the actual EMTs." Dean shot the doctor a wry smile.

"They give you grief?" Gilane frowned. "I can speak to them if you'd like."

Dean shook his head. "It's fine."

But the doctor didn't let it go. "Anything you need, Dean. You let me know." He nodded. "No matter what it is, I'm here to support you."

"Thank you." What else would he say? He'd expected to have to fight for what he wanted in order to convince the doctor this was the right thing. "I just need a location and the resources to pull it off."

It wasn't like Dean had the money for something like this lying around. He was comfortable, and he had good savings, but wiping out his resources and living at the edge wasn't wise. What he needed were financial donors. Charity events. Annual fundraisers. People in town pulling together.

"I've had some thoughts about that, as well." The doctor pulled a business card from his shirt pocket. "This is the paralegal at Holmford and Watts. She's done fundraising for the local schools and for the hospital. I think she'd be a great resource. And that's only if she doesn't jump in with both feet to help you."

Dean took the card. "Thank you."

"I already sent her an email, so she knows you'll be headed her way."

"I actually have an appointment to see Holmford in an hour. I'll talk to her while I'm there."

"You're seeing the lawyer?"

"He didn't say why he needed to talk to me." Dean blew out a breath and leaned back in his chair. "I feel like I'm totally out of my depth, but I want to do this so I figure that's a good thing."

It was important. He could help people, long term. Make a difference in their lives past just putting a bandage on their injuries and telling them to see their doctor.

He *should* feel like he was taking on too much responsibility to start up a therapy center. That would help him move cautiously and consider the weight of what he was doing.

"Well, then." The doctor stood. "I won't keep you if you're headed to another appointment."

He still had half an hour, but Dean was pretty shocked and needed some time to just think. He shook the doctor's hand and just sat back to absorb it all. He was really going to do this.

"Anything you need, Dean." The doctor said, "You let me know."

Dean blinked, then watched him walk out. Full support with no convincing wasn't exactly what he'd imagined this meeting would be. Now that it was done, and so easily, he didn't know what to do with himself.

Anything you need.

Because the doctor believed in him? Dean had grown up with a father who said what he thought would get you to do what he wanted you to do. That level of manipulation made him sick now. He couldn't stand it. Dean wanted to believe the doctor was just supportive. That he believed a therapy center was a worthy cause. But something just didn't sit right.

After all, nothing in life was free.

Continue reading *Expired Cache* now!
https://lastchancecounty.com/last-chance-county

OTHER BOOKS IN THE LAST CHANCE COUNTY SERIES

Find ALL of the books at:

LastChanceCounty.com

In this Series:

Book 1: Expired Refuge

Book 2: Expired Secrets

Book 3: Expired Cache

Book 4: Expired Hero

Book 5: Expired Game

Book 6: Expired Plot

Book 7: Expired Getaway

Book 8: Expired Betrayal

Book 9: Expired Flight

Book 10: Expired End

Also available in 2 collections!

Books 1-5

Books 6-10

ABOUT THE AUTHOR

Follow Lisa on social media to find out about new releases and other exciting events!

Visit Lisa's Website to sign up for her mailing list to get FREE books and be the first to learn about new releases and other exciting updates!

https://www.authorlisaphillips.com

www.ingramcontent.com/pod-product-compliance
Lightning Source LLC
Chambersburg PA
CBHW020055310726
48970CB00002B/328